ERIN MALLON

Sharkbait

Dedicated to Jiva, the modern-dancing,
water-pouring life force who unites our family in love.
I'm so excited to see all the things you will do.

Prologue

TWO MONTHS AGO
LOUISE

*T*his guy is a talker.

And not exactly a *dirty* talker. Just a straight-up talker.

"What's your name?" he rasps as he slams me up against a huge ice-cold keg.

Holy crap, that's frosty.

My shirt buttons are undone. The skirt I'm wearing is hiked way the hell up, and the hot Henley he was wearing is nowhere to be found. I tore that thing off him the moment we got in here, which was excellent thinking on my part. It turns out this man's abs are insane.

"Actually, let's not do that." I wince.

"You okay, beautiful?" He hikes my leg around his thigh. "I'm sorry. That was rough, wasn't it? And cold."

His warm hand cups the curve of my chilled ass cheek like it's asking for my forgiveness too.

Damn, this guy is hot.

Chatty but hot.

"Oh no, I'm fine. I didn't mean that I didn't want to... what I meant was I'd rather not—"

I take a moment to gather myself and then get way too clinical sounding for a random hookup in a bar. Because let's be clear. That's what this is.

"Rough is good. And I don't mind the cold. Let's just not do the name thing. Okay?"

He releases my leg and leans back a few inches. "You don't want to do 'the name thing'?"

"Also..." I silence him with the classic put-your-index-finger-on-his-lips move that I've seen countless times in movies. And what do you know? It works in real life too.

Wow. Are those golden flecks in his brown eyes?

"You were saying...?" he laughs.

"*Also*, my friends think I'm in the ladies' room right now, so I only have a few minutes before they come looking for me. That means we should probably skip all this small talk and get right to the good stuff, yeah?"

"Fine by me, Cold Brew."

He cups my face with both hands and dives into another out-of-this-world kiss.

What did he just call me?

Who cares. He can call me whatever he wants so long as he keeps kissing me like that.

Who am I right now? Because I am not the girl who hooks up with hot bartenders inside walk-in beer refrigerators at a local bar. I feel like I'm watching some other girl saying and doing all these things tonight. This girl is impulsive. She's rowdy. She's a girl who knows what she wants.

And tonight? She wants this guy.

And he wants her.

I do an internal cheer.

Because up until this point, I've always been a relationship girl. Basically, if I kiss you, I'm *with* you. For *years*. Even if you're a douche. Maybe especially if you're a douche. It seems the douchier you are, the quicker I'll give up all my needs and wants to keep you happy.

I don't know where the hell I learned how to operate that way.

Correction: I know exactly where I learned that from, but that's all in the past.

I'm free now, and it's freaking glorious.

Did I mention sexy bartender man has a buzz cut? That style is not usually my cup of tea. But on this guy? I'm obsessed. I want to run my hands all over his prickly, sexy skull.

So I do.

Let's rewind for a moment. How exactly did I end up making out with a sexy-as-hell, buzz-cut bartender in a walk-in beer refrigerator?

It was some kind of magic.

After hours of sly glances across the bar, we locked eyes and... *boom*.

No words were necessary.

Instant same page.

Things happened fast from there. I mumbled something to my friends about the bathroom. He threw his rag down on a rack of pint glasses. Then before I knew it, we were facing off in a dark hallway, breaths synced, bodies drawn to each other like magnets.

And I'm not being poetic about the magnet thing either. This honest-to-God energy I've never experienced before literally pulsed through my body and *dragged* me to him.

I resisted it for a hot second, but then that voice in my head—the one that's usually so freaking loud—surprised the hell out of me when it whispered, "Fuck it, Lou."

Fuck it, indeed.

Tonight I'm not "smart girl" Louise who weighs every decision over and over until her brain is ready to burst. Tonight, I'm not "responsible girl" Louise who everyone counts on to do the right thing.

Tonight, I am Lou: the girl who does whatever—or whoever— she wants.

James. His name is James.

James breaks from the kiss and runs the backs of his fingers down my cold cheek. "You're really not gonna tell me your name?" His whisper sends delicious chills across my skin.

"No, I am not," I whisper back.

"Alright." His deep voice vibrates as he rains kisses down the column of my throat. "I guess I'll keep calling you Cold Brew then."

"I don't like that."

"Oh no?" He tears his lips away.

"Resume what you were doing, please!"

I'm giving him mixed signals.

"What I meant was I like *that*." I point at his mouth, then jut my neck out in his direction. "The uh, that thing you were doing just now to my neck? *That* was good. But I'd prefer it if you didn't call me... Cold Brew."

He dives into my neck again, and I think we're back on track until he murmurs this madness between kisses, "That's too bad. A hot thing like you slowly pouring over me and effortlessly spiking the temps in my refrigerator? A strong, concentrated woman like you who won't be diluted with water for other people's comfort? A delectable drink of a girl like you who isn't afraid of a coarse grind when everyone else is pummeling themselves into soft, palatable powders to please the masses? Cold Brew is the perfect nickname for you."

What the hell is he talking about?

So he's weird. That's fine. After tonight, I'll never see him again.

Looks like I need to take matters into my own hands.

I cup the bulge in his jeans and feel him respond.

Now we're getting somewhere.

I think.

"You said you don't mind the cold," he breathes. "Are you into winter sports then? Skiing, snowshoeing, mountain climbing?"

"Not into winter sports, no." I desperately work to undo his pants.

"So what *are* you into?" he rumbles as he helps me with the button.

"You mean sex-wise? The regular stuff. The regular stuff will do."

He laughs. "Good to know. But I meant what are you into in *life*? Like hobbies and stuff."

Alright. Now buddy boy here is starting to test my patience.

"Not really a hobby person. My hobby is my work, and my work is my hobby."

Score! Jeans are officially down. He kicks them, and they land on top of an icy growler, almost like he choreographed it. You would think a woman getting him pants-less would be enough to curb this guy's relentless inquisition, but no.

"What's your work then?"

"Marine biology," I huff. "Can we—?"

"Oh wow, the ocean and I are like *this*." He crosses his index and middle finger in that universal sign of closeness. "I'm a swimmer! A diver too!"

"Cool, cool," I say and try to get his focus back to the physical. The fact that we have both been in a body of water at some point in our lives does not bind us together in any meaningful way.

"I've been told I have the lung capacity of a whale." He pats his chest. "Yeah, these guys certainly served me well when I free dived in Sri Lanka. Wait. Is it 'dived' or 'dove'? 'Dived' always sounds wrong to my ear, but I think that's actually correct. Doesn't matter. Point is, I love extreme sports! And speaking of marine biology, get this, once a week I volunteer at—"

"Hey, James!" I shout.

He stops speaking.

Hallelujah!

I soften my voice to a husky tone. "It *is* James, right?"

"James, yeah," he confirms with a dazzling smile.

I reach into his pants and find him more than ready for me, so I start to stroke.

"You're fucking gorgeous, James," I whisper in his ear and shiver when his stubbled cheek brushes against mine. His olive skin smells like ivory soap and shaving cream.

He tightens his strong arms around my back and pulls me closer.

I continue my ministrations below.

"Thank you," he says. "You're also—"

"And you seem like a nice guy." I interrupt.

He smiles. "I appreciate that. You seem like a—"

"But I'm not looking for a nice guy."

"No?"

"No. I'm not looking for *any* guy."

He looks down and laughs good-naturedly. "So why are we—?"

"I'm using you."

His laughter stops.

He removes my hand.

His dark eyes land on mine.

Whoa.

When he looks at me like that, I feel completely naked. In fairness, I *am* practically naked right now, but I mean more in the emotional sense, in the oh-my-God-he-can-see-deep-into-my-soul sense.

He stays completely still and silent, giving no clue as to what he's thinking or what he's going to do next.

"I'm not interested in anything beyond what we do here tonight, okay, James?" I continue. "Listen up because this is very important."

His non-response seems to say, "Go on."

"After tonight? If you ever run into me again, we pretend this never happened."

No reaction.

I repeat myself. "We pretend this never happened."

Still nothing.

Geez. For a guy who couldn't shut up a few minutes ago, he's now fully committed to his silence.

"Got it?" I say with more force than necessary, but suddenly, I can't get myself to look directly at him.

He closes the distance between us, climbs his fingers into my hair, and gives it a tug, gently forcing me to look up at him.

Tingles cascade down my spine.

He tilts his head slightly.

His lips are barely an inch from mine.

His warm breath caresses my skin.

"Then I guess we'll need to make tonight count, won't we?"

Now I'm the silent one.

All I can do is nod.

"Let's do this, Cold Brew."

Chapter One

*D*ing! *Ding! Ding!*

The clang of a buoy reverberates in my head.

Is it right next to me? Or miles away?

The sound rattles my brain one minute, then my ears strain to hear it the next.

My whole body startles.

"Oh my God, what was that?"

Something slithered against my leg. Was that an eel? A jellyfish? Aah, it just did it again. I'm freaking out. Under normal circumstances, I find all ocean creatures fascinating, thrilling even. But these are not normal circumstances.

Because right now, I'm treading water, surrounded by pitch-black sky, lost in the literal middle of nowhere with no clue how I got here.

Ding! Ding! Ding!

My heart starts to pound.

How long have I been in this spot? How deep is it?

"You need to start swimming," a voice says.

"You think I don't know that!?" I shout. "I *know* I need to start swimming. But you never tell me which way to go!"

The only response I get is the clang of the buoy.

Ding! Ding! Ding!

I could choose to swim in one direction and hope it leads

me back to shore, but what if I pick the direction that takes me farther out into the black water? What if I never find a place to land?

Wait a second.

This is familiar.

All of it.

The water. The black sky. The sounds. The confusion. This has all happened before. How do I keep ending up here? What is wrong with me? Why can't I…?

Eeeeng! Eeeeng! Eeeeng!

I shoot up in bed with a gasp.

Like every morning, I instinctively smack the crap out of my alarm clock until it stops blaring.

I know plenty of people who swear on those sweet bird-call alarms. Or the fancy light-emitting ones that simulate the glow of the rising sun, making your room steadily brighter and brighter until you crack your eyes open with a smile, give a little stretch, then yawn and pitter-patter down the hall to happily start your day.

Yeah no.

If bird sounds or sunshine did the trick for me, I would just open my damn window.

This girl needs her old-school alarm with the glaring red numbers and the blaring *eeng eeng* sound to rattle her bones and catapult her to consciousness.

I blink my eyes and steady my breath as I scan the unfamiliar room. It takes a few moments for me to realize where I am.

I'm in my new apartment—my friend Calliope's old apartment—in Philadelphia. I took over her lease a few weeks ago when she and my brother made the decision to cohabitate. They are disgustingly in love. This place is just on the verge of being out of my price range, but it was too great of an opportunity to turn down. Clearly, it doesn't quite feel like home yet. I make a mental note to hang up some artwork and photos this weekend. Putting my own touch on the place will help, right?

I roll over and reach for my phone. I know all the Zen experts say to never check your phone or social media first thing in the morning if you want any semblance of inner peace, but I just I can't seem to break this particular habit.

Ugh. Another text from my mother.

> **Mom:** Honey. Please call me back. It's been way too long since I've heard your voice. I'm starting to get worried.

I fire back a quick text just so she knows I'm alive.

> **Me:** Doing fine. First official day of work. Gotta go.

There's no way I'm calling and getting into a whole thing with her. I minored in psychology in college. The fact that these nightmares came back with a vengeance right after Mom started reaching out to me again is no coincidence.

I already know what she'll tell me. My serial monogamist mother has no doubt broken up with yet another Steve, and now she's craving some "girl time." Seriously, they're all named Steve, with an occasional Frank on the side. Different guy, same story. Every single time.

After a cold shower and a yogurt, I'm out the door and powerwalking toward the waterfront.

When I was a little kid, and my dad still cared enough to do overnight visits with us, I told him once that I had a nightmare. He shrugged and said, "Next time, just tell yourself it's a dream and wake up." It blew my mind that he was able to do that. Still does. But hey, he was also able to leave his family behind without a second thought—another thing that shouldn't be possible. So clearly, my dad is capable of great things.

I pick up my pace, turn a corner, and...

There she is.

The Philadelphia Aquarium.

A beautiful beacon surrounded by sparkling water.

Sunlight bounces off the glass exterior. Brightly colored flags on poles wave in the parking lot, advertising all the delights housed inside: Sea Lion Shenanigans! Penguins on Parade! Jelly Fish Jamboree!

For the past few months, I've been a volunteer. But today, I start my new, full-time position as an education specialist, manning the touch pools and leading "Creatures of the Coral" workshops for kids.

I take a deep breath when I realize once again how busy I'm about to be. I'm used to staying busy, but this is next level. Starting in just a few days, whenever I'm not here at the aquarium, I'll be working my tail off as a grad student at the University of Pennsylvania in their marine biology program, where I'm on scholarship. Two years of that intensity and I'll land my dream position at the world-renowned Coral Conservation Center in the Florida Keys.

That's the plan, and I'm sticking to it.

The aquarium is closed to guests on Mondays, so the lot is speckled with cars belonging to the staff and volunteers only. I exhale. It's the perfect day for me to ease into my new role without the pressure of caring for guests.

I press through the main doors with a huge smile on my face, only to feel it drop instantly when I spot Brendan Fraser beaming back at me.

No, not the guy from that *Mummy* movie. This Brendan Fraser works at the aquarium. His official position is Penguin Supervisor—yes, that is a real job title—but he's also one of the senior members on the team, so he's the one who's going to show me the ropes today. Can't say I'm thrilled about that. He's always given me vibes. And irritating nicknames.

"Louisiana!" he booms and opens his arms wide.

"Oh. Are we hugging?" I ask.

"We are," he says, then thinks better of it and retracts his arms slightly. "That is, if you consent to hugging. I am your superior, so you're correct. It's probably best to pause before we make any physical contact."

He goes completely still. Doesn't even blink.

"Brendan, what are you doing?" I ask.

"Waiting for your consent."

"To hug?"

"Yes."

I hesitate. "Uhhhhhhhh."

"Excellent." He takes my grunt as an affirmative and dives in for the embrace, smooshing my face directly into his neck stubble. "Congrats on the first day of the rest of your life, Louis CK."

"Um... Louis CK?"

"Ha. Yeah. I heard once that giving people nicknames is a good way to show them you care," he says into my hair.

Is it me, or is this hug endless? And sweaty. They pump the A/C in here like crazy. So why is this man so sweaty?

"Hm. Maybe that particular nickname isn't the best one to give me? Especially since you're my superior and all. And we're still touching." I mumble that last part under my breath and try not to choke on the scent of his Axe body spray.

"Did I hear you're into coral?"

"Can we, uh—can we be done with the hug now?" I blurt.

"Oh. Sure," he says, seeming surprised by my request.

He finally pulls back. My nostrils sing a song of joy at being released from his cologne-soaked stubbly neck.

"And, yes, I am *into* coral. I did my thesis on Coral Reef Research and Restoration. After I finish school, my goal is to head to Florida and—"

I cut myself off. I recently heard on a podcast that it's best to keep your goals quiet if you want to accomplish them.

Don't *tell* people your plans. *Show* them your results.

"Did you know that coral reefs cover less than one percent of the ocean floor but support about twenty-five percent of marine life?" he asks.

"Yes," I respond.

"Did you know that contrary to what many people assume, coral aren't plants—they're animals?"

"Yes." Is he for real right now? I just said I did my thesis on this exact topic.

"Did you know that coral reefs play a vital role in managing the planet's carbon dioxide levels and thus are crucial to the survival of life on Earth?"

"Dude, yes." I exhale, not doing a great job of hiding my exasperation.

His eyes dart around, and his voice lowers. "Probably best to only call me 'dude' after work hours, Louise. People might get the wrong idea." He gives me a weird wink.

Why this man thinks he will ever be seeing me outside of

work hours is beyond me.

"Understood, Brendan. I will refrain from calling you 'dude' in the future."

"I think that would be best."

Let it go, Lou, let it go.

Nope. Can't help myself.

"Hey, Brendan. You might not be aware of this, but I have my bachelor's degree in biology with a minor in psychology from UCLA. I also completed four summer internships during my college career: Aqua Quest, Camp Coral, The Center for Marine Mammals in Monterey and Cretaceous Mantua. And I just began a two-year marine biology graduate program at UPenn this week on full scholarship. Yes, I'm young and new to the aquarium, but

I'm well-versed in our field and not in need of lessons in Ocean Trivia 101."

"Yeesh," he huffs. "Was just trying to make conversation. Everyone is so touchy these days."

He tosses a small rectangular badge at me that spells out 'STAFF' in big, bold letters, then stomps away without waiting for my response.

Damn, why is it so hard to walk that line between being the "go with the flow" girl and the bold girl who's unafraid to stand up for herself?

I slip the lanyard over my head and jog after Brendan. He leans against the wall next to an unmarked steel door.

"Ready for your tour?" he says with far less enthusiasm than he had a moment ago.

"Sure." I flash him an apologetic smile. "I don't want to waste your time, though. I've been volunteering here most of the summer, so I do know my way around."

"You know what we want you to know, Louis Vitton."

"Hahaha another nickname," I burst out, attempting to get back on friendly terms with him.

He doesn't join me in the laughter, but for better or for worse, I do sense his mood improving now that he's resumed his perceived power over me.

"There are plenty of places the volunteers never go," he says with a conspiratorial lean in my direction. "Bet you didn't know that, did you, Louis Armstrong?"

He straightens, and I watch his chest puff out. Just like his penguin friends.

"I did not know that." It's a lie. I totally knew that.

"Well, today you get to see it all, lady."

"Very coooooool," I say and find that I actually mean it. Because I truly am excited to see the corners of the aquarium I've yet to experience. "Let's do it."

Brendan nods to the blinking light on the pad next to the door. "Alrighty then. Let's see if your badgey badge is working."

I lift it to the pad, and the door unlatches. He holds it open for me.

"Up we go, madam."

We stomp up the long flight of stairs and reach an open area with rubber flooring and large pools. I can't help it. A big cheesy grin spreads on my face as I take in all the various aquarists busy with their morning tasks.

"This is where the team has access to feed and care for the sharks and rays," he explains.

To our left, a woman gives me a small salute as she preps a small raft for a feeding. I wave back.

"This is also where our divers access the tanks to do maintenance and cleaning."

Brendan points to the right, where a suited-up diver is securing his mask and goggles.

Something about him grabs my attention.

His build.

The way he moves.

It all feels... familiar.

Goggle guy grabs a small brush and an algae scraper in one gloved hand and gives us a "hand symbol" sign with the other, then disappears under the water.

Weird.

"This smaller tank over here is off exhibit," Brendan continues, like nothing out of the ordinary just happened. "Mostly used for rehabbing injured animals. If you follow me through this hall here, you'll find..."

But I don't hear the rest of what he says.

Because my attention is captured by the gorgeous California Sea Lion in the rehab tank.

Her nose is pressed against the glass.

Her gaze is fixed on me, and I can't take my eyes off her.

For some reason, the moment I see her, it feels like coming home.

The skin on my face softens.

My shoulder blades slide down my back.

A warmth grows in my chest.

My breathing steadies.

And time itself seems to slow way, way down.

This must be what love at first sight feels like.

If I believed in such a thing.

I lift my palm to touch the glass, and I almost can't believe it, but she places her flipper right against mine.

My eyes well with tears.

How magnificent can one creature be?

"You coming?" Brendan's voice is suddenly right in my ear.

I startle, but my eyes stay glued to the sea lion. "Yes, in a minute, I'm just—"

"She likes you," a female voice says. I turn to see a silver-haired woman approaching with a smile.

"Oh. Hi. Dana, right?" I give her my full attention and reach out my hand. "Sorry, I've been volunteering for a few months, but there are still plenty of people—and animals—I haven't officially met."

She takes my hand and gives it a friendly squeeze. "No problem. Big place. Takes a while to get to know everyone. I started as a volunteer too. Many years ago." She chuckles. "But now I'm Head Aquarist, so it's sort of my job to know everyone."

My cheeks heat. "Oh. I didn't realize—I mean, my interview was with Andre, so—"

She waves off my embarrassment. "Recent development. Andre retired last week. I got promoted."

"Congratulations! So you're my new—"

"Hey! Lady! Try to keep up, will ya?" Brendan bellows from where he's pacing by the exit sign.

"Boss, yes," Dana finishes my sentence for me. "I'm your new boss." She jerks her head in Brendan's direction. "His too. Whether he wants to accept it or not." She keeps her back to him when she asks, "How's the tour going?"

"Great," I say, a plastic smile in place.

She places a warm hand on my shoulder. "Say no more. I'll take care of this."

"Dana, he's fine," I whisper. "I don't want to cause any—"

"Brendan?" Dana tosses her voice toward the exit. "Carry on. I'll take Louise on the rest of her tour."

"But," he sputters.

"Carry. On," she repeats in a tone that brooks no argument.

"Whatever," he murmurs, then pushes through the door without another word.

"Ah, Brendan." Dana sighs. "Amazing with penguins. People? Not so much. Come on. Let me show you the ropes."

Chapter Two

JAMES

"Hi. I'm James, and I'm an alcoholic."

"Hi, James." A chorus of voices rumbles off the white plaster walls of the community center. It's one of my favorite sounds on the planet. Those two words spoken by a few dozen people—some I know well, others not at all—translate to "we've been there, man" and "we're listening."

It's a relief every damn time I hear them.

I wipe a smudge of algae off my forearm. Normally, I'd shower right after my volunteer shift at the aquarium, but after the surprise of seeing Cold Brew there this morning, I skipped the suds and hauled ass to this meeting as fast as I could.

I really should stop calling her Cold Brew. Even in my head.

My buddy Kathleen gives me an encouraging nod from the learning chair at the center of the semi-circle. That's the name for the seat the meeting leader takes. She's absolutely killing it this month, supporting the hell out of everyone, which is a surprise to absolutely no one. Everyone knows Kathleen is the best.

"Sorry if I smell like seaweed, friends." I chuckle. The leathery-skinned, hairy new guy to my right leans in for a quick sniff, purses his lips, then gives me a thumbs-up. Not sure if that means I *don't* smell like seaweed or that I *do,* and he doesn't mind. Either way, he seems like a nice guy. I look forward to hearing his story at some point when he's ready to share.

I continue, "So uh. Quick update. A decision has been made.

I'm officially making the move to the Big Island to be with my girl."

"Hey!" Kathleen claps. "Good for you, boyo. We'll miss you of course, but good for you!"

"Thank you. But you're not getting rid of me completely. I'll be back every month or so, checking in on the businesses, popping into these meetings. I figure someone has to keep tabs on you, lady."

She smiles. "When do you leave?"

"After the holidays. The plan is to start the new year fresh."

"So you have a few months. That's good." Kathleen nods in acceptance. I may be imagining it, but are her eyes getting a bit misty?

I shake my head when I consider how much Kathleen has overcome. Back in the nineties, she somehow managed to leave her "good for nothing husband" in Dublin, moved to the States with her *seven* children, and raised them here all on her own. All this while getting and staying sober. She's in her sixties now, and the kids are grown, so she spends her days radiating her no-nonsense mom energy to anyone who needs it and running meetings like these. She's been a real gift in my life.

I continue, "So. The past few meetings I've been hemming and hawing about my family drama, but now that the move has been decided, I'm hoping you'll indulge me today as I get a little more... personal."

Kathleen lets out a good-natured chortle. "Personal? Boyo, last week I stood here and told you all how I showed up to a PTA meeting in the late nineties with no pants on." That gets a laugh from the room. "In this group, we're all about the personal."

I laugh too. "True. That's true."

"We're here to listen, Jamesy. You can't shock or embarrass us. Trust me."

Leathery new guy gives an affirmative grunt and slaps me on the shoulder.

"Thanks. Alright. Here goes then." I take a deep breath and let it all out. "Two months ago, the woman of my dreams walked into my bar, gave me fuck-me eyes all night, then dragged me into the walk-in refrigerator and proceeded to rock my world against some cold-ass beer kegs. Now I keep seeing her around town, I can't say a damn thing to her, and I feel like a total and utter chump."

Kathleen gasps. "Holy shit, boyo. I wasn't expecting that."

"Me neither," I say. "Believe me."

"You think you can just waltz into this meeting and spew your carnal filth all over the place?" she scolds.

"I'm sorry! I thought this was a safe place to—"

She cackles. "Course it is! Just yankin' yer chain, baby. Spill it. All yer filthy details are welcome here."

When I look around the semi-circle, I see a whole bunch of wide eyes and goofy smiles. Things can get real serious in this room. We hear so many tales of how alcohol brought people to their knees and how they've fought tooth and nail to get their lives back on track. Seems like me sharing salacious details from that night in the bar would provide some much-needed entertainment today.

Too bad I'm about to disappoint everyone.

"I'm sorry to say, that's as detailed as I'm going to get about the incident itself."

"The *incident*?" Kathleen scoffs. "Is that what the kids are calling it these days? In my day, we called them one-nighters. Booty calls. Road gigs. Wham, bam, thank you, ma'ams."

"Alright, alright." I hold up a hand.

"I could go on." Her eyes twinkle.

"I know you could. I'm just desperately trying to keep things classy right now."

She snorts. "Hard to keep it classy when you start your story with 'fuck-me eyes' and 'rocked my world against some cold-ass beer kegs.'"

"An excellent point. Regardless, out of respect for my... 'wham-bam-thank-you-ma'am' partner, I'm going to refrain from sharing further details. What I need is some guidance on how to get her out of my system."

"The Sex Addicts Anonymous group is down the hall, pal," Leather Man huffs.

"Thanks for that. Not addicted to sex, though." I turn to

Kathleen, "But hey, since he brought it up, permission to go further down the sex trail?"

"You don't need my permission. But what the hell is a sex trail, and how do I get on one?" Kathleen laughs at her own joke, then drops into a more serious tone and addresses the group. "Before we continue, friends, I feel like I should mention for the new people in the room that we're not exactly following meeting protocols right now. It's clear, though, that our pal Jamesy needs a little back-and-forth on his dating drama, and we do try to give people what they need when they need it. Okay by everyone?"

She holds for any objections. When she doesn't hear any, she gives me the floor again.

"Thanks, everyone. Alright, here's what I'm struggling with." I clear my throat. "Aren't guys supposed to be the ones who are cool with the love 'em and leave 'em approach?"

The men in the room give a collective shrug.

Not exactly illuminating.

"Because I've been in my share of locker rooms, and most guys will tell you that one-night stands are the best thing ever. A girl wants to have sex with you and never see you again? That's the dream!"

Kathleen opens her mouth to speak, but I cut her off before she can.

"Well, I'm telling you it's *not* the dream! It's a nightmare. Don't get me wrong, the sex itself was awesome, but the rejection afterward? Damn!"

I flash back to how she left the bar that night without a word. Like she does this sort of thing every day and I was just an amusing way to pass the time.

"Are you sure the sex was awesome?" a quiet woman with glasses asks. She comes to every meeting, but this is the first time I've actually heard her speak.

"Excuse me?"

She nervously braids and unbraids her side ponytail. "I don't mean to overstep, but you said the sex was awesome. For *you*. Are you sure it was awesome for her?"

"Yes! Absolutely!" But then my stomach drops out. "Oh shit.

You think maybe it wasn't awesome for her?!"

"Hard to say. I guess you'd have to ask her."

I shake my head. "Impossible. When I said I can't speak to her, I meant that literally. She said if I ever saw her again after that night to act like we'd never met."

"Ho ho ho!" Leather man laughs and slaps my back again. "Looks like you have your answer right there. You ain't got the goods, kid."

"I have the goods!"

The woman in the glasses gives me a doubtful look.

"No! I really think I do! She gave me all the signs! She was very—" I stumble over my words. "She definitely had several, um... Let's just say... she was into it."

Another look.

"She was! And I feel I should clarify for my own pride and reputation; she laid down the 'never speak to me again' rules *before* we..."

"Went all the way?" the woman fills in my blank.

"Sure. Yes. 'Went all the way' will work."

I feel like an awkward teenager talking about his first time, which is ridiculous. I am a thirty-two-year-old man. Obviously, I've had plenty of "times." I'm a father, for fuck's sake. Part of me wants to abandon this topic and let someone else take the floor, but I've already gone this far, and I need to get to the bottom of this for my own mental health. So I choose to continue with the semi-public humiliation.

Kathleen steps in. "I'm sure you're lovely in bed, Jamesy."

"Thanks, Kath."

"But even if you're not, you know everything we say in this room is confidential, so your secret is safe with us." She pauses a moment. "Want my opinion on the matter?"

"Always."

"Forget her. Any girl who can't recognize the wonderful man that you are isn't worth your time or energy."

"That's the thing, though. I can't forget her! It feels like the universe keeps putting her on my path."

"Or on your sex trail," Leather Man chortles.

I ignore him and continue, "First, she showed up at my bar. Then, the day after our... 'road gig,' I ran into her at Summer Fest, where my bar was serving brews. I waved to the woman, and she acted like I was insulting her simply by existing. And just before this meeting, while I was doing my regular volunteer shift diving at the aquarium, there she was again!"

"Alright. Jamesy, I gotta stop you there. I know in this group we all believe in a power greater than ourselves, but don't go full woo on me now," Kathy says.

"Full woo?"

"Yeah, boyo. You can't really believe 'the universe' is putting you two together for some sort of meant-to-be rendezvous, do you?"

"I do. I do believe that. It feels like the universe consciously put her in front of me—"

"Or *under* you..." The woman in glasses giggles then quickly schools her features. "Sorry."

"That's fine. To be clear, though, we were mostly standing that night. But the few times we did find a surface, she was on top of me."

She gives me a thumbs-up.

Why in the world did I feel a need to clarify that?

"Anyway, positions aren't important. What's important is that I've never felt a pull to someone like I do with this woman. I don't pretend to understand it. I just know it's there. The second I saw her, it was like we already knew each other—like our souls recognized each other. Like this was the moment the planets agreed many millennia ago that they would align just right so she and I could land at the time and same place to join hands, sync hearts, and walk the journey of life together."

"Oof." Leather man shakes his head and can't make eye contact with me.

"See?" I say and slam my ass back in the seat. "I'm a chump!"

"You're not a chump, boyo," Kathy says and gives my shoulder a squeeze. "I do think you could be putting the cart before the horse on this one, though. Perhaps you could have an actual conversation with this woman before you imagine you two are married and walking into the sunset?"

"She specifically asked me not to speak to her again. I feel like I have to respect that."

"True."

"Besides, we talked plenty that night."

Correction: *I* talked. I wince when I remember how much I talked.

Female friends have told me the guys in their lives shut down when they're nervous or uncomfortable. They go silent. Me? I'm the exact opposite. When I'm nervous, I will talk your fucking face off.

I let out a big breath and scrub my hands over my face. "This is nuts. I'm sorry for wasting your time, everyone. I just got done telling you all that I'm moving five thousand miles away in a few months. It's not like I can start something with someone new anyway. So what is the point of even stressing over this?"

Kathleen gives me a bright smile. "Never a need to apologize here, Jamesy. And the point is, you're a sensitive soul with a big, romantic heart. You're allowed to get swept away from time to time. Just don't let it bring you down."

"You're right, you're right." I've already taken too much of these people's time. "Thanks, everybody."

"Always a pleasure, boyo. Alright, friends, who would like to share next?"

Chapter Three

LOUISE

Calliope: Hey, women. Free tonight? I need your brilliant brains.

Mabel: I'm free, bitches! #MabelUnleashed

Me: Sure. What do you need?

Calliope: Planning session for Ralph's Surprise 29th! Woohoo! Where should we meet?

Mabel: Oh hellllllllllllz yes! My new place, bitches! 7pm! Housewarming AND Brainstorming, bitches! I'll take care of all refreshments! Be there, or be square, bitches! #MabelUnleashed

Wow. That was a lot of "bitches."

I'm in the lunchroom at the aquarium, checking my texts while Dana fields a phone call.

Ever since Mabel moved out of her parents' house last month, her vibe has been... interesting. She ends every text message with #MabelUnleashed. And apparently, she can't go a single sentence without gleefully calling us "bitches." I've been so tied up with prepping for school and moving that I haven't seen her in a while. It'll be good to catch up tonight in person.

Dana rushes into the room just as I'm pocketing my phone.

"Hey. Thanks for your patience," she says. "One of our big

donors for the AZA Philly Arts Fest was on the phone. She had some questions about the auction that the front desk couldn't answer. So cue me!"

"There's an AZA Philly Arts Fest?"

"Yep! Each year, the week before Thanksgiving the aquarium, the zoo and the science museums in the city come together and throw a big arts festival to raise money for an animal-related cause. This year it's called 'Brew at the Zoo.' We're especially excited about this one since all proceeds are going to combat ocean pollution."

"That sounds amazing."

"Well, we'd love to have you contribute."

"I'd be happy to," I say. "I just don't do... art."

That same pang of sadness I feel whenever I say some form of "I don't do art" moves through me.

I ignore it.

Like I always do.

She waves me off with a hand. "Oh, that's fine. We call it an arts festival, but people offer up all kinds of things! Carol from Accounting commissions an artist she loves to paint her favorite animals on exhibit and we auction them off. Jamie in Education creates these narrow quilts with beautiful green and blue fabrics for people's dining room tables. She calls them wave runners! Last year Brendan created these little accessories for kids' sneaker bottoms so they can walk like penguins. Calls them waddlers! And those of us without a creative bone in their bodies"—she points at herself and laughs—"we rip tickets, man the raffle table, assemble gift bags... you get the idea. Feel free to give it some thought and let us know down the line what you might want to do."

"Sounds good," I say.

"Want to follow me back up to the shark tank? I was thinking you might enjoy assisting me with something before we officially wrap the tour."

"Of course. Whatever you need, I'm your girl," I say. We exit the break room and make our way up the stairwell to where we can access the shark tank. "I have to thank you again, Dana. It's been really cool spending the morning with you."

"Oh, it's been my pleasure," she says, then laughs when she turns to the smaller rehab tank on the other side of the large space.

I follow her gaze and see that same beautiful sea lion working hard to get our attention again. My attention specifically. She zooms to the top of the tank and spirals down. Then repeats the motion. Then again. She presses her nose against the glass like she doesn't want us to walk away.

It's then I realize she's missing part of her right flipper.

Dana laughs again. "Wow, you're really showing off for Louise today, aren't you, Meilani?"

"Meilani?" I say. "What a beautiful name."

"She's named in honor of Bethany Meilani Hamilton."

I rack my brain for a moment.

Dana answers my unspoken question. "Pro surfer? Lost her arm in a shark attack?"

"Right, right. Of course. Incredible story." I pause. "Is that what happened to Meilani here?" I nod toward her torn flipper.

"Well, I haven't seen her on a surfboard yet," she jokes. "But yeah. Shark bite. She's a tough little lady, though. She survived the bite but washed ashore in California pretty malnourished in the spring. NOAA sent her here to rehabilitate."

Dana smiles warmly at the animal, but Meilani still only has eyes for me. I'm struck by how elegant she is—how openhearted she seems—despite what she's been through and what she's lost.

"Are there any plans for her to be released back into the ocean?"

"We're hopeful. But Mei-Mei has a lot of work to do here before that can happen."

I place my palm to the glass again. Meilani lifts her flipper in response. A little laugh escapes me.

"Hah. It's almost like we're holding hands," I say.

Dana tilts her head to the side. "Hmm."

"Hmm what? What hmm?" I snap out of my sea lion-induced stupor.

"Kind of a crazy idea over here. I know you'll be busy with

the touch pools and teaching classes for the kiddos, but maybe you'll make a point to come up and spend time with Meilani when you can?"

"Wait. Are you serious?"

"Completely serious, yes. You interned with the CMM team in Monterey, right? So you have a little experience with pinnipeds?"

"Some pinnipeds, yeah. I assisted with our walrus exhibit, and I ran the Q & A session after the Seal Life documentary they had running. Can't say I worked with any of the sea lions directly, though. My focus has always been more on echinoderms and coral life." "That's fine. Meilani has a team of trainers dedicated to her care. There would be nothing you'd need to do other than offer her your focus and friendship."

"Sure. Oh my gosh, I'd love that!" Tingles of excitement roll through me.

"Good. Seems she'd like that too." Dana's gaze toggles between Meilani and me. "She's been slow to trust our team. Hasn't been responding as well as we would like. But she certainly seems smitten with you. Maybe the extra time and attention would be helpful."

As if on cue, Meilani does a flip, then nuzzles the glass right beside me again, making us both laugh.

"I'm pretty smitten with her too," I say and press my nose briefly against hers. "I'll see you again real soon, sweet girl. Okay?"

I blow her a kiss, then immediately feel like a doof. Because I have no idea what the appropriate signals are when working with a sea lion.

I have a lot to learn if I want to work with Meilani in any official capacity.

"Alright," Dana says. "You ready?"

"Ready for what?"

She guides me over to the shark tank, removes a long red pole from a hook on the wall, and hands it to me.

My mouth goes dry when she gestures to the raft the other aquarist was prepping earlier.

"Time for me to feed the crew. Hop in! You can give me an assist."

Ding!
Ding!
Ding!

I'm transported back to my dream, treading black water, my heart pounding a staccato rhythm in my chest.

"You want me to get on that raft? In the water?"

"Well, yeeeeeeah." She stretches the words like she's speaking to a timid creature. "I know this isn't an official part of your role here, but I thought you might enjoy the opportunity to feed the animals with me. First up is Boris, our whale shark."

I'm still and silent.

She softens her voice even more. "Louise, is there a problem?"

"Nope!" I insist. "No problem. I have no problems whatsoever!"

But my feet remain frozen to the rubber floor.

Because there most definitely *is* a problem. A *big* problem. And try as I might, I can no longer ignore it.

I am a marine biologist who is petrified of the water.

Chapter Four

LOUISE

I'm standing outside a newish apartment complex in Manyunk later that day, staring at a red door flanked by stone flowerpots filled with yellow chrysanthemums.

"Thanks for meeting me here," Calliope says.

"Sure," I respond. "Happy to help."

"Speaking from decades of experience, though," I continue, "My brother is a pretty tough one to surprise. So I have my doubts that this birthday plan of yours is ultimately going to work."

"He'll be surprised," Calliope responds with her usual abundance of confidence. "The fact that we're going all out for twenty-nine is surprising in itself. You expect a surprise party for thirty! But twenty-nine? Nah." She rises up on her tiptoes and peers into the small rectangular window, then lowers her heels and rubs her hands together like a cartoon villain. "I'm uber curious to see her new digs. Aren't you?"

"Uh. I guess so?"

I'm distracted by the cutesy wooden sign hanging on the door. I take a step back to ensure I read the hand-painted cursive correctly the first time. Yup. It actually does say "Home is Where the Pants Aren't."

I look over my shoulder and spot Mabel's green VW bug in the lot. "You did ring her doorbell, right?"

"What kind of a question is that?" Calliope scoffs.

"A reasonable one?" I shoot back.

Calliope has only been dating my brother for a few months so we're still getting to know each other, but we already squabble like sisters.

Truth be told, I love it.

"Let me guess," she continues. "You're also that punk who walks up and presses the elevator button like she's doing everyone a favor when five people are already standing there waiting for it to arrive."

"Of course," I say. "I'm not counting on other people to get me where I want to go in life. The only person I can count on is me."

"That's a depressing life motto if I ever heard one. Bad day?"

I consider how to answer that question and come up with, "*Challenging* day."

"Want to talk about it?"

"Nope."

"Of course you don't. Anyway"—Calliope sighs—"to answer your question, yes, I rang her bell just as you pulled up. She shouted, 'Just a minute!' but that was..." She checks the time on her phone. "Four and a half minutes ago."

"She's probably doing that speed-cleaning thing people do when they have last-minute guests," I offer. "We should have just met at a bar."

And not for the first time—or even the hundredth time—in the past few months, James the handsome bartender's face flashes in my mind. And for the hundredth time, I shove that image right back out.

Calliope shrugs. "You saw her texts. She wanted to host."

"Where the hell is this girl?" I throw my hands up and give the door a hearty pound. Something I should've done five minutes ago.

When I turn back to Calliope, she's staring at me like it's her job. You'd think as a scientist, I'd be cool with being studied, but I'm not.

"What?" I huff.

"Your vibe tonight is tweaked."

"My vibe is not tweaked."

"You're tweaky deaky eggs and beaky, baby."

I give her a look. Because what in the world do you say to

something like that?

"Just trying to get you to laugh, Anderson."

She pushes my shoulder, and I stumble. Calliope is the definition of 'small but mighty.' She's got freakish strength hiding in that itty bitty body.

We both turn to face the door again.

"What did you mean before when you said, 'Of course you don't?'" I ask.

"Huh? And ew, I do not like that impression you just did of me."

"Sorry. You asked me before if I wanted to talk about my day. When I said 'no' you got all snarky and said 'of course you don't.'"

"Oh. You never want to talk about your own issues. You're awesome at encouraging and counseling your friends, but you'd never in a million years let us do that for you."

"That is completely..."

True, the voice in my head says. *That's completely true.*

Do I tell her that on my very first day as a full-time staff member at the aquarium, I completely froze when my boss asked me to join her in the water? That my heart pounded like crazy, and I stood there in complete wide-eyed silence until she absolved me from joining her on the raft?

When it becomes clear I'm not going to finish my statement, Calliope pats me on the back and smiles.

She's letting me off the hook.

"I'm sorry to be... tweaky." I sigh. "I'm just hangry."

"Well, say no more, sister friend! Hanger we can handle!" She whips out her phone and scrolls. "Mabes said she was ordering food. Check out this text she sent me an hour ago."

I take the sparkly purple phone from her and read the end of their text thread out loud. "I like my wings like I like my men. Spicy! Hope you do too. #MabelUnleashed."

Calliope takes her phone back and chuckles. "Just my opinion, but if Mabel was *really* unleashed, she would already be living with Wally. We know it's only a matter of time before they move in together, so why delay the inevitable?"

"The point is that Mabel is smart," I counter. "And moving in with a man too fast is the death knell of a relationship. She's an independent, bug-loving woman who doesn't need a man to take care of her."

Calliope takes a deep breath and launches into her rebuttal. "Excuse me, sister friend—"

"Please stop calling me 'sister friend.'"

"Aw," she whines. "It's so cute!"

"Is it, though? It makes me feel like we're in a plural marriage. And the fact that your beloved is my brother makes that scenario hella creepy."

"It's a term of endearment, ya dork! You're my friend. And for all intents and purposes, you are my sister-in-law. Hence, you are my sister friend."

"Fine."

I've learned that giving up is the easiest option when sparring with Calliope.

She smiles triumphantly. "Fantastic. May I return to my outrage at your asinine insinuation about female freedom?"

"You may."

"A woman's decision to cohabitate has nothing to do with her intelligence or independence. I too am an independent woman, but I moved in with Ralph right away. And that decision certainly hasn't been the 'death knell of a relationship' for us. And for the record, he does not 'take care of me.'" She purses her lips and reconsiders what she just said. "Well, *sexually* speaking, he does. Obviously. I mean, who would waste their time with someone who didn't take care of them sexually? Oh Lou, can I tell you the brilliant thing he did to me this weekend with his—"

"No, you cannot!"

I nip the brother sex story in the bud. I've already heard way too many of those.

She shrugs. "Your loss." She does a few bunny hops in another attempt to peek through the window. "Okay, this wait is excessive. I'm ringing the bell again."

She does, and we stand in silence for a moment.

I sigh. "I just think—*in general*—we women need to be careful. If we get too comfortable with a guy too soon, we're in for a world of trouble more often than not. That's why I am one-hundred-percent off relationships. Been there, done that. From here on out, it's flings only for me."

At that, the door flies open, revealing Mabel wearing a saucy smile.

And nothing else.

She croons, "Did someone say trouble?

Chapter Five

LOUISE

"Ahhh!!" Calliope screams.

"Ahhhhh!" Mabel shouts back. "Why are you yelling at me!?"

"Because you're naked!!"

Mabel casts her eyes down her completely clothes-free body. "Huh. I am! Cool, right?"

"You seem surprised," I offer. "Did you not realize that you are one hundred percent in the buff?"

She giggles. "I guess I momentarily forgot? Nudity is my natural state now, so believe it or not, *wearing* clothes actually feels odd."

"I take it this is a new development?" I ask.

"Yup! I'm a nudist now," Mabel says proudly. "Ever since I got my own place! I can't stop reveling in the freeeeeeeedom!" She accompanies freeeeeedom with a shoulder shimmy that keeps on giving long after she intentionally stops shaking. "Oh, hi, Mr. Reynolds!"

She waves happily to an elderly man a few doors down who is frozen by the unexpected strip show he's receiving. The key in his hand is frozen in midair.

"That's Mr. Reynolds," Mabel explains as she turns back to us. "He's so nice. All of my neighbors are!" She waves to him again as he finally shuffles his way inside, eyes wide as saucers. "Well? What are we waiting for? Let the party planning begin!"

"After you." I bow my head toward Calliope.

This may be the first time I've ever seen her speechless.

We dutifully trail behind Mabel's bare bum as she leads us through the door and into her open concept kitchen.

Once we land, she whips around with the flourish of a game show host. "So? What do you think?"

"About the apartment? Or your genitals!?" Calliope bursts.

"Oooooooooh," Mabel shudders. "Can we not? The word 'genitals' makes me feel weird."

"Genitals!" Calliope wields the word like a weapon.

"Oooooooooh," Mabel shudders again. "I would think the lady who writes dinosaur porn could come up with some sexier terminology for the lady land, no?"

Calliope ignores the dig—as much of a dig as you'll get from kindhearted Mabel—and parrots back way louder than necessary, "The word genitals makes *you* feel *weird*."

"Oooooooooh."

"Stop shuddering!" Calliope scolds. "You know what makes *me* feel weird, Mabel?"

"What?"

"Showing up at my friend's new apartment to find her hoo-hah and gazongas flapping in the breeze!"

"Oh, is it too breezy in here for you?" Mabel whips her body left and right, trying to gauge the airflow. "Hm, you may be right. I'll turn up the A/C. It is September, after all."

Mabel sashays to the thermostat and makes the adjustment.

At this point, I feel the need to step in and back Mabel up. I nudge Calliope. "Gazongas? Flapping? Are you sure you're a writer, sister friend?"

"How are you so comfortable with this?" Calliope marvels.

I shrug. "Can't say I relish the opportunity to socialize with my friends while they're in their full naked glory, but whatever. I took a ton of figure drawing classes in college, where nude models were the norm, so I'm used to it."

"Louise!" Mabel enthuses. "I didn't know you're an artist! Why did you never say something?"

"Because I'm not. Not anymore."

"Once an artist, always an artist, isn't that what they always say? What's

your medium? Pencils? Paints? Pastels? Ooh! Change of plans!" Mabel squeals and claps. "I have a chez lounge thingy-ma-bobby in my mantis room! I'll go lie down on it so you can paint me! We'll be like Rose and Jack in *Titanic*!"

"No, thank you, Mabel," I say with as much calm as I can muster. "And dare I ask what the hell is a mantis room?"

Calliope nudges me and whispers, "You don't want to know."

"But I'll commission you!" Mabel pleads. "With money! I don't expect you to work for free."

"Mabel, no."

"Pleeeeease, Lou? As a gift for Wally! He'll love it!"

"I am not a painter. I do not paint anymore. Ever. For the love of God, can we please change the subject!?"

You could hear a pin drop after that.

They count on me to be the cool friend.

The reasonable friend.

The one who keeps calm under pressure.

Well, not today, apparently.

Mabel eventually breaks the silence.

"It's because I'm naked, huh? All this tension? You're right. I absolutely should have warned you that I'm a nudist before you came over. If you would like, I can absolutely go put on a thong and some pasties."

"That would be a *start*," Calliope says diplomatically.

"Fantastic. That's what I'm going to do then. Back in a flash!" Mabel hustles toward what must be her bedroom. Before she's out of sight, though, the doorbell rings, and she calls over her shoulder, "Could one of you get that? I ordered some goodies for us! #MabelUnleeeeeeashed!"

"I'll get it!" I shout and leap for the door.

As soon as I open it, though, I wish I hadn't.

Because standing on the other side is my one-night stand.

Chapter Six

JAMES

"Hey, Cold Brew," I say and instantly regret it when I see the blank look on her face. "I mean Louise. Lou? Which do you prefer? Never mind. Look, I'm just as surprised to see you as you are to see me." I lean back to double-check the house number. "This is Mabel's place, isn't it? Do I have the wrong address? Also. How, uh, how have you been?"

Christ, man. Stop talking.

"This is Mabel's apartment. She's just, um—she's putting her thong and pasties on."

I swallow. "Who's doing what now?"

The sound of heavy footsteps come from inside the building. A voice calls out, "You know what? I'm thinking our pal Mabel Unleashed may actually be on to something with the—Whoa! 'Adventure Bar James!' What's up, fella?"

"Calliope," I say with a slight bow of my head. "Good to see you again."

"Likewise."

Louise whips her head back and forth between us. "Wait. How do you two know each other?"

"Ralph and I go to Adventure Bar all the time," Calliope says. "James makes the best drinks. You have to try one sometime. Oh, duh! You already had some. Don't you remember over the summer when you and Mabel came with me and—"

"Yup, yup, I remember." Louise looks at the ground. Anywhere but at me, it seems. "The drinks were… fine."

"Better than fine, if you ask me," I mumble.

Calliope cocks her head to the side, watching our interaction. "Anywaaaaay, I have to say, James, it's kinda weird seeing you outside of the bar."

"Is it?"

"Yeah. You know that feeling when you're a kid and you unexpectedly see your middle school teacher buying Hanes-Her-Way low-rise briefs at Walgreens, so you immediately dart to hide behind the cardboard cutout of Rihanna endorsing CoverGirl Wetslicks Fruit Spritzers? And then your prepubescent brain explodes and spins out of control because you're thinking, 'whoa, I never considered the fact that Ms. Henderson buys underwear! Or even has a butt, for that matter?' So you hope like hell she doesn't catch you quaking behind that cardboard cutout of Rihanna because you honestly don't know who will be more embarrassed: you, the cowering kid, or her, the granny-panty-purchasing educator?" She takes a breath. "It's kind of like that."

I laugh. "Can't say I've had that *exact* experience, but I think I hear what you're saying."

"Basically, I've never imagined you exist outside the bar, so this is trippy!"

"Well, if it makes things less trippy for you," I offer, "I am here on bar business."

"Oh yeah?"

"Yup. Mabel hired us to set up a spread for your get-together tonight."

"Score! I love Adventure Bar food!"

I reach down for the silver cooler at my feet.

"No, thank you," Louise says.

I rise back to my full height.

"No, thank you?" I repeat.

"Yeah," she shrugs. "We're not that hungry."

"Speak for yourself, missy!" Calliope admonishes. "Besides, you told me like two minutes ago how hangry you are."

"Oh, hanger is the worst," I say. "Can't have you ladies hangry when there's something we can do about it."

"You know what? I'm actually gonna go," Louise says. "I have a bunch of reading I need to do for school."

"No way! I need you to party plan!" Calliope says. "Just give me an hour and then I will release you to all your fish studies, promise. Mabel, James is here!"

Calliope heads into the apartment, leaving Louise and me facing off in the doorway.

She's physically blocking me from entering.

"May I?" I look her directly in the eyes and nod toward the entrance.

Louise stays as still as a statue.

"Sister friend!" Calliope shouts from inside the apartment. "Would you let the man in, please?"

I know she said she was only interested in that one night, but damn, was it so bad that she's embarassed to be in my presence now? Was the new guy at the AA meeting right and I don't "have the goods?"

No. That's impossible. I was there that night and neither of us was complaining.

She blows out a breath and finally steps aside.

"I thank you," I say and pick up the cooler.

So, she has regrets about what happened between us.

Fine.

I certainly don't.

I was hired to do a job here today, so I'll get in and get out.

But apparently not without getting a little saucy. A surprising energy rises up in me, one that says she's not going to dismiss me – or this spark between us – so easily.

"In case you're wondering," I say to Calliope, but my awareness is focused entirely on Louise, "like your middle school teacher, I, too, have a butt. I also wear underwear." As I slide past Louise, my hip brushes against hers, and I whisper in her ear, "Sometimes."

Chapter Seven

LOUISE

I'm left alone in the foyer, holding the door open for no one.

Goose bumps ripple across my skin.

Did this guy just show up to a work engagement commando?

Before I can think about what I'm doing, I whip around and shoot my gaze directly to his man region—as if I have X-ray vision and can confirm what is or is not under his jeans. It's only a split-second glance, but when my eyes shoot back up to meet his, it's clear I've been caught.

He winks.

I scowl and slam the door behind me.

He heads deeper into the apartment while I begrudgingly follow.

"James!" Mabel breezes into the room and dives straight into James's arms like they're besties. "Thank you so much for doing this."

"Of course!" They rock back and forth in a warm hug. "Anything for my buddy's girl."

I breathe a sigh of relief when they pull apart, and I see that Mabel is fully dressed now.

She's sporting her typical tank top and skort. I don't even know where she finds these things. Until I met Mabel, I thought skorts were left back in the nineties. Unless you're a professional golfer or tennis player. And Mabel is neither of those things.

Calliope watches James and Mabel, confusion etched on her

face. Then the proverbial light bulb goes on. "Ohhhhhh, you and Wally go way back, right?"

"That's right," James says. "I wouldn't be standing here today if it weren't for that guy."

"Wally saved his life!" Mable chirps.

"Ha. Okay," I say.

"No, really," James says. "Wallace saved my life. Summer after senior year of high school. I nearly drowned, and he pulled me to the surface."

"How's that possible? You're a swimmer! You free dived in Sri Lanka. You have the lung capacity of a whale! You love extreme sports!"

He smirks. "Someone's been taking notes on me, I see."

"No, I have not been taking notes, *James*. I just—I remember you said that you—ugh, forget it."

Calliope's brows scrunch together. "What the hell is going on here? Have you two hung out?"

"No!" I shout at the same time James says, "Yes."

Calliope chuckles. "So is that a 'no' or a 'yes'?"

My eyes fly to his in a you-better-not-say-a-single-word stare.

After a moment of silence, James clears his throat and turns his full attention on Mabel.

"Is this a good place to set up?" He gestures to the kitchen island.

"Yup. Here is perfect!"

Mabel frantically clears the surface of candles and potpourri. Potpourri: another thing I thought was a thing of the past until I met this new friend of mine.

Welp, if he's going that way, I'm officially heading in the opposite direction.

I plop myself down on a floral-patterned loveseat, which has to be a hand-me-down from Mabel's parents.

From across the room, I watch as James lines up a series of silver shakers and small liquor bottles. He dumps a bag of lemons and limes into a bowl and starts slicing fruit and mixing drinks.

I try my darnedest not to watch his forearms flex while he works.

"Can I help?" Mabel asks him. "You know I'm a helper."

He chuckles. "I know you are. Why don't you unwrap that charcuterie board and line up those crackers for me?"

"Sure thing, dingaling!"

Dingaling?

Mabel and James are operating like a weird, well-oiled machine. I guess they've gotten close since she started dating Wally.

"Love the new place!" James says while he slices.

"Aw thank you, friend!" Mabel chirps.

I startle when Calliope sits next to me.

"Staring much?"

"What? Who? I don't know what you're—"

She smiles. "Come on. Gimme the scoop, woman! What's the story with you and James? You've been all sorts of jittery since he arrived."

"I'm not jittery."

She places a hand on my bouncing knee then smirks when it settles.

"I need a cracker." I hoist myself from the couch and sidle next to Mabel at the counter, making her the delightful buffer between James and me while avoiding further inquisition from Calliope.

Two birds. One stone.

"A pro tip for you, James," Mabel says as she assembles meats and cheese on the wooden board. "In the future, if you're looking to compare yourself to a creature with incredible lung capabilities, what you really want to reference is a scorpion."

"No way," I interject mid-cracker bite. "Blue whales have the largest lung capacity in the world."

"Well, yeah! Whales are massive. They *should* have the largest lung capacity in the world. But a scorpion? A tiny little scorpion can hold its breath for six days. Now *that's* impressive."

"Agreed," James says. "Hey Mabes, could you grab me some ice?

"You bet!"

Why am I so irritated by this easy rapport he has with Mabel?

Mabel moves to the freezer, leaving an open space between James and me at the kitchen island.

He immediately steps closer to me.

Or did I step closer to him?

I swear I can hear my own heart pounding.

Mabel continues to chatter away from the opposite side of the kitchen, totally oblivious to the tension between the two of us.

"Scorpions can also live a full year without food, they glow under ultraviolet light, and they perform one hell of a dancing ritual before they mate."

"Thongs and pasties!" Calliope shouts from the couch. "That's what we need to make Ralph's birthday special!"

I nearly choke on my cracker.

We all stare at her in confusion.

Calliope explains, "Sorry. Mabel said dancing ritual, then I thought back to the nudity thing, and voilà, an idea was born!"

"You want to hire *strippers* for my brother's party? No thank you."

Calliope joins us at the kitchen island and pops a slice of cheese in her mouth.

"What's up, prudey with the attitudey? A few minutes ago, you were all, 'I grew up painting people in the nude. Naked bodies are no big deal.'"

"I am not a prude. And did you just mock me in a British accent? I don't have a British accent."

"True, but sometimes it feels like you should."

"What?"

She shrugs. "You have this fancy, all-knowing vibe. You could totally be British."

"She totally could!" Mabel plunks a bowl of ice cubes down on the counter in front of James. "Here ya go, buddy."

"Thanks, lady." He gives Mabel a wink and adds the ice to the silver cup he's been filling with liquor and lime juice.

"That makes absolutely no sense," I murmur to no one in particular.

James slaps another silver cup on top of the first one and shakes with gusto.

He takes the noisy opportunity to lean close to me and whisper, "We both know you're not a prude. Should I speak up?

I'm happy to defend your honor if you'd like."

Tingles cascade over my body when his breath skates over my skin.

"That um, that won't be necessary."

Distance. I need distance.

I hop onto a barstool next to Calliope.

"Strippers?" I say. "Really?"

She scoffs. "No, Louise. I will not be hiring strippers for your brother's surprise party. That would be super inappropriate."

I exhale. "Good. Glad we can agree on that much."

"But *burlesque*! Burlesque would be amazeballs!"

"Oooooooooh!" Mabel shudders with delight. "Burlesque!"

James rims three chilled glasses with salt, places them in front of us, and fills them to the brim with pale-green frothy goodness.

"Yum! Thank you, James!" Mabel squeals and lifts her glass high. "Cheers, friends!"

"Cheers!" Calliope and I lift and clink with her.

"Ohmuhgah this drink is amazing," Calliope moans after a sip.

She's not wrong. This is all sorts of delicious.

So is the man who poured it.

Not that I'd ever admit that out loud.

"Pour one for yourself, James!" Calliope says. "We could use a man's perspective on the party planning."

"Actually, I, uh… I don't drink."

He steals a quick glance at me.

"A bartender who doesn't drink?" Calliope says. "That's surprising."

"Yeah well, I'm a surprising guy."

He leans on the counter like he intends to stay a while.

"Don't you need to get back to work?" I ask.

"Sure. But I have a minute or two to bounce some ideas with you ladies. So Ralph is your brother, huh?"

"Maybe."

"I've met him a few times at the bar with this one." He gestures to Calliope. "Solid guy."

"The best guy!" Calliope corrects.

"He's fine, I guess," I mumble.

Geez. Leave it to me to choose the one guy on the planet who is incapable of a one-night stand. All I wanted was one night to be reckless and fun with no strings attached.

But this guy seems determined to get to know me.

"And we're hiring strippers for his birthday?" James asks.

"No," I correct and point at myself and the girls. "*We* are not hiring strippers."

"Alright, people." Calliope gets her stern voice on. "Let's get one thing straight. There is a big difference between stripping and burlesque-ing."

"Ooooooh, burlesque-ing." Mabel shudders again and claps her hands.

"Mabel. Are you going to do the shudder thing every time I say the word burlesque?" Calliope scolds.

"No. No, I'm not. Sorry."

Calliope continues, "Not that there is anything wrong with stripping, of course, they're just two very different practices. Louise, are you familiar with burlesque?"

"Yeah. It's a variety show, typically involving a striptease. It's usually comic in nature and seeks to make social commentary of some kind through parody and exaggeration."

"Exactly!"

"Whoa," James cocks his head at me.

"Oh yeah," Calliope says, "Lou here knows all the things. FYI, if you're ever doing a trivia night at the bar, you want this woman on your team."

"I'll keep that in mind." James smiles.

I stare down into my drink.

Calliope slaps her hands on the counter. "Alright, that's settled. Burlesque it is! Comedy and nudity are two of Ralph's favorite things, so it's perfect."

"He's an astronomer," I remind her. "Isn't astronomy one of his favorite things?"

"True. Ooh, I wonder if there are any outer space-inspired troupes out there! Imma research!"

Calliope starts scrolling on her phone.

"You know, my college offered an Intro to Burlesque class," Mabel says between sips of her drink. "And I have to say, now that I'm a nudist, I'm kicking myself for never taking that course."

"Colleges offer burlesque classes?" I ask.

"Sure! Didn't yours?"

"I don't know. I stayed focused on what would make me a marine biologist. Didn't do many extracurriculars."

"Well, it's good to be well-rounded. That's what I keep telling Chloe. Now that she's a junior, we've started looking at schools for her, and let me tell you, the smorgasbord of studies out there these days is just wild! Did you know NYU has a Taylor Swift course?"

We collectively shake our heads.

"It's true!"

Chloe is Mabel's teenage half sister. She just found out about her a few months ago. But because she's Mabel and wonderful, she dived headfirst into building an awesome relationship with her.

"Ah! This troupe looks perfect!" Calliope squeals. "I'm sending them a message."

"So." James drums his fingers on the countertop. "Where will you be having this striptacular surprise birthday party?"

"That's an excellent question," Calliope says while emailing. "Pretty sure we'll need a place with a private room."

"How about having a whole place to yourselves?" he suggests as he shakes up a fresh batch of margaritas.

"I mean, yeah, we'd love that." She presses send. "Not sure something like that is in the budget, though."

"How about free? Is free in the budget?" James asks. "Because I know a guy with a place."

Calliope gasps. "You're offering us your place?"

"Sure."

I shake my head. "Uh-uh. No way."

"Why not?" Calliope asks.

"Because it was only supposed to be one night!"

My voice echoes through the still mostly unfurnished apartment.

The margarita shaking stops.

Well, that certainly shut everyone up.

Shit.

"What was only supposed to be one night?" Calliope says with a smile.

Mabel just stands there, shifting her gaze back and forth between James and me like she's watching a tennis match.

James gestures to me, giving me the floor to explain myself.

He thinks I'm just going to spill the beans on what happened between us?

No way.

I clear my throat. "Sorry for yelling just now." I pause. "Um. Thank you for your generous offer, James, but no thank you. We need somewhere closer to Philly. Your bar is in Doylestown. That's quite a hike from Ralph and Callie's new place in the city. It'll be way easier to surprise Ralph if we stay local."

"So we'll have it at my other location," he says as he pours the drinks into a pitcher.

I stare at him. "You own two bars now?"

"I do. One in Doylestown. One in Manyunk. I'm also working on creating an excursion tour company focused on mountain climbing and deep-sea diving."

"How old are you?" I marvel at him.

"Thirty-two."

"Wow. You've accomplished so much for being so—I mean, that's really..." I don't have the words for how impressive that is, so I settle on another breathy, "Wow."

"Glad you're impressed."

"Didn't say I was impressed," I retort, full-voiced this time.

"Didn't have to." He smiles.

Ugh. This guy.

Mabel chimes in. "His excursion company is going to be called 'The Highs and Lows.' Isn't that cute? You know, because of the high mountains and the deep ocean? And just... the ups and downs of life?"

"Hmm." That's all I manage to say.

"Gosh, Lou, you didn't think I asked James to deliver food and drinks to us all the way from Doylestown tonight, did you?

I may be #MabelUnleashed, but I'm not #MabelEntitledAsshole! At this time of day, it would take him fifty minutes to get here from the original location. That is if he went west on 276. Pretty sure he could shave off a full minute, though, if he opted to take Lower State Road and then merge onto 309 going south. But merging onto 309 South can be a real bitch no matter what time of day, so I actually wouldn't recommend that even with the one-minute win."

Is Mabel already drunk after only a few sips?

Ask me how I know all this," Mabel says, bubbling over with giddiness.

"No, thank you, my friend."

"I *know* this because Wally and I are always trying to lessen the travel time between here and the arboretum. You know, for the plentiful booty calls we engage in." She pauses mid-giggle. "Wait. Can you call it a booty call if you're in a loving, exclusive relationship? I guess so, right? Booty is still booty with or without a commitment, yeah?"

"I like that," James says. "Could be a tee shirt slogan. 'Booty is still booty with or without a commitment.'"

He gives me a wink and moves the extra food and drinks to the refrigerator.

"Anyway," Mabel continues, "I'm so lucky Wally's supportive of my choice to live here because lordy, I love living here! It's hip and fun and safe and way more affordable than living in the city proper. I get to enjoy the charms of small city life without all the hustle and bustle of downtown. And it's convenient! All I have to do is hop on 76 East for a cool nineteen minutes and boom! I'm at the museum for work!"

"You're still an entomologist, right?" I ask, knowing full well that she is.

"Of course! Bugs for life!"

"So why do you sound like a cross between a hyped-up real estate agent and a human GPS demonstration right now? PS, you don't need Wally to 'support' your decision to live here. Your decisions are yours and yours alone. Who cares what he thinks? Who cares what any guy thinks?"

"Easy Lou," Calliope says under her breath.

You know it's bad when Calliope warns someone they're crossing the line because that girl crosses the line like it's her job.

"Me," Mabel says in a small voice. "I care what he thinks."

Her cheeks are bright pink.

"Of course you do," I backpedal. "I'm sorry, Mabel. Wally is wonderful." I turn to Calliope. "And you and Ralph are wonderful. It's just," I stammer. "Personally, I'm just…"

"Only interested in booty," James murmurs and shuts the freezer door.

"What did you say?" Calliope whips her head around. "What did he say?"

"Nothing!" I shout. "He said nothing."

My stare dares him to say more on that subject.

"Well, ladies, I think that's my cue to go."

I move to the door and fling it wide open for him, then wait.

He's such a nice guy and I'm beyond attracted to him, but I need him to leave so I can think straight.

He shakes his head, places the last of his equipment inside his cooler and joins me at the door.

He speaks to Mabel, but his eyes stay steady on me. "Mabes, I put another batch of drinks in the freezer for you when you're ready for round two."

"Thank you, James," she says, still sounding confused as to what's going on between us.

"Can we speak outside for a minute?" he asks me softly.

"Sure. Fine. Yes," I rattle. Anything to get Mabel and Calliope's eyes off me and to put this thing between him and me—whatever it is—to rest.

I hurry onto the front stoop without looking back at my friends. He presses the cooler out with his foot and shuts the door behind us.

Gotta hand it to the guy, he certainly doesn't shy away from conflict. He dives right in.

"Did I do something wrong that night?" he asks. "I mean was it not good for you or something?"

"No James, it was great for me," I say.

"That sounded sarcastic. Are you being sarcastic?"

"No! I'm being sincere. It was fucking fantastic."

A brilliant smile lights up his face.

"Okay, so what's the problem?" he asks.

"The problem is, we were supposed to leave it at that. One night. Wham, bam, thank you, ma'am."

He leans on the wooden post of Mabel's mailbox. "Shit, so is that like an official term now?"

"Is what an official term?"

He shakes his head. "Never mind. You were saying?"

"It was a fun and unexpected night, and while I thank you for it..."

I thank you for it? What the hell am I saying?

"... I am not interested in a repeat of said night. I don't want to learn about you, and I don't want you to learn about me. The nature of a one-night stand is that you don't have to talk about it afterward. Dramatic discussions are for relationships, and there is no relationship here. There should be no post-game wrap-up. We played the game and scored some goals. Done."

"Who won, though?"

I sigh. "What?"

"Just playing along with your metaphor. Who won the game?" he asks.

"Has anyone ever told you you can be annoying?"

"Sure. Lots of people. Part of my charm."

"You sure about that?" I narrow my eyes at him.

"I was." He takes a deep breath. "Until I met you."

There's a vulnerability in his eyes I find totally disarming.

I need to end this and go back inside.

"Please don't make this personal, James. It's not about you. It's men. In general. I'm just not interested right now. Or maybe ever."

The sudden need to backpedal overtakes me. "I don't mean it like I'm not *interested* in men. Well, actually, I did try being with a woman once, but that wasn't really the right way to go about fixing the feelings I was—" I interrupt myself with a deep breath. "Anyway..."

"You're absolutely right."

"I'm what?"

"You're right," he repeats. "Like I said before, you've been extremely clear. Tonight, and also the night we, um—"

He's distracted by something at the window.

I turn and see Calliope and Mabel peeking through the curtains, but I'm exhausted at this point and don't have the energy to care. Mabel, ever the good girl, immediately darts out of sight. Calliope takes the opportunity of being caught to give us an enthusiastic thumbs-up, then she disappears from the window as well.

James continues, "I should have taken you at your word the night we met. I apologize."

My mind flashes back to that night. The way he kissed me. The way he took care of me.

"Which, um, which word are you taking me at?"

He rubs a hand over his head.

I remember how it felt when I ran my own hands over it.

Like I wanted to do it again and again.

He takes a step closer to me. "When you said if we were to ever to run into each other again that I should pretend we never met."

"Right. That."

"This is not an excuse, but, well, you said that *before* we— And I guess when everything between us was so—I thought that—"

He's so close now his breath caresses my skin.

"You thought what?"

"When it was so amazing between us, I assumed you'd change your mind about not wanting to see me again. Because..." He brushes a lock of hair out of my face. "Damn, we were good together."

"We were, weren't we?" My voice is the softest it's been all night.

"But you didn't change your mind, did you?"

He's close enough that I could kiss him.

But I can't.

I won't.

"No," I say. "I didn't."

He nods. "Then I have to respect that. No. I *will* respect that."

"Good. That's um—" I swallow. "Thank you."

"You bet." He pauses. "Though it sounds like you're going to throw one hell of a strip show birthday party for your brother at my bar. So maybe we can work on *tolerating* each other? At least for one more night?"

I laugh. "Maybe."

He does a hand symbol, says, "I'll take that 'maybe,'" then starts to walk away.

Where did I see that symbol recently?

"You into heavy metal or something?"

He stops and turns back to face me.

"Not particularly. Why?"

I nod to his hand. "That thing you just did. Isn't that a sign for heavy metal?"

"Oh no, you're thinking of devil horns. Like this." He lifts his index and pinky finger and mimes like he's head banging.

I laugh. "Right. Gotcha."

"*This...*" He walks forward and takes my hand, then seems to think better of it. He looks deep into my eyes. "May I?"

I can only nod. There's so much electricity pulsing through me right now.

He takes my hand again, extends my thumb and pinky, then curls my other three fingers into my palm.

"This," he repeats, looking down at our hands, "is a shaka." He traces my hand shape with his finger. "It's—"

"A gesture of friendly intent often associated with Hawaii and surf culture," I finish the sentence for him.

"That's right. Damn, Calliope wasn't kidding about you and trivia, huh?"

I shrug. "Growing up, Alex Trebek was basically my de facto dad. I racked up a lot of hours watching *Jeopardy*." He opens his mouth to say something about that, but I cut him off before he can. "Are you Hawaiian?"

A soft smile crosses his lips. "Sort of."

He continues to hold my wrist and trace my hand. I let him.

"We lived there until I was thirteen, and my dad's job transferred us to Philly."

"Do you ever get back there?" I breathe. My eyes are locked on the sight of his hand caressing mine.

"Careful, Louise."

"What?" My eyes dart up to his.

"Ask me too many questions and we might just get to know each other." He gives my hand one soft squeeze, then gently releases it by my side.

I'm more turned on than I've ever been in my life.

And all he did was touch my hand.

He jogs down the steps, tosses the cooler in the back of his Jeep, and drives away, never once looking back at me.

I quietly shut the door and tap my forehead against it. A whole bunch of times.

"What. The hell. Was that."

I startle. "Callie! You scared me."

Calliope and Mabel are standing in the foyer, pure puppy dog energy emanating from them.

"Ooooh! What's the story with you and James?" Mabel practically squeals.

"Nothing," I say. "No story."

"You just had hand sex on Mabel's stoop," Calliope says. "There's definitely a story."

Mabel hightails it to the kitchen, pours me another margarita, and runs it back to me.

I grab it without a second thought and knock it down.

Calliope kicks back on the floral sofa and says, "Sister friend? Start talking."

Chapter Eight

LOUISE

The following day, I'm on the UPenn campus, trying to stay dry under a plastic bus stop awning while rain pours all around me. It's weirdly peaceful. Like my own personal fishbowl.

I'm on a video call with my pseudo-therapist, Gail.

"Slow down, slow down, would you?" she says.

"Sorry. You're right. I've been talking a mile a minute." I take a breath and consciously slow my pace. "Thank you for taking my call, by the way. I realize I don't have an official appointment. That therapist guy I was working with a while back just wasn't feeling right, so I cut the cord. And listen, as soon as the health insurance goes through with my new job, I *will* find a new therapist, so you don't have to worry about me bothering you all the time."

"An appointment. Bah! You know you never need an appointment with me."

"Seriously, I can't keep taking advantage of you! Soon you'll have real clients lined up and—"

"Real clients? Bah! You're a real client."

Before I met Gail, I thought 'bah!' only came out of the mouths of old man curmudgeons in Charles Dickens books. But Gail is one of a kind.

"We both know I'm not a real client. A real client would pay you money for your therapy expertise."

"Bah! Who needs money?"

"Um. Everyone?"

"Bah!"

"Alright." I laugh. "Can we cool it with the 'bahs' now please?"

"Fine. Yes. The 'bahs' are banned. But let's get something straight. With only four years of psych classes under my belt, no license yet, and plenty more education to go, the jury is still out on whether or not I have any therapy expertise. You're doing me a favor just as much as I am doing for you." She zooms close to her screen, giving me a comically enlarged view of her left eyeball. She puts on a weird, cartoony voice. "I'm looking you direct in the eye, woman. You see me?"

"Yes, I see you. And your cornea."

"This is a win-win, okay? A. I need the practice and B. You're my girl."

There's a split second of awkward silence.

"By 'my girl' I meant that you're my completely platonic friend who I would never in a million years think of in 'that way' ever again. You are my friend who is a girl." She continues like she's coaching herself. "My actual girlfriend is an actual lesbian who actually loves me in 'that way.' And ya know what? I'm finding out that works a whole lot better for me than dabbling with girls who are just 'trying it out' between shitty boyfriends."

I squeeze my eyes shut for a few seconds.

As much as I'd like to think that sophomore year is fully behind us, it still rears its awkward, ugly head from time to time.

"Louise. I'm trying to make you laugh. Don't worry, we can blast right past the weirdness like we usually do."

I exhale. "Awesome. Thank you. How is Hannah doing?"

"She's great, thanks." Gail beams. It's an honest-to-goodness contented smile. I love seeing her happy. "But this is about you." She puts her "professional" voice back on. "When we texted last night, you mentioned an annoying-as-hell guy powering into your butt. Are we talking about Penguin Boy or Refrigerator Sex Man?"

I laugh. "'Refrigerator Sex Man.' Though his name is *James*, and I did not say he 'powered into my butt.'"

"Pretty sure you did," she teases.

"No, I said he felt *empowered* to butt into my life."

"Oh, right right. My bad."

Two-by-two, people in their semi-formal attire huddle under umbrellas and tromp their way up the stone steps into the Arts & Sciences building.

Ralph should be here by now. He's never late. Or he never used to be late. Apparently love means you're always running behind.

"Your makeup looks fancy today. What's up? You have a date with Refrigerator Sex Man?"

"No, I do not. Tonight is the big Arts and Sciences Department cocktail party for scholarship recipients. We're supposed to meet our donors face-to-face and thank them for their generosity. I'm waiting for Ralph. He's my plus-one."

"Good idea. He'll help you stay calm."

"Yeah, that's what I figured."

"Hey." Her voice softens. "You'll be fine. Just don't do the *Jeopardy* thing, and you'll be fine."

"I'm not going to do the *Jeopardy* thing."

"Okay," Gail says like she doesn't quite believe me.

"And for the record, Refrigerator Sex Man –James—and I will not be dating."

"Ya know, that's the part I'm not really understanding. Sounds like you're into him."

"You think with a new full-time job and a master's degree course load I have any time whatsoever for dating?"

"Bah! What a cop-out." She pauses. "Sorry about the bah. But seriously. Lou. You really think I'm going to let you off the hook that easily?"

I shrug.

"You said your mom's been calling again. Does that mean the nightmares have started up again too?"

I nod.

She knows me so well.

Gail's voice softens. "Louise. You're not her."

My eyes well up, but I won't let them spill. "So why have I gone from one serious relationship to another since I was fifteen?"

"Because you're a young woman, and you were dating and figuring things out? In other words, you're completely normal?"

I don't let her words register. "And why do I always adopt

the guy's interests like they're my own? Why do I lose myself in a relationship every single time? With Mark, it was football. With Aidan, it was D & D. With Trent, it was art."

"Alright, hold up. We both know you were never into D & D. And art does not belong to Trent. You, Louise Anderson, were born an artist. Trent didn't introduce you to it. If anything, he was the one who beat the art out of you." Her face twists. "Ugh. Poor choice of words. See? This is why you should not be paying me for my services yet. Or ever. I know he didn't *beat* you. Right? Oh my God, you'd tell me if he ever did anything like—"

"No," I assure her. "Of course not. Trent was never brutal like that. Just 'brutally honest.' His words, not mine."

Gail scoffs. "Yeah, people are always 'brutally honest' when they want an exemption from being a good human being."

I murmur, "It was actually Ralph who gave him a good beatdown."

"Right. Who could forget?"

After all this time, I still cringe when I think of it. Ralph came to visit me in California junior year. He was pissed at the way Trent was treating me and lost his damn mind. I didn't speak to him for a year after that.

"Hey. You want my expert opinion?" Gail asks.

"Always."

"I think being single for a while is a worthy mission. You should absolutely focus on work and school and whatever else makes you happy. I just don't want you to shut yourself off to the opportunities—and people—who may be good for you along the way. Life has a way of surprising us when we give it some room. So maybe... keep an open mind?"

"I'll try." I give her a salute.

"Oh! Also! Don't discount any animals who cross your path over the next few weeks. There are animal love symbols everywhere we look! FYI, starfish are symbols of salvation during hard times *and* signs of infinite divine love."

"Gail. I will literally be handling starfish at my job every single day."

She gasps. "See? What did I tell you? Love is on its way!"

"*Or*," I emphasize, "it could just be that my job is to handle starfish and sea urchins in the aquarium's touch pool."

"Whatever. I'll give you that one. If you see a ladybug, though, you gotta let me know. It's widely believed that if you catch a ladybug and then free it, you will be its master, and it will continuously whisper your name into your lover's ear."

I laugh. "Stop it, will you?!"

"Oh but holy shit, if you see a beaver? Then forget it, friend. A beaver means you've found your mate for life."

"You really need to cool it with the animal spiritualism."

Her energy instantly deflates. "Really? I thought you enjoyed that."

"I *did*. For a little while. But maybe it's not something you need to add to the therapy toolbox when you start your actual practice."

"Your feedback is noted, madam."

"Okay, I gotta go. My brother is pulling up in his vulva."

"It's a Volvo, Louise. A Volvo."

"Old habits die hard, I guess." I gather my bag and stand. "Thanks for the chat, Gail. I appreciate it. I appreciate *you*."

"You know I love ya. Have fun at the shindig!"

I blow her a kiss, and we hang up.

Ralph jogs over in a classy trench coat and creates space for me under his umbrella. "Hey!" he says, a bit out of breath. "Sorry to cut it so close. I had to get the last few chapters of Callie's new book recorded today, or she was going to miss her deadline." He brushes a few raindrops off his forehead and offers me his arm. "Shall we?"

I hook my arm around his elbow, and we make our way toward the steps.

I give him a nudge. "I was about to head in without you."

"No, you weren't." He chuckles.

"You're right. I wasn't. So what's this one called?"

"Callie's book? *Tempting the Pterodactyl*."

I laugh and shake my head. "I still can't believe my astronomer brother is now a porn star."

"Louise. We both know that statement is completely inaccurate."

"My apologies. My astronomer brother is now a *vocal* porn star."

"I have *narrated* several of Calliope's dinosaur *love stories,*" he corrects.

"Alright. So is this really going to be the main thing now? Are you even applying for museum jobs anymore after everything that went down?"

"I don't know. Applying for another museum position would likely mean moving to another city since I blew my chance at the only natural history museum in Philly."

"Literally and figuratively." I snort.

"Huh?"

"You *blew* your chance literally and figuratively."

"Hardy har har."

"Don't say hardy har har. It's lame."

Last spring, Ralph and Calliope had psychedelic mushroom sex in the dinosaur room at the natural science museum where he worked as an astronomer in the planetarium. This would have been bad enough after-hours when the museum was closed. But these two geniuses decided to get their groove on while chaperoning a family sleepover event. Security cameras caught the footage, and he was fired. Obviously.

"Anyway," Ralph continues, "We like where we are. We don't want to leave Philly. We're looking to put down roots here."

"Wow. So many 'we' statements are happening."

"What's wrong with 'we'?"

"Forget it. Let's head in."

We reach the top of the grand stone steps that lead to the event.

"Ugh. I'm nervous," I whisper as we pick up our name tags at the check-in table.

"Nothing to be nervous about." He gives my shoulder a squeeze. "I went to my share of these things when I was in grad school. Think of it this way. You already have the scholarship, right? This is just the thank-you part of the transaction. Easy! As long as you..." He trails off. "Never mind."

"No. What were you going to say? You give great advice, and I need great advice right now."

"I was going to say… as long as you don't do the *Jeopardy* thing, you'll be fine."

"What is wrong with you people?" I whisper-scold him. "Gail just said the same thing. I'm not going to do the *Jeopardy* thing. I haven't done the *Jeopardy* thing since I was a teenager. Why the hell would I start doing it again now?"

"Well, you used to do it whenever you got nervous in big groups of people. And here we are." He gestures to the crowd milling in the lobby. "You're nervous and…"

"We're heading into a big group of people," I finish the sentence for him.

"Here's all I'll say: If you can stop yourself after the trivia, that would be ideal. That trivia aspect of it is generally adorable. It's when you get indignant and belligerent immediately afterward to cover your embarrassment that things get tricky. So just… skip that part if you can."

"Great. Now I'm terrified. Of myself."

"Forget I said anything." He rubs a hand up and down my back a few times. "You'll do great, and I'll be by your side the entire time."

I take a deep breath, plaster on a smile, and we enter the event space.

"Ralph! Ralph Anderson!" a male voice calls from a cocktail table across the room.

"Oh, wow! It's Otto! I know him from my museum days! Be right back."

With that, he tears across the room.

"By my side the entire time, huh?" I say under my breath. Leave it to my brother to immediately find a friend. Everyone loves Ralph. They always have.

I take a moment to get my bearings. Everywhere I look, servers in black pants and white tuxedo shirts scuttle around with trays of hors d'oeuvres and drinks. One passes by with a crab rangoon tart thingy. At least, I think that's what he called it. I politely decline. As I always do when someone offers me seafood. For obvious reasons.

The flute of champagne, though? That I happily accept.

I scan the room as I sip and quickly realize that something is off about this supposed social event.

The left side of the room is a sea of gray and black suits. The right side is full of jewel-toned cocktail dresses.

Men to the left. Women to the right.

Bizarre.

It's like a seventh-grade school dance, but instead of preteens and chaperones, the attendees are grad students and wealthy alumni.

A silver-haired woman in a magenta sheath dress spots me standing by myself and gives me a warm smile. She waves me over to her cocktail table. Not wanting to be rude, I nod and slowly make my way over to her and her friends.

Our invitation to this event included photos and bios of all the benefactors. I studied the hell out of that thing this weekend in hopes of lessening my inevitable anxiety by recognizing a few names and faces. I'm surprised and relieved to find that so far, at least one person resembles her photo.

"Mrs. Carmello, hi!" I zoom toward the woman and jab my arm at her like a knife. She startles but shakes my hand anyway. What a nice lady.

She tilts her head to the side. "Have we met before, dear?"

"Not in person, no. But I've read all about yours and your husband's contributions to the University. Thank you for all you do for the arts." I take an ill-timed sip of champagne that goes down the wrong way and leaves me sputtering and coughing.

"My goodness, dear. Are you alright?"

I whack myself in the chest a few times. "Fine, thanks," I wheeze, then get a wave of unwelcome nostalgia when I remember my family's nickname for me as a child: Wheezy.

"You're very welcome, dear. It's our great joy to give back to this wonderful school. After all, it was here on this campus where my husband and I met and fell in love."

At that moment, she catches eyes with her husband across the room and gives him the most adorable smile.

"That's so sweet!" I say and search the place for Ralph. I'm reaching the end of my ability to be socially charming and could really use an escape at this point. It's as if the sea of suits swallowed him whole.

Mrs. Carmello pulls me back to the conversation. "Are you in the arts or the sciences, dear?"

A pit forms in my stomach. "Well, I was in the arts. Then I wasn't. Then I was again. Now I'm really, *really* not again. Why, uh, why do you ask?"

She rubs her neck like I've given her whiplash. "Because all the students here tonight are either in the arts or sciences?"

I laugh. "Right, yes. Of course. I am one of the sciencers."

One of the sciencers? Get it together, Lou.

"What I meant to say is I am a marine biologist. I mean, I'm studying to be a marine biologist, which I also love. As much if not more than I loved art! Because when you think about it, the ocean is one big, beautiful work of art all on her own, yeah? And I get to spend my life studying her and all her beautiful creatures while making a living. A modest one, of course, but what are webcams for, am I right? Hahahaha."

Mrs. Carmello smiles politely, but her eyes swim in confusion.

The *Jeopardy* theme music starts playing in my head, softly at first, like it's steadily traveling toward me through a very long tunnel.

Uh-oh, shit's about to go down.

"What I'm saying is, it became clear that I was never going to make a living in art, and—I'm sure you know this, Mrs. Carmello— sometimes in life, we must make choices. Decisions. Did you know that the word decision comes from the latin root decidere?"

"Hm. I may have heard that at some point…"

She's growing tired of me. I can tell.

The *Jeopardy* music gets louder.

As do I.

"It's true. Decidere is the combination of two latin words, 'de' which means 'off' and 'caedere' which means 'cut.' That's right, Mrs. Carmello, the word 'decide' literally means to 'cut off.' When you make a decision, you are cutting off all other options in favor of what's the best possible choice for you at that moment. So that's what I did: lopped off my artistic balls in order to go balls deep into science and only science, and I've never been happier."

"That's... lovely," one of Mrs. Carmello's friends warbles, momentarily saving me from myself. She tucks a stray hair back into her French twist and changes the subject. "How are you liking UPenn so far?"

"Oh, I love UPeen!"

Shit, did I just say UPeen?

"Did I just say UPeen?" I whisper in horror.

"You did," Mrs. Carmello says, a tinge of pink rising on her cheeks.

"Hahahahahaha!" I don't recognize the sound of my own laugh. "Gosh, I'm so sorry. Slip of the tongue. I mean mouth. I mean—"

I take one look at the classy silver-haired women surrounding me, and all I see are wide eyes and dropped jaws. My own face is positively flaming now, I'm sure of it.

I take a deep breath and try to salvage this situation.

The *Jeopardy* music is blasting in my brain now.

We've reached the point of no return.

"Obviously, I meant the University of *Penn*, not peen. Penn, as in Pennsylvania. As in William Penn, English colonial leader and member of the Religious Society of Friends, otherwise known as The Quakers. Though if you ask me, I don't know how *friendly* it was of him to own a plantation run by slaves. Yeah, yeah, you could argue that this was the 1700s and Willy P didn't know any better, but come on! It's never too early in history to value your fellow human beings! Also, dude was gifted what would become the state of Pennsylvania. Can you imagine? Being gifted an entire state? Without working for it? And then naming it after yourself like an egotistical maniac?"

I crane my neck in the direction of Ralph's last known location and spot him this time, but he is chatting and laughing away, totally oblivious to me digging my own grave over here.

As quickly as the music rattled its way into my brain, it just as abruptly cuts off.

I'm left staring at a small crowd of shocked older women, stewing in my own embarrassment.

And now... the indignant phase.

"You know what? On second thought, maybe there *should*

be a University of Peen. I would totally enroll!"

They gasp.

"Hear me out, ladies. If there was an actual University of Peen, then perhaps we could learn how to deal with those penis-wielding creatures we call men once and for all, yeah? Who's with me?"

No one.

No one is with me.

But plenty are gawking at me.

"No. Scratch that. On second thought, the whole world is already the University of Peen! We all know it was built for those sausage swingers!"

Sausage swingers? Someone save me from myself.

"She's not wrong," one of the women murmurs.

"Thank you, random elegant lady. If only we had no need for the peen, ya know? Like physically speaking. These days, I make time for occasional recreational peen only. That's it! That's where I draw the line—"

"Louise?"

I turn to find my brother standing next to me, his eyes wide, his posture rigid.

"Oh hey, *bro*!" I sneer. "Where ya been, buddy?"

"Having a quick drink with an old friend. Sorry I got caught up." He nods politely at the women I've scandalized. "Hello."

"Ladies, this is my brother Ralph, one of the few peeners who's worth his salt. Usually. Tonight I'm not so sure."

Ralph smiles and speaks out the corner of his mouth. "Corbin Bellows is asking to meet you. Is this a good time?"

"It's the best time, yes. Thank you for the chat, ladies," I say and punctuate it with a weird half bow/half curtsey.

Ralph ushers me a few feet away. "Did you just call me a peener?"

"Sure did! Way to leave me, dude!" I hiss.

"I'm sorry. My old pal Otto is here. I haven't seen him since—"

"The incident?"

"Basically, yeah. So we had a lot to catch up on."

"He's the one who got you hyped up on shrooms, right?"

"Not on purpose. But yeah, his thermos of mushroom tea

sent Callie on the sexy spiral that led to my demise."

"Don't pin it all on the woman. From what I've heard, you were quite the active participant."

That gives me a horrifying visual I want to instantly bleach from my brain.

His eyes go all lovey-dovey. "Well, 'the incident' led to a beautiful relationship with my dream girl, so you won't ever hear me complaining."

"Think Otto has any shrooms on hand tonight? I could really use something like that to help me relax. I went full contestant on those women just now."

"Ugh, I'm sorry. Well, look at it this way. You got it out of your system, right? Now, you can be fully on your game when you meet Corbin. That's the whole goal tonight, isn't it? To make a good impression on him and get on track for the Florida internship?"

"Yes. Yes, yes, yes. That is the goal," I say.

We reach a buffet table with tiny sandwiches and pitchers of lemon-infused water.

Ralph pours a glass and hands it to me.

I proceed to chug.

"Hey, just a thought," Ralph says softly. "Maybe we should steer clear of general drug and peen conversations tonight. From my experience, this kind of crowd leans toward the conservative side of things."

"Uh, ya think?"

I spot Corbin Bellows across the room, chatting with another grad student.

I take one last gulp of the lemon water and slam the empty glass into Ralph's waiting palm, like he's my coach and I'm a prize fighter getting ready for the big match. I wonder if he could hype me up with one of those vigorous shoulder rubs you always see them doing in the corner of the ring. That might help.

Hearty male laughter crests over the crowd.

I nudge Ralph in the arm and nod toward my benefactor. "And Corbin is as conservative as they come. You know, if you don't count his five divorces, multiple baby daddy dramas, and the questionable 'contributions' to his foundation. But hey, he's making the oceans cleaner and safer for the next generation, plus he's singlehandedly funding my education right now, so we'll let all that slide for the moment, yeah?"

Ralph smiles at an austere couple nibbling on a prosciutto sandwich next to us and murmurs, "Lower. Your. Volume. Lou."

"You're right, you're right," I whisper. "Let's say hello and thank you to Corbin and then get the hell out of here. Sound good?"

"Sounds great, yes."

We make our way through the room, offering our "excuse me" and "pardon me" as we go.

"How did you know he was asking for me?"

"I recognized him and said hi. Told him I was here with my sister Louise Anderson and how honored she is to be one of his scholarship recipients." He shrugs. "Figured it may help your nerves to crack the door to conservation open a bit."

"You're the best, thank you." I give his hand a quick squeeze.

We plant ourselves next to where Corbin is still chatting with that student. We do that awkward thing where we make it clear we want to say hi but don't want to interrupt. My knee starts to bounce.

I try smiling at the beautiful but bored woman standing beside him. She's his most recent wife. I think her name is Jane. Or is it June? Joan maybe. Shit. I'll just wait for him to introduce her by name.

I'm struck by how Corbin looks just like he did on TV when I watched him as a kid, only now he has whiter hair and a few more wrinkles on his skin. I'd be lying if I said I wasn't starstruck. This man has been an idol of mine since I was six, and I spent the majority of my days devouring every ocean-centric show on the Discovery Channel. Corbin was always going on epic ocean adventures and making the world a better place: scuba diving to study the Great Barrier Reef in Australia, swimming with sharks in Florida, organizing beach cleanups in New Jersey.

I wanted to be just like him.

Still do.

Corbin spots us waiting, politely wraps up his conversation and turns to me with open arms.

"The elusive Miss Anderson!" he beams.

His arms are still wide open.

Are we hugging?

Well, all signs point toward imminent hugging, so I dive in.

He wraps his arms around me in a warm, fatherly squeeze.

Dreams are coming true.

"Hi, sir! I mean hello! Good evening. It's so nice to meet you in person after all this—thank you for all the inspiration you've given me over the—Wait. Elusive? Am I elusive?"

"Well, for good reason. With one internship after the next, you were a constant blur on the map last year during the interview process. You know, you're the only student I've ever awarded a scholarship to without meeting them in person first."

My face heats. "Wow. Thank you for that. I guess I was pretty busy this past year. I'm sorry I could only ever do video calls."

"Not a problem. Your brilliant essay and exemplary record and recommendations spoke for themselves. Oh, allow me to introduce you to my wife, Jean."

Jean. So close.

"Hello, Jean." I reach my hand out to her. She can't be much older than I am. She just nods and sips on her champagne.

I lower my hand.

"I hope you're applying for my Keys to the Coral Kingdom internship this spring?"

"Oh, hell yes! I'm on your website every damn day. And I've been obsessing over my statement of purpose for months and—"

Ralph hands me another glass of water.

Where the hell did that come from?

I take a gulp and hand the glass back to him, then say much more professionally, "Yes, sir. I'm pressing send on my application tomorrow."

Corbin reaches out and gives my hand a hearty shake.

"Fantastic. I look forward to reviewing it. I have a very good feeling about you, Miss Anderson. I can't wait to see all the wonderful work you're going to do."

Chapter Nine

JAMES

"Daddy!" my favorite voice in the world peals through my phone.

"I gotta take this," I say to Mabel and my buddy Wally. As Tuesday night regulars here at the new location, they are currently making googly eyes at each other, so they don't seem to mind.

I put the glass I was wiping down on the bar to give the video call my full attention. I've been waiting for this all day.

"Baby girl! How was the first day of school?"

"Good, I guess?" Her little brow scrunches up.

"You guess? Oh man, I was hoping for a bit more enthusiasm than 'I guess.'"

"It was sorta fun, but just super different, ya know? I've concluded that first grade is bonkers."

"You've concluded that, huh?" I place my phone on its stand and try to keep my face serious. Not easy when this kid is constantly so damn cute. "What made it bonkers?"

"Well, for one thing, there was way more singing last year in kindergarten. And fingerpainting too! We didn't sing or fingerpaint once today! But we did walk on the beach, which was cool. And not all the kids are the same as last year. Also, now we have desks instead of floor cushions, and pencils instead of crayons, and double recess instead of a rest hour, and Chromebooks instead of whiteboards and—"

"Alright, baby." Eva comes into view with a laugh and ruffles Iris's hair. "Take a breath, girlfriend. Let me talk to Daddy for a minute, okay?"

"Mom, I need my snack A-sap! I'm ravenous."

"Your gummies and granola bar are waiting for you on the kitchen table."

"Yes!" Iris does a fist pump in the air and runs off-camera.

Stomping six-year-old footsteps fade into the distance.

Eva's face fills the screen. "Sup, Jay Bear?"

"Not too much, Evie B. Slow night tonight. But that's just how I like it when my girls call. That way I can focus on you. Tell me everything. It went well? Kills me to miss the first day of school."

She tilts her head to the side and gives me a look. "It's not even four o'clock here. We called you on our walk there this morning and now again the minute we walked in the door. You basically only missed the actual hours she was in school. Same as me."

"I know. Thank you. I'm not criticizing, I'm just...This is hard." I sigh. "Really fucking hard."

That's the understatement of the century.

But I'm trying not to make her feel guilty.

"Have I thanked you enough for making this work for us?" she asks.

"You thank me plenty. But hey, you know how I feel. What's best for my ladies is what's best for me. And it's only four more months of this, right?"

"Four more months," she repeats.

Up until about nine months ago, Eva and I had been happily co-parenting here in Philly while I got my bar business up and running. We traveled as often as we could and got back to Hilo once a month to visit with her family. Iris was going to this cool nature school nearby that Wally recommended, and all was well.

Or so I thought.

I didn't realize how homesick Eva had been for Hawaii. For years. She has a big family, and they're native to the island. I've missed it too, but I have no family left there, so it's a different kind of missing for me. After a handful of discussions, we realized putting down permanent roots on the Big Island would be the best thing for our little modern family, especially Iris. As an only child who missed out on quality parenting, it's a top priority for me that my own kid is surrounded by all the love she can get. That means letting her grow up with grandparents, aunts, uncles, and cousins close by, and ensuring that she has a happy, contented mom. So my girls moved home, and I'm tying up loose ends here so the bars can operate without me when I join them.

"How're things going with Ron?" I ask.

Her smile beams as bright as I've ever seen it. "Things are great. I think I'm…" She hesitates. "I love him, Jay. I really love him."

"That's—Wow." It blows my mind when I consider all we've been through these past seven years. Our path may not have been the 'norm' or 'traditional' in any sense, but it brought us Iris—the absolute best part of both of our lives—so even if I could go back, I wouldn't change a damn thing. "I'm happy for you. Truly."

"Thank you."

The bell jingles, signaling that another customer is coming in.

"Callie in the hayouse!" Mabel shouts toward the door.

Calliope curtseys, tears off her raincoat, and plops herself down on a barstool with a flourish.

I give her a silent wave.

Eva notices the commotion and says, "I'll let you go, Jay Bear."

"I'm not rushing you."

"I know, but you have work to do."

"See if our girl will come back to the phone real quick, will ya?" I ask.

"Rissy?" she calls off-screen. "Daddy wants to say goodbye to you."

Iris comes back in view with lightning speed, gnawing on her granola bar. She grabs the phone from her mom and holds it at the perfect angle so I can see directly up her nose.

God, I love this kid.

"Hey, Daddy-O!"

"Hey, girly. You game for another chapter of *Marla the Mermaid* tonight before you go to sleep? I can call you at eight thirty your time."

"Totally! I brainstormed a new adventure for her."

"Oh yeah?"

"Yeah. I think in chapter six, Marla and a scuba diver meet in a sea cave, and they get married and have hybrid mermaid scuba babies."

"Interesting!" I try to keep a straight face. "But hey, in our last chapter, don't we have her in mermaid school playing with her fish friends?"

"Yeah. Next chapter is a time hop. Life moves fast, Dad. Try to keep up."

It sure does.

"I'll try. Listen, I booked my flight today for my next two visits, so we're all set for some fun in the sun. And... Mommy and I finally worked out the details for your Thanksgiving trip. I'm counting down the days until you're here with me."

"Yay! 'Iris and Daddy's Two Weeks of Philly Fun!'" she squeals.

"Is that what we're calling it?" I smile.

Iris nods. "That's definitely what we're calling it."

"Awesome. Ask Mom to give you some extra hugs for me until I can give you a real one myself, okay?"

"Okay."

"Love you, Rissy baby."

"Love you too. Peace out, cub scout!"

She kisses her fingers, shoots me a peace symbol, then ends the call.

I let out a long exhale and face the liquor shelf for a moment.

I close my eyes.

She's changing every damn second.

And she's right. Somehow, I gotta keep up.

"How you doing, hottie?" Calliope calls over the bar. "You okay?"

I turn to face her. "Me?"

"Yeah, you, Hottie McKegstand. Sounds like you've got some moves."

I place a menu down. "She told you, huh?"

"Oh, she told us, alright."

Wally perks up. "Told you what?"

Mabel whispers something into Wally's ear.

"Eh. Old news," Wally says before taking a sip of his beer.

Mabel punches him playfully on the shoulder. "You knew, and you didn't tell me?"

He shrugs. "Not my story to tell."

I tap Calliope's menu and put a place setting down in front of her. "What'll we be having tonight? Can I get you some food?"

"Surprise us!" she says. "Whatever you've got that's app-tastic and vegan-friendly for Ralph-alpha. And we'll both have an IPA. Oh, and can we have two more place settings when you get a chance?"

"*Two* more?"

With that, the door jingles again, and in walks Ralph.

And his sister, Louise.

As I put the extra place settings down on the bar, Calliope gives me a wink. "You're welcome, big guy."

Chapter Ten

LOUISE

"**D**id it really have to be this place?" I whisper to Ralph as we make our way over to the bar.

"Callie and I like it here. Plus, you really need to unwind after that event."

"Don't tell me what I need."

"Sorry. You're right. You're totally chill." He pats me on the back, letting me know I'm the opposite of chill right now.

I take a seat on the end and feel the immediate need to bolt. Beside me, Ralph and Calliope suck face in greeting. Next to them, Mabel and Wally's limbs are intertwined like squid.

It's couple central in here.

James gives me a little salute, then addresses the whole group.

"I get to see your motley crew two nights in a row? What an honor."

"Oh, do you know my sister, Louise?" Ralph asks James.

James looks at me.

I look at James.

Neither of us answers the question.

So Mabel does it for us.

"Yup! They raw dogged it in the refrigerator."

"Raw dogged in the refrigerator?" I screech and whip my head toward James. "Is that what you told them?"

He puts his hands up. "*I* didn't tell them anything! I have been sticking to your rules as much as humanly possible."

I turn to Ralph, whose face is stark white. "There was no 'raw dogging.'" Not that I owe my brother any explanation for my own sex life. "We absolutely used protection. I was trying to be impulsive, I guess, but I'm not an idiot!"

Mabel bolts from her stool and gives me a too-tight squeeze. "I'm sorry! Is that what raw dogging means? No condom?"

"Uh, yeah!" I say.

"Gotcha. That makes total sense now that I think about it. I always thought it was a position and a vibe thing. So I totally thought it applied here to this situation. You know, because you guys were so *raw* and intense, and you did it doggy—"

"Got it, Mabes!" I cut her off. "But yeah, no. That's not what it means."

"Gotcha. Consider me corrected." She returns to her seat and wraps an arm around Wally. "Life, am I right? You learn something new every day."

A silence descends on all of us. I avoid eye contact with anyone and everyone.

Out of the corner of my eye, I see Calliope holding back her laughter.

James slides two IPAs onto the bar.

Ralph glares at him.

I lean closer to Ralph and speak low. "For the love of God, do not make a big deal about this. I am a grown woman and don't need my big brother being weird and macho on my behalf. Remember where that got us last time?"

A whole year of not speaking to each other.

Ralph's shoulders visibly relax.

He takes a deep breath.

I slide his beer closer to him.

He doesn't say a word, but he still eyes James over the rim of his glass while he takes a sip.

"Can I, uh—can I get you something to drink?" James asks me.

I stare into my menu like it's the most fascinating thing I've ever seen and ramble, "Water will do. I had way too much champagne already tonight. Besides, we're not staying long anyway, and I should probably hydrate."

"You got it."

He pours me a glass of water and goes to place it down.

I reach for it too fast and end up with my fingers touching his.

I snatch my hand back like I've been burned.

"Sorry," he says.

"No, I'm sorry. My bad." I pause and finally look up at him. "It was all... my bad."

James's brown eyes search mine.

"So!" Calliope breaks the silence. "How was it?"

I shrug. "It was fine. I've had better."

Ralph chokes on his beer.

Calliope laughs and pats him on the back.

James's eyebrows furrow.

"I meant the champagne! Not the sex! The sex was fine! I mean, better than fine! It was probably the best I've—"

Oh my God, stop talking.

"The *champagne* wasn't so great. That's what I meant when I said I've had better. You were asking about the champagne, right Callie?"

"I was asking about the *event*," she says smoothly.

"Oh."

"Let me clarify, though," Calliope continues, "in case there's any confusion. The *school* event, not the sex event between you two cuties." She flashes a smile at James. "But hey, I'm all ears if there are further details either of you would like to share about that."

How many details does the woman want? I already told her and Mabel way more than I was comfortable sharing last night.

I was trying to be a more generous friend.

Sharing is caring and all that.

Ralph puts his head in his hands and groans.

"What? I write romance! Everything is fodder. Even your sister's sexcapades. "

"You write romance, huh?" James asks while wiping the bar down. I do my damnedest not to watch his forearms while he works.

"I do." Calliope beams. "The dinosaur kind."

"Huh. I wasn't aware there was a dinosaur kind."

James gives me a quick, knowing look. One that says "Don't worry. I got this."

He's taking the focus off me, like he instinctively knows exactly what I need.

"Oh, there's every kind!" Calliope says. "The possibilities are endless in romance, the subgenres infinite."

"So do you think you two will do it again?" Mabel fires an enthusiastic question at James and me.

Well, that didn't last long.

"Because how awesome would that be?" She squeals, then full-on gasps. "Oh my God! We could triple date! Yes! Yes, yes, yes! Please raw dog again, guys! Please?"

The music in my head doesn't ramp up this time. It goes full blast right from the get-go.

Mabel stands and grabs her purse. "Wally, why don't we head out, so they can close up early and do their thing."

"'Come, for I am drinking stars!'" I shout.

Everyone stares at me and my weird outburst.

I continue, "According to legend, these words were spoken by this seventeenth-century French monk the first time he tasted champagne."

It's silent.

I watch several seconds tick by on the "It's Miller Time" wall clock across the room.

"You're doing the *Jeopardy* thing again," Ralph says on the sly from the corner of his mouth.

"You think I don't know that?" I hiss.

"Ooooh, the '*Jeopardy* thing!'" Mabel claps. "That sounds fun!"

It's not.

The '*Jeopardy* thing' is the opposite of fun.

Earlier, when Ralph said it flares up when I'm in crowds, that wasn't entirely accurate. I've learned it has less to do with how many people are in the room and more to do with the pressure I feel to please them.

Gail says it has to do with my childhood.

Doesn't everything, though?

But I'm a twenty-three-year-old woman now.

I shouldn't need coping mechanisms anymore.

"Who is Dom Perignon?" James says.

"What?" I ask.

He's leaning his elbows on the bar, a soft smile on his handsome face.

"The answer to your question is Dom Perignon. He's the seventeenth-century champagne-drinking monk. Except, this is *Jeopardy* we're talking about, so I suppose I should say that's the 'question to your answer.'"

"That's correct!" I say with wonder.

People don't usually participate when I slip into this mode. They mostly stare and stammer, like the fancy ladies did at the event tonight. Not that I can blame them. But it made me want to run home and hide.

"What else you got?" James rises to his full height and gives me the universal gesture for "bring it."

I straighten my spine and continue with less shame this time. More confidence.

"This Grande Dame of Champagne took on her husband's wine business when she was widowed at age twenty-seven."

"Who is Barbe-Nicole Ponsardin, aka Widow Clicquot or Veuve Clicquot?" he says. "I'm sure I just murdered those French pronunciations, but you get the idea."

"Correct!" I high-five him, suddenly feeling like he's the only one here who truly gets me. "The accent was awful, but you basically got the pronunciation, so I'm pretty sure Alex would cut you some slack."

"Gimme another," he says.

This is surprisingly fun.

"The following line: 'Champagne, with its foaming whirls, as white as Cleopatra's pearls' is from *Don Juan*, a poem by this eighteenth-century English poet."

"Who is Lord Byron?"

"Yes!" I say. "Wow!"

Mabel laughs. "Look at them! They could go all night!"

"Sounds like they already did," Ralph mumbles.

"I've only been asked booze-related questions so far, and booze is basically my biz," James says as he waves to a group of regulars coming through the door. "So don't be too impressed."

"You know, 'jeopardy' is one of those words I always spell wrong on the first try," Wally says between sips.

I'm still getting to know Wally, but Mabel is head over heels in love with him, and that's enough for me. Plus, he has this dry sense of humor and no-nonsense attitude about him that I really like.

"We all have words like that." James gathers four pint glasses, lines them up under the spouts, and begins to pour for the folks who just came in.

He knows what people need without them even asking.

Wally continues, "Oh yeah, I have a buncha those. Broccoli is one of them. Is it double C's? Double L's? Both? Neither? Fuck if I know. Bureaucracy is another. I mean, what the hell are they doing with that one? They're gonna put an E and A and a U before a C and tell us to pronounce it 'ock'? Fuck that shit. Oh and goddamn, the word 'rhythm' gets me every single time. How many H's are there, and where the hell do I put them? You're seriously telling me there is no vowel in the second syllable? Shit."

Calliope offers, "In the case of no official vowel, the letter Y becomes an honorary vowel."

"Eh." Wally takes another sip. "That's some bullshit."

James pours the last glass with care and ensures it has just the right amount of foam on it. Who am I kidding? I don't know if it's the right amount of foam. I don't even know if it's called foam in this instance. Beer people have some beer language I don't pretend to understand. But it's clear he takes special care with each glass.

He slides them past me, where two of the four guys are waiting at the end of the bar.

I help hand the glasses to them before they head to their table.

"Those glasses were kind of warm," I say to James. "Isn't beer supposed to be cold?"

"Stouts are more of a warm brew, Cold Brew." His voice is

low and rumbly.

"Are you still calling me that?" I ask in a near whisper.

"Depends."

"On what?"

He leans a little closer. "Are you still calling me Hottie McKegstand?"

I shoot daggers at Calliope, who I can tell is hanging on our every word.

She shrugs, not at all apologetic.

"Hey, Wally." Ralph gets up and moves to the opposite side of the bar. "If it helps? I always sound out jeopardy to get the spelling right. It's like geo party but with a J instead of a G and a D instead of a T."

I guess he's done with the protective older brother stuff. Or maybe his drink has just loosened him up. He's always been a lightweight.

"That does help. Thank you very much."

"Ralph used to be all about geo parties." I laugh.

"What's a geo party?" Calliope asks.

"Oh, you'd love it, babe." Ralph pulls her up to stand and wraps her in his arms while he talks. "My geology professor in college always threw us an end-of-semester celebration. Served us Earth-inspired food like rock candy and little dirt pudding cups with gummy worms. Oh man! One time, she even constructed this volcanic fondue dispenser that erupted with chocolate every ninety seconds!" His eyes roll back in remembered ecstasy. "Blew my mind and coated my strawberries."

Calliope cocks her head to the side and looks up at him. "That's not a euphemism for...?"

"No, baby, it's not." Ralph strokes her cheek and drops his voice to a purr. "You know the only one who coats my berries is—"

"Stop speaking," I blurt. "Stop speaking right now."

Ralph scoffs. "Oh, I see how it is. You draw your line at 'coats my berries,' when I say it, but you can say 'raw dogging' in the presence of your brother, and that's just fine."

Mabel raises her hand. "Ralph, in fairness, I was the one who said raw dogging. I've learned my lesson, though, and I won't say raw dogging again. Except for just now. And the time before that. But I'm done now, and I will not say raw dogging again."

"When are we getting a dog, Ralph-alpha?" Calliope croons.

"This again?" Ralph looks over at me. "She's been gunning for a dog ever since we moved into the new apartment."

Calliope says, "Well, we have more space now, and there's a cute little dog run right down the street..."

"Dogs are just so much work." He strokes her hair and tries to change the subject.

"How would you know?" she says.

"We had one when I was little," I answer for him.

"You did?" Her face scrunches in confusion. "You've never mentioned that."

"That's because she was my dog," I say. "But Ralph helped out with her quite a lot."

Because Ralph helped me with everything. All the things parents are supposed to do for their kids. I probably don't thank him enough for everything he did for me.

"Her name was Muse. She was my best pal. Slept in my room, followed me around..."

"Inspired your paintings," Ralph adds.

"Yeah." I can't help but smile any time I think about Muse. "She did."

Ralph reaches into his pocket and pulls out his phone. He starts scrolling. "Here, I'll show you all one of their collaborations."

"Oh God. Please don't."

"Why not? If I've said it once, I've said it a million times. The whole world should see your art."

"No. They should not," I fire back.

"You're an artist?" James asks as he places a bunch of appetizers in front of us.

Here we go again.

I sigh. "No. I am not."

Mabel whisper-shouts to James, "Warning: don't call Louise an artist. It really pisses her off. I tried to commission her to paint me nude as a sexy surprise for Wally last night, and she yelled at me."

"I didn't yell at you."

"You yelled," Mabel and Calliope say together.

"A nude commission, huh?" Wally waggles his eyebrows at Mabel.

"Oooooh. You're waggling." Mabel pauses. "The waggle is good, right?"

"Yes, milady. The waggle is very good."

"Speaking of waggling, Wally," Calliope says. "Maybe you could have given us a heads-up that your lady is a nudist now. I saw all her nooks and crannies last night against my will."

"I'm only a nudist at home," Mabel corrects. "As you can see, I am fully clothed while in public."

"Looks like we need to get home then." Wally picks her up caveman style over his shoulder.

She squeals in delight.

"Perfect timing!" I say and start gathering my things. "Could I have a ride?"

I've got to get out of here before—

"Wait, wait, wait. I found it! Here is one of Lou's best," Ralph holds up a screenshot of one of my paintings.

I haven't seen this one in so long.

It's always been one of my favorites.

"Wow," James breathes.

"I know, right?" Ralph says. "It functions on two levels, though. You can take it in as a wide view, like you're doing now. But then, get closer and..."

Everyone moves closer, including James, who leans over the bar to get a better look.

Ralph slides two fingers outward on the screen, zooming in on a small section of the painting. The section gets wider, revealing another image of Muse.

"It's like paintings within paintings!" Mabel says as she slides down from Wally's shoulder.

Looks like I lost my ride.

They're not going anywhere now.

"Sister friend." Calliope's mouth drops open. "This is fucking gorgeous. And impressive."

"That's what I've been saying! For years!" Ralph says. "She

has an incredible gift."

"Alright, simmer down, sir," I say and try to laugh.

"No! I'm not going to simmer down. Not about this! That asshole made you feel like you were less than. An asshole who couldn't paint his way out of a cardboard box!"

"That makes no sense," I murmur. "Can anyone paint themselves out of a cardboard box?"

"You know what I'm saying. My sister is goddamn amazing. And no artsy, asshole punk is going to make her doubt herself. Not on my watch!"

Calliope rubs his back and faux fans herself. "My goodness. You're putting the alpha in Ralph-alpha right now, baby."

My normally kind, gentle brother turns all Hulk-like whenever Trent comes up in conversation.

It's an issue.

"I'm sorry," he says softly. He scrolls through more of my work and holds up another screenshot. "But don't you miss it?"

"Sometimes, yeah," I say.

More like all the time.

I continue, "But come on. It's not like I have time to paint with a new job, a new apartment, grad school, and applying for an internship. I'm maxed out with no room for anything else."

I can't help but peek at James from the corner of my eye.

He's serving someone at the opposite end of the bar, chatting up a storm, a warm, friendly smile on his face.

"Plus, I don't have Muse anymore. I don't have *a* muse."

"Excuses." Ralph shakes his head.

"Okay." I get to my feet and grab my raincoat. "It's been a long day. I'm tired, and I've had enough public psychoanalysis for one night. I'm heading out."

I'll walk if I have to.

"Here." Calliope reaches into Ralph's pocket and pulls out his keys. "I brought my car. You can take Ralph's Vulva."

She tosses the keys to me with no complaints from Ralph.

Say what you want about the girl, but Calliope always comes through when you need her.

I say quick goodbyes to everyone, then stop in my tracks as

James comes back to our end of the bar.

"Thanks for the, uh—the water, and the um. Thanks for..."

Making me feel normal?

Relaxed?

Like myself?

I settle on, "Just... thanks."

"Anytime." He pauses, then nods toward Ralph's phone lying face up on the bar. My painting is still lit up. "For what it's worth... your work? It's really beautiful."

My cheeks heat. As do other parts of me.

"Thanks," I say one more time, then turn and push through the door.

I stand outside for a moment and tip my face up, letting the cool raindrops land on my skin.

After a few deep breaths, I look back through the bar window and see James holding Ralph's phone.

He looks closer.

Closer.

Even closer.

He smiles.

And just like that... I want to paint again.

And I know exactly who my new muse is going to be.

Chapter Eleven

LOUISE

"Hey, beautiful," I say as I set up my easel next to the rehabilitation tank. "Mind if I join you?"

Dana never specified *how* I should spend time with Meilani, just that I should feel free to keep her company whenever I could.

And ever since last night, I can't stop thinking about painting her.

So I'm going to give it a go.

Meilani swims right over to the glass and looks me squarely and securely in the eye.

A sensation of calm washes over me, just like it did the other day when we first met. I can't explain it.

But I guess I don't have to.

All I know is my breathing gets deeper.

My heart seems to beat slower.

She feels like home. Just like Muse did back when I was a kid.

I dip my brush into the paint and touch it to the canvas.

Meilani responds with a twirl, like she knows progress is being made on my side of the glass.

Like she's proud of me.

Pretty sure I'm projecting, but whatever. If I learned anything from my time studying marine animal psychology, it's that they are sensitive creatures. The way they experience loss, love, and connection isn't as different from humans as we may initially believe it to be.

Time flies as I fill the canvas with color. I'm in the flow for the first time in what feels like forever.

I'm not sure how long I've been at it when I'm startled by a familiar male voice.

"What's her name?"

I look up, bleary-eyed and confused.

Why is James standing across from me in full scuba gear?

He's dripping wet and holding his goggles like he just got out of the tank.

"Her, um—her name is Meilani," I say, my head cocked to the side. "What the hell are you doing here? In scuba gear?"

"Heavenly beautiful," he says.

"Oh my God." I put my paintbrush down and stand. Is he really flirting with me right now?

"Meilani," he explains. "It's a Hawaiin name. It means heavenly beautiful. Or heavenly flower."

"Oh."

And now I'm disappointed he's *not* flirting.

"You thought I was saying *you* are heavenly beautiful?" He smiles.

"No," I scoff. "Of course not."

"For the record, you are," he says. "Beyond beautiful." He scrubs his hand over his head, and some water droplets fly. "But you didn't hear that from me. I'm trying not to dwell on your beauty too much these days."

He has to try?

"So." His tone shifts dramatically, and he's back to being a jokester. "You new here?"

My head rears back. "Am *I* new here? No, I'm not new here, James. This is where I work." I flash him my badge. "Clearly, *you're* the new one. What's going on?" I lower my voice and lean closer to him. "Are you here because of me?"

He laughs. It's this deep throaty sound I want to hear again and again.

"You have a healthy ego on you, huh?"

I don't know what to say to that.

He continues, "It's okay. You should. But, no, I'm not here

because of you."

"You sure?" I say slowly. "Because it kind of feels like you're everywhere this week." My mind flashes back to the diver doing the "hang loose" sign the other day. And then to him holding my hand on Mabel's front steps. "Oh my God, that was you in the shark tank the other day, wasn't it?"

"It was. I'm a volunteer tank diver on Wednesdays. My trusty algae scrubber and I make sure everything's clean and clear for the animals. And the guests. Been doing this shift for about nine months now. But I also pop in on Mondays once a month for a deeper clean."

"I don't mean to be a jerk, but you're a bartender. What qualifies you to be in that tank?"

"Whoa! What a jerk!"

"I'm sorry! I didn't mean—"

He's still laughing. James seems impossible to offend. Or rattle. In any way.

"Come on, Louise. Surely, you know people are capable of being more than one thing."

I shrug.

"Take you, for example." He points toward my easel. "You're a marine biologist who also paints. Yeah, I'm a bartender. But I'm also a diver. Not many opportunities to dive in Philly. This way, I get to swim with these beautiful creatures and help out at the same time." He holds up the algae scrubber in his hand.

"So why didn't you say hi when you saw me here Monday?" I ask.

"Well, one reason was you seemed busy."

I nod. "It was my first day as official staff."

"But the main reason was that I was under strict orders to never speak to you again."

I wince. "Right. That."

He scans my body. Not in a creepy way but more of a curious way. I'm not wearing my official aquarium uniform.

"Today is my day off," I explain. "And school let out early. Hence the reason I'm—" I gesture to my clothes. "And also why I'm—" I nod toward my easel and paints.

He smiles. "Well, it's good to see."

"Yeah. I've always avoided hump day when I can."

"Excuse me?"

"When I was making my aquarium schedule, I asked for Wednesdays off. I hate that whole 'Hump day' thing."

"You hate the hump?" he says with a smirk.

I cringe. "I certainly hate that *word,* James."

"What? Hump?"

"Yes! Will you stop saying—" I blow out a breath. "I don't hate the *act* of—You of all people should know I—" I stop myself from saying anything further and throw up my hands. "I give up."

"Deep breaths, Louise. Just trying to make you laugh. Break some of the tension between us."

"There's no tension between us."

"Oh, there's tension, alright." He laughs. "But listen. I agree. The whole hump day thing is annoying. So is 'I got a case of the Mondays.' Though, that's more of an office and academia thing, yeah? And I try to stay out of those two environments as much as possible."

My phone dings from the easel with an email notification.

I pressed send on my application for the Florida internship this morning. It's not possible they already got back to me, is it?

"I need to check that," I say.

"Sure, sure. I should get back to it, anyway." He holds up the algae scrubber in his hand.

I tear over to my phone and open my email.

It's not from Corbin's team.

It's from my Mom.

> *Hi, sweetie! I'm so excited to see you in a few weeks to celebrate Ralphie's birthday! Shhhh, moms the word about the party! I mean mums! Ha! Get it? I'm just so excited to see my babies and feel like a mom again, so expect to hear a lot more Mom jokes during my visit. I can't wait to do ALL the girly things with my Wheezy. Love you!*

"You okay?"

I startle. "Oh, you're still here."

"Your face just..." James clears his throat. "You okay?"

"Fine, yeah. I'm fine. Go! Happy diving!" I wave him off.

"Thanks. Okay, I'll..." James hesitates, then says, "I'll see you around."

He turns to go, but it suddenly feels very important that I tell him something.

"I don't usually do things like that!"

He turns back to face me but doesn't say anything.

"I need you to know that."

"You're referring to..."

"The humping, yeah," I fill in the embarrassing blank for him. "Or maybe we should call it the one-night..."

"Kegstand?"

I laugh.

He's good at that. Getting me to laugh.

"Yeah. I know I seemed pretty... confident. And I had all those rules for afterward, but it wasn't because it's something I usually do."

He's just standing there, silent, giving me the proverbial floor.

"They say the definition of insanity is to do the same thing over and over again expecting a different result, right? Well, ever since I started dating—which, in hindsight, was way too early for me to start dating in the first place—I have had a string of serious, not-so-great relationships, and I'm trying to break the chain. So that night, with you, I was... trying something different."

He nods.

His feet stay steady on the ground.

Meilani catches our attention from her tank, and we watch her swim for a few moments.

He finally speaks.

"Well, listen. Even if you did make a habit of... one-night keg stands, you wouldn't owe me—or anyone—any sort of explanation for that. It's absolutely no one's business."

He's right of course.

I've just so used to explaining myself to the guys I'm with.

But I'm not *with* James.

Not at all.

"I have to admit, though, the caveman part of me is a wee bit happy to hear I was an exception to your standard proceedings."

"A wee bit?" I laugh.

"A wee bit, yeah." He smiles.

"I think it's safe to say there is no caveman in you."

"Don't kid yourself, Louise. There's a little caveman in every guy."

"Alright, noted. I just meant that—" I pause. "Well, I may regret saying this, but... I'm not mad that I met you."

A brilliant smile spreads across his chiseled face.

"High praise, Cold Brew."

"Yeah, well, Cold Brew is a bit of a slow burn when it comes to getting to know people, I guess."

"That's alright. I'm not going anywhere." He starts adjusting his gear and making his way toward the entrance to the shark tank. "Just don't go thinking now you're being nice to me and we're technically co-workers that I'm going to sleep with you here at the aquarium."

I know we're the only two people up here right now, but that doesn't stop me from whipping my head around to make sure, then whisper-yelling, "Um. Who said anything about having sex here at the aquarium?"

"Not me," he winks. "Get your mind out of the gutter, girl."

I follow him toward the tank and keep my voice low. "It's not my mind I'm worried about, caveman. FYI—you know, in case you decide to hook up with anyone else here—my brother lost his job at the Natural History Museum this summer for getting down on company grounds. I'd advise against it."

"Ralph? Really? Seems like such a straitlaced guy. Well, cheers and condolences to him! But I assure you, making love to you on museum property is the last thing on my mind right now."

So why am I suddenly thinking about it so much?

He gets in the water and leans his arms on the edge, his twinkling brown eyes tipped up to me.

I kneel on the rubber flooring right in front of him.

We're so close now that anyone who walks in would know something is going on between us.

"'Making love?'" I whisper. "Is that what you think we did in your refrigerator this summer?" I get even closer. "News flash, fella. That wasn't making love. That was fucking."

"Agreed," he whispers back. "But if I'm ever lucky enough to find myself in that situation with you again? I assure you, we'll be making love."

With that, he pulls on his mask and disappears under the water.

Oh boy.

I am in so much trouble.

Chapter Twelve

JAMES

"I assure you, we'll be *making love*?" Wally repeats my words through the phone. "You really said that to her?"

"I did!" I shake my head in shame. "What am I, some schmaltzy soap opera dude?"

I squint toward the ocean where Eva and Iris are putting the finishing touches on our epic sandcastle while I make some quick business calls back home. At least that's what I'm supposed to be doing. Instead, I'm being mercilessly mocked by my best friend.

"I have known you more than half my life, and I've never heard you say something so corny."

"Believe me, I know." I slide my sunglasses on. "Wall, this girl does something to me. I'm a fucking mess around her. I say all this stupid shit, like I can't stop running my mouth whenever she's near me."

"Well, you've always been a talker."

"True, but this is a whole other level." My mind flashes back to that first night in the bar. "Oh, I almost forgot this insanity. The night we met?"

"You mean the night you boinked?"

"Did you seriously just say boinked?"

He snorts. "I did."

"A guy who says boinked has no right calling me corny. Dude, you used to be my classy friend. What's happening to you?"

Wally laughs. "I don't know, man. Mabel unleashes my silly, I guess. Anyway, boinked is just a fun word to say, isn't it?"

He's not wrong.

"Fine. So the night we... boinked, I couldn't shut the hell up."

"Dirty talk?"

"Not exactly."

"So what were you talking about? The weather?"

I sigh. "I busted out a weird impromptu monologue comparing her to coffee grinds."

"Excuse me?"

"I said she was a strong, concentrated woman who won't be diluted with water for other people's comfort."

"That makes absolutely no sense."

I frown. "Come on. It makes a little bit of sense, doesn't it?"

"No, it does not."

"Fine. I didn't even stop there, though. I also told her she was slowly pouring over me and effortlessly spiking the temps in my refrigerator. Oh, and I gave her the nickname Cold Brew."

"Damn, you hit that metaphor hard. And FYI? Cold Brew is a terrible nickname. Especially for someone you hope to sleep with again."

"I know, I know." I dig my toes into the sand.

"Well, this is what you get when you don't date for six years, friend. You've got no game."

I do some quick math. "Seven years. I haven't dated in seven years. And I've got game, ya jerk. It's just... rusty."

Iris and Eva gather our buckets and shovels and start making their way over to the umbrella.

Seven years.

From the moment I learned Eva was pregnant, everything changed. I quit women. I quit drinking. And I placed my entire focus on them.

Seems like a lifetime ago and also the blink of an eye.

"So how's the visit going?" Wally asks. You making progress with The Highs and Lows?"

I'm halfway through my once-a-month trip back to Hawaii to spend time with my daughter and get things squared away for the new excursion company.

"It's going great. Business-wise, everything is on track for launching in January. And Rissy-wise…" I sigh. "One week is never enough."

Iris plops her sandy butt in my lap and whips her wet hair in my face. I make a big production of sputtering and spitting the strands out of my mouth. She laughs. "Who are you talking to, Daddy?"

"It's Uncle Wally. Want to say hi?"

She nods vigorously.

I put him on speaker.

"Say hi, Uncle Wally."

"Hi, Uncle Wally!" Iris squeals.

"Hey, Rissy Roo!" he says. "We miss you in these parts."

"Miss you too! But I'll see you soon when I fly to Filthadelphia for Thanksgiving."

"Oh no, are your grandparents still calling it Filthadelphia?"

"They are," I answer for her.

Eva's parents haven't fully forgiven me for taking their daughter away for so many years. I'm thinking I deserve some major brownie points now, though, since she and Iris are back.

"Hey, Wally!" Eva shouts as she reapplies some sunscreen.

"Hey, Evie B! Our boy was just telling me about his lack of prowess with the ladies."

"Oh, believe me, I know all about that!" she cackles.

I take off my sunglasses and glare at her. "Coming from the woman I've procreated with, I take offense to that."

"Mommy? Can I listen to *Magic Tree House*?"

"Sure, baby." Eva digs Iris's waterproof iPad and pink headphones out of our beach bag and hands them to her.

Iris lays down on her mermaid towel and starts listening to her book.

I love what a beach kid she's become.

Eva sits beside me and rests a hand on my back. "Jay Bear, I mean no offense. But we both know you used zero 'prowess' on me. Our particular potion that night was Seagram's 7 and sadness."

She speaks the truth.

"Whoa," Wally says. "You guys talk this way around your kid?"

"Relax, she's got her headphones on," I say. "But generally, yeah. Iris knows her parents have always been best friends, but never were and never will be a couple."

Eva nods puts her head on my shoulder. "Modern parenting at its best."

Eva and I grew up together here on the island until I was thirteen and moved to Philly with my dad. We stayed in close touch over the years, and when she visited me during a particularly sad and drunken time, well, the result of that visit is now lying beside us on a mermaid towel and licking a lollipop.

No regrets.

"So are you all caught up on the drama, Wally?"

I nudge Eva with my shoulder. "Drama? Come on, there's no drama."

"Says the guy who spouts off lines like 'I assure you, we'll be making love.'" Wally laughs.

"Ooh!" Eva says. "Did he tell you he also said 'Don't kid yourself, Louise. There's a little caveman in every guy?'" She's literally rolling with laughter on the beach towel now.

"There's a little caveman inside you, Daddy?" Iris pipes up from behind us. Her headphones are draped around her neck.

"Uhhhhhh." I hesitate. "Sort of? How's the story going, baby?"

"It's okay, but I think I wanna switch to music now."

"Go for it, kiddo!"

She pops her headphones back on.

"All busting on James aside," Wally says, "from everything he's told me and from the energy I observed between them at the bar the other night? Louise is not as opposed to him as he thinks."

Eva takes the phone out of my hand and speaks into it directly. "So why shouldn't they have some fun, right?"

"Oh. Have we reached the point in the conversation where you two speak about me as if I'm not here? Also, Eve"—I tilt my head and really take her in—"is this you encouraging me to date?"

"Why not? I am." She shrugs. "And don't you think it's time? You're a great guy. You deserve to have some fun! Whether it's with this girl or someone else."

I watch the waves rise and fall a few times.

"Alright, but what's the point when I'm leaving in a few months?"

"Fun, my friend. Fun is the point," Wally says.

These two are giant pains in my ass, but I know without a doubt they want the best for me.

And—as much as I hate to admit it—they're also always right.

Because one thing is for sure. With the exception of the one-night keg stand, my little caveman has been out of commission for way too long.

Chapter Thirteen

LOUISE

Ralph: What's your ETA?

Me: I've been around the corner for twenty minutes debating whether to ring your bell or not.

Ralph: Lou, come on. It'll be good. I promise.

Me: Don't make promises you can't keep.

Ralph: She's in a much better place now.

Me: You mean she's dead?

Ralph: Damn, that was dark.

Me: Sorry. You know my humor gets dark when it comes to the parentals.

Me: I didn't mean that.

Me: Ralph, seriously. I didn't mean that.

Ralph: I know you didn't.

Me: Ugh. I feel bad now.

Ralph: Don't. It's okay. Come up. I'll try my best to keep the focus off you. She's on a get-to-know-you mission with Callie since she arrived last night. And if anyone is a good buffer, it's Callie.

Me: True. Alright, give me another minute and I'll be there.

Ralph: CU soon.

*I*t's Ralph's birthday week, and the mother figure has descended.

I was surprised at first that Ralph and Calliope are down to host her for an entire week, but in hindsight, I shouldn't have been. Ralph is generally a better person than I am. And Calliope? Calliope likely doesn't know the extent of what she's in for.

Well, strap in, sister friend.

This family is a wild ride.

The past few weeks have been a blur. Between my shifts at the aquarium that are in full swing now, the intense workload I find myself under for grad school, and squeezing in whatever space I can find in my schedule to bond with Meilani, thankfully there hasn't been much time to stress over Mom's impending visit.

Somehow, though, I have managed to stress over the lack of James in my life.

Which is ridiculous, I know.

After all, I was the one who told him I wasn't interested.

But after that interaction next to Meilani's tank a few weeks ago, I felt something shifting in me, like I was softening toward him. And I guess I assumed he'd keep popping up in my life.

I spotted him once on hump day while he was scrubbing the tank—I'm ashamed to say I popped into the aquarium on my lab lunch break in hopes of seeing him—but he just gave me a little wave and was out of there as soon as he finished.

The diving team was doing deep cleans again on Monday, but he didn't show up at all.

Maybe he's out of town?

Maybe he's avoiding me.

Maybe he finally took me at my word and moved on.

I take one last look at the Schuylkill River, roll my shoulders back, and speed walk toward Ralph and Calliope's building before I have the chance to change my mind.

Plenty of people give the Schuylkill a hard time. Sure, it's impossible to spell, confusing to pronounce, and it often looks more like a brown, wet, winding road than a sparkling river, but I love it. I feel peaceful whenever I'm near it. I looked up where its name comes from once. It's a Lenni Lenopi indian word for "slowly moving river." I think that's what I love about it. It doesn't care that everyone can see its muddy bottom constantly rising to the top. It takes its time and keeps moving forward, steady and strong.

Whereas I feel like I'm always rushing.

Rushing and hiding.

But not today.

Today I will do my daughterly duty and face my mom.

No matter how much emotional energy gets stripped from me.

I ring the bell, and the outside door immediately unlatches. I forgo the elevator and stomp up the five flights instead. A little internal tantrum is exactly what I need right now.

The door to their apartment is propped open for me.

Here goes nothing.

As soon as I enter, I'm hit with the pungent scent of my mother's perfume. And not three seconds later, I'm tackled with her tiny, tan body in an explosive hug.

My mom's personality may be in perpetual flux, but her Elizabeth Arden perfume and projectile hugs always stay the same.

"Baby!" she shouts into my shoulder.

"Hi, Mom." I squeeze out the words with very little air left in my lungs.

She pulls back and places her hands on my face. "How's my baby? Is she doing okay?"

I look around, confused. "By *she*, do you mean me?"

"Of course! Who else?"

"I'm okaaaay. How are you?"

"Never better!" She weaves our fingers together and pulls me by the hand into the living room. "You have a funny look on your face, Wheezy baby. What's going on?"

"I guess I'm curious why you're using third person when I'm right next to you. And can we skip calling me Wheezy? I've never loved that."

"Oh really? You never told me that."

"I did. On the daily."

"I don't remember that." She juts her lower teeth out. It's this weird habit she does when I call her on her shit. "Here. Sit, sit, sit." She flops back on the modern loveseat by the window and slaps the cushion to her right. "Sit next to me and tell me everything."

I silently lower myself beside her as she prattles on and pats my thigh.

"When I used the third person while addressing you just now, I did that quite intentionally. I asked how my *baby* is doing. Not *you*. But my *baby*. Clearly, I was referring to your inner child."

Clearly.

And the emotional whiplash begins.

"Sweetie, relax your forehead. If you're not careful, you're going to get an eleven. All the women in our family get an eleven when they turn forty."

"I'm twenty-three."

"Exactly. You're more than halfway there." She rubs her thumb between my eyebrows until I swat her hand away.

Calliope sweeps in then with a forced smile on her face and places a ring of shrimp cocktail on the coffee table in front of us. "Hey, girl, hey! So glad you're here! Ralph will be out in a bit. He's just assembling the salads."

"So? how is *she* doing?" My mother stares into my eyes, ignoring that Calliope just entered the room.

That's weird.

"My inner child?" I ask.

"Yes."

I'm not surrrrre." I hesitate. "Though if I had to guess, Mom, I'd say my inner child is probably pretty fucked up."

"Well, then you better get to work, missy! Only you can heal your inner child. That's the work that no one else can do for us. I've been healing the hell out of mine, I can tell you that!"

"Cool, cool," I say and crane my neck toward the kitchen in hopes that Ralph is almost done.

Should I mention the fact that she is the one who messed up my inner child in the first place?

No. Not worth it.

I've learned over the years that when dealing with my mother, it's best to let her words wash over me like water. I don't need to make sense of them. I don't need to take them to heart. Because next month, whatever is driving her now will be forgotten. This month it's this inner child mumbo jumbo. Next month? Who knows. But whatever it is, it will be directly influenced by whoever she happens to be dating—or getting over—at the time.

"Is this a Steve thing?"

"A what thing?" She tilts her head to the side.

"A Steve thing. Did Steve get you into the whole 'inner child investigation' thing?"

"No. Steve and I parted ways ages ago. My new friend Dave introduced me to it.

Have a shrimp, sweetie," Mom says. She dips one in cocktail sauce and lifts it to my mouth.

I lean back. "No, thank you. I'm not much for seafood. Sort of feels like eating my friends."

She shrugs and pops it into her own mouth instead.

"Shoot!" Calliope shouts. "I knew that! Ralph mentioned Theresa loves shrimp cocktail, so I got some, but I totally forgot that you hate it, and—"

"It's not a problem. I don't plan on staying long anyway. I'm just dropping in to say hey before I head home and hit the books."

"Oh baby, please stay," Mom whines.

"I would, but I have a lot of studying to do."

"For ocean school? How's it all going, sweetie?"

Ralph comes in then with a tray full of drinks and places them on the table.

"Hey, Lou. Good to see you," he says with a crisp nod.

Wow.

So formal.

Seems Ralph might not be as cool and collected about this visit as he would like me to believe.

I turn to find Mom still staring at me, waiting for my answer. Is there tension between the three of them? First, she ignored Calliope. Now she's barely looking at Ralph.

"Um. The *marine biology* program at UPenn is going great, thanks. We're only three weeks in, but it's already really intense."

"Well, make sure you're making time to rest, Wheezy. You

look exhausted." She strokes my hair. "You're way too young to have those dark circles under your eyes."

My fingers automatically rise to touch my face.

Calliope shakes her head, silently telling me my mom is full of crap.

"I'm getting plenty of rest," I say, which isn't exactly the truth. "But even if I wasn't, I don't mind the intensity at school. It's what I signed up for."

Mom picks up a glass of chardonnay and takes a sip. "You were always an intense little girl. Always so passionate about things. You give your all to whatever is in front of you."

Did my mother just give me a compliment?

"Must've gotten that from me," she continues. "Because we all know you certainly didn't get it from your father. I mean, really. What kind of a man—?"

She cuts herself off like she's trying to restrain herself, but h er breathing picks up, and

the anger rises in her like a volcano.

"The man had a beautiful family right in front of him, but did he give his all to us? Did he have passion for us? No. Apparently, he could take or leave us! I mean, what kind of a man—"

"Hey, Mom?" Ralph pulls up a chair and places a hand on her arm. "We haven't been together like this in a long time. Maybe we can skip the Dad stuff tonight?"

Her breathing steadies. Her eyes focus on Ralph, like she went somewhere else entirely for a few seconds, and now she's back.

"Sure, baby. Sure. We can skip all that. You know, if I could go back in time, I'd skip that man entirely. But then I wouldn't have my two beautiful blessings, now would I?" Her voice chokes up. "You two are the only good things that man ever gave me. I don't know what I'd do without you. If you two ever left me, I'd—"

"I think I'm going to head out." I'm on my feet and slinging my bag over my shoulder in a flash.

"You just got here, Louise. Sit back down!"

And just like that, her crocodile tears are gone, and the anger is back.

"Yeah, I know, but these books aren't going to study themselves."

I pat my bag and attempt a chuckle.

She takes a silent sip of her wine.

"Have a good night, Mom. I'll see you at the party."

"What party?" Ralph asks.

Calliope scrunches her eyes closed.

Dammit.

"There's no party!" I blurt.

"So why did you mention a party?"

"Whew! Mom's right. I'm exhausted. I'm getting all my commitments mixed up. I was just thinking about this... social thing I have to do next month. More of an art fest fundraiser thing at the aquarium and—"

What the hell am I saying?

"And you want me to attend?" Mom's hand rests on her chest over her heart. Now she's back to over-the-top loving Mom mode. "Oh sweetie, I'd love to! I was only planning on visiting for the week, but of course I'll be there for you! I'll extend my stay!"

Calliope's eyes practically bulge out of her head now.

How is Mom not picking up on the fact that I made a dumb slip about Ralph's surprise party?

"No, no, no, that's alright." I wave Mom off as I make my way to the door. "Forget I said anything. I know you're busy. And you know what? Now that I'm thinking about everything I have on my plate, I'm not even sure I'm going."

Mom starts, "Don't be silly, baby. I'd love to go with you."

"You're off the hook!" I haul ass out of the apartment and shout over my shoulder, "Going to get some of that rest you suggested! Bye!"

"I'll walk you out!" Calliope says and makes it into the elevator beside me right before the doors close.

I stab the down button, lean back on the wall, and close my eyes.

I shouldn't have come.

My gut told me not to come.

So why didn't I listen?

"I know you're having a moment right now, but I need to ask you something," Calliope whispers.

I groan. "I'm sorry about the party slip. I just get all up in my head around her and—"

"Oh, I don't care about that. You were right. I should have known better than to try to surprise a scientist. Every day, your brother looks for clues to prove his 'you're throwing me a surprise party' theory. It's exhausting. If he knows, he knows. I give up. But he'll never guess the sexy details. The sexy details are unguessable."

"Dare I ask?"

"Probably not." She smiles, then softens her voice. "Are you okay? I'm starting to understand why you and Ralph-alpha are the way you are about your parents. That whole scene was—"

"Our childhood in a nutshell," I finish her sentence for her. "If you don't mind, though, I really don't want to talk about it right now."

"Understood."

The elevator lets us off into the lobby.

"Are you still following me?" I joke.

"Yeah. Like I said, I need to ask you something. But after witnessing that whole thing upstairs, I feel all sorts of conflicted."

"Why are you whispering?"

She peers up the stone staircase. "Your mom has supersonic hearing. Case in point, I think she heard Ralph and me getting it on last night. Correction: she definitely heard us getting it on last night."

"Yikes. Couldn't you guys cool it for one night until she got settled?"

Her face goes deadly serious. "No. We could not."

These two are wild.

"Anyway," Calliope continues. "I think she's mad at me for defiling her baby."

"That's ridiculous."

"No. It's not. This morning at breakfast she said, 'I'm mad at you for defiling my baby.' She hasn't looked at me since."

"Ugh. Sorry."

"So can she stay with you?" she asks sweetly.

"What? No! No way."

"I figured you'd say that. Forget I asked. I totally understand."

"I don't know why you guys agreed to this family experiment in the first place. Ralph should have told her to get a hotel."

We push out the main door and reach the street. The leaves are starting to turn, and that crispy fall smell is in the air. I take a moment to breathe it in.

"Yeah, well, with his birthday coming up, I guess he's feeling sentimental."

I scoff. "For what? All the good times we didn't have?"

She places a hand on my shoulder. "He's entering the last year of his twenties. Our parents are all getting older. I think he just wants to have as good a relationship as possible with her moving forward." She shrugs. "We're adults now. Maybe we don't need to hold on so tightly to the mistakes our parents made with us along the way."

"When did you get so introspective and wise?"

"I guess your brother is rubbing off on me. Literally and figuratively." She winks.

"Ew. I should have seen that one coming, ya perv." I pull her in for a hug. "Thanks for trying the whole dinner thing. And good luck with Mom. She's... unpredictable with her moods. But she'll warm up to you, and everything will be fine."

"Thanks. You're still good to arrive early on Monday night to get things ready to rock with James?"

I step back from the hug.

"What am I rockin' with James where?"

Calliope laughs, then speaks very slowly. "The party. You're arriving first to set up with James, so I can bring Ralph an hour later for the not-surprise, yes?"

"Right. Yes. I will be there early."

"Great. Thank you."

I give my head a scratch and try to look nonchalant. "Have you, um... Have you seen him lately?"

"Who, James? Nah. He's been out of town. But I've emailed with him plenty about the party. Why?"

"Has he... asked about me?"

Man, I sound pathetic right now.

"Oh constantly! Dude won't shut up about you!"

"Really?"

"No." She laughs and places a hand on my arm. "We've mostly stuck to party business."

"Of course, yeah. Okay, catch ya later, sister friend."

I start walking.

She calls after me, "You've got it so bad for that guy!"

"Do not!" I toss back.

I hear her giggle, but to her credit, she doesn't say the obvious.

She doesn't have to, though, because the voice in my head is saying it loud and clear. *Do too, do too, do too.*

Chapter Fourteen

JAMES

This is already proving to be quite an interesting night, and it hasn't even officially begun.

For the past half hour, I've been treated to an odd but delightful parade of scantily-clad, heavily made-up people sauntering into the back room of Adventure Bar with sequined wardrobe bags slung over their shoulders with the initials "BBB" printed in bright-blue bubble letters.

Several of them have invited me to "help them warm up" before the show. One woman gave me a literal wink wink, nudge nudge when she extended her invite.

Hm.

I politely declined.

I may be a guy with many skills and interests, but acting or... burlesque-ing—that's what Calliope called it, right?—is not one of my talents, so I'm not exactly sure how I can "help." Besides, I've been plenty busy making sure the food and drinks are ready.

I want everything to be perfect for Louise.

I mean her brother.

Whatever. I just want it to be perfect.

After the most recent arrival—a man smeared in what appears to be head-to-toe metallic body paint—I start hearing some surprising sounds from the back room.

What the hell are they doing back there?

I consider going in to check on them, but then I remember

when I did stage crew junior year of high school to get close to Sabrina Waltrich. The vocal warm-ups they did were pretty damn weird, so I'm not going to worry about it.

A light knock sounds.

"You with BBB?" I shout in the direction of the door.

"Uh, no. I'm—Calliope asked me to come early?"

Louise peeks around the doorframe with a shy smile.

Since when is this woman shy about anything?

"Hey! Of course, come on in!" I say. "Pull up a stool."

She doesn't take a seat. "No, I'm here to help. What can I do?" She bounces on her toes.

"Nothing, really. Everything's done, so seriously, you can relax. Cake was delivered about an hour ago. Weird cake, by the way. Have you seen it?"

She shakes her head. "No. Weird How?"

"Spherical? With a whole list of serving instructions? You'll see. Anyway, food and drinks are pretty much ready. Just need to slice some more garnishes, and we're good to go. Guests should be arriving shortly."

She looks around at the place. "Alright then."

The vocal warm-up sounds from the back room get louder.

Louise's blue eyes widen.

"Those noises you hear are coming from the performers. They seem to be a bit... eccentric," I say.

Tiptoeing toward the private room, she puts her ear to the door, then whispers, "Did she really hire burlesque performers?"

"Seems so."

The noises get even louder.

"Well, this should be interesting," she says as she moves back to the bar and finally takes a seat.

"I've been so busy lately, I haven't been keeping up with the party planning." She takes a deep breath. "Thanks so much for hosting us."

"It's my pleasure."

I take her in fully. Damn, this woman is gorgeous. She looks more tired than the last time I saw her, which somehow makes her even more beautiful. There's an openness to her tonight that

I haven't seen before. Her lips are painted a pale pink, and the ocean blue of her eyes has me drowning in their depths.

"Drowning in their depths? What the fuck, dude?" I say out loud.

"Excuse me?"

I scrub a hand over my head. "Sorry. I'm a little... distracted all of a sudden."

She smiles.

"Can I get you a drink?"

"Sure. Soda water with lime?"

"You got it."

Get it together, man.

"So," she says as I pour her drink. "Where have you been?"

"Been looking for me, have you?" I smirk.

"No," she emphasizes. "I just happened to notice you weren't at the aquarium this past week, and before that, when I saw you there, you seemed like you were..." She tucks her hair behind her ears. "I don't know. Never mind."

I was trying like hell to keep my distance from her, that's what I was doing, but I skip talking about that.

"I was in Hawaii this week."

"Oh yeah?"

"Yeah." I place her glass down in front of her. "Miss me?"

"Nope." She skates right past my flirtation and takes a sip. "What brought you back to Hawaii?"

"I go back monthly, actually."

"Wow. That's a long trip to take once a month."

I hesitate, then go with, "Yeah well, that diving and mountain climbing excursion company I mentioned—The Highs and Lows?—I'm basing it in Hawaii."

Is it terrible I don't immediately say my daughter lives there?

That she is the main reason I travel back so often?

I don't know why I withhold that information when everything inside me scrambles to say it. For some reason, it doesn't feel like the right time.

"Why are you creating a company in Hawaii when you live here?" she asks.

"Well." I swallow. "I'm moving there."

"To Hawaii?" Her voice goes up a few octaves.

"Yeah."

Am I imagining it? Or did her face just fall?

"Wow, that's—When is that happening?"

"Few months. The plan is to start the new year there fresh."

She takes a long sip of her drink and puts her smile back on. "Good for you. Making moves is always a good thing, right?"

"Eh. Not always," I argue. "I mean, in this case, yes, I hope it will be good. But I've seen people bounce around the globe their entire lives trying to avoid themselves, ya know? To outrun themselves. But that never works. Because we take ourselves with us wherever we go. Eventually, we have to deal with whatever is inside us that's making us want to run."

Her eyes lock on mine, but something about them still feels distant.

"Can I say something?" she asks.

"Sure."

"Don't take this the wrong way, but—"

"Uh-oh." I laugh. "Whenever someone says, 'Don't take this the wrong way,' you know you're about to be dissed."

"No! No diss! I was just thinking, you're..." She shifts in her seat. "You're deeper than I initially thought."

Not the first time someone has said that to me.

"I get that a lot." I shrug. "When you're a bartender, you hear a lot of stories. Gives you perspective, I guess."

She shakes her head. "It's more than that."

A quiet comes over the bar.

Even the backroom crew seems to have settled down.

"You okay?" I ask.

She takes another sip and nods. "Mm-hmm."

I clear my throat.

"As the resident bartender—at least for a few more months— and someone who's been told they have 'surprising depth' on more than one occasion, I'd like to hazard a guess as to why you look so down right now."

"That's not necessary, James."

I barrel ahead. "I'm thinking that maybe you're sad because

the guy you're catching feelings for just told you he's moving..."

"Whoa, whoa, whoa. Catching feelings?" She laughs. "Wow. And you said I have a healthy ego?"

"And that means you'll never have another one-night keg stand with him, which is a real heartbreaker because who's going to show you that kind of a good time again?"

Her jaw drops, but I keep going.

"I mean, a guy who goes on and on about the size of his lungs? Begs you to tell him about your hobbies? Then tries to sweet-talk you by comparing you to coffee grounds? Come on! How could you not mourn the loss of that?"

She cracks up. "Don't flatter yourself, sir. I've got a lot on my mind right now, and not all of it involves you."

"But some of it does?"

Her laughter quiets. "Maybe."

"I'll take that maybe," I say.

I turn my back and busy myself at the bar because I'm sure I have a cheeseball grin on my face right now that I'd rather she didn't see.

I almost don't hear her when she says, "That night with you was fun."

"Oh yeah?" I keep wiping down the bottles on the shelves, not ready to look at her yet.

"Yeah. The most fun I've had in a long time, actually. Even with your incessant blabbing."

"Incessant blabbing?" I turn and confront the insult head-on. "Ouch."

She laughs some more.

It's the best sound.

"I won't admit to being sad you're leaving," she says. "I am a bit surprised, though."

"Why is that?"

"Well. The other day at the aquarium, when I said it takes me a while to get to know people?"

"Yeah?"

"You literally said 'That's alright. I'm not going anywhere.'"

She's right. I did.

"So," she continues, "call me crazy, but I thought you weren't going anywhere." She pauses. "I thought we had time."

Did she just use a "we" statement?

I nod in understanding.

Her fingers trace the knotted wood of the bar top.

"Listen," I say after a moment. "I should be more careful with my words. I'm sorry about that. And this is not an excuse, but I do think you should know—when you're around—my brain is generally a walking, talking clusterfuck."

"What? Really?"

"Big time. I'm a mess around you, Cold Brew. I mean, Louise. Sorry."

Deep breath, dude. Slow down.

"Basically, I spend a full day after each of our interactions cursing myself for my motormouth and trying to conjure up some sort of self-protective filter for the future, so I'll have my shit together if or when I run into you again—because it does seem like the universe keeps putting you on my path. Have you noticed that? So far, though, no dice. I am filter free now and forever, it seems! But—for what it's worth—I am working on it."

"Well, don't work on it too hard," she says. "As I recall, your motormouth came in handy that first night."

Her cheeks immediately turn pink.

"Oh my God, did I just say that?" She covers her face with both hands.

I laugh, but quickly school my features and get faux serious. "You did. But I am willing to accept the compliment. I'm pretty sure that was a compliment...?"

"It was, yeah." She nods quickly and waves her hands like she wants to keep the conversation moving.

"And move along to another topic if it makes you feel better," I finish.

"I would appreciate that, thank you."

"Cool, cool. I did want to say one thing, though. You said before that you thought we had time. Well, we do. We have twelve weeks."

"Twelve weeks," she repeats.

"Yeah. Plenty of time to become friends, don't you think?"

She smiles.

"Yeah. That—That sounds nice."

How the hell I'm going to be just friends with this woman is beyond me, but I will do my damnedest.

The bell over the door jingles.

"Speaking of friends!" I nod toward the entrance where Wally and Mabel are making their way in, followed by a stream of other punctual party people. "Hey, everybody!"

An hour later, the party is in full swing. We're just waiting on the birthday boy. Louise has been keeping me company this whole time, drinking and laughing with Mabel and Wally. Her usual edge has softened, and I like seeing her more relaxed side.

When Wally and Mabel get up from the bar to dance, I'm surprised she sticks with me.

I'm certainly not complaining.

"The coolest thing happened the other day at the aquarium," she says with a sparkle in her eyes. "Want to hear about it?"

"Course! Tell me." I finish a pour and slide the glass to a guy with Clark Kent glasses and a sweater vest. I'm loving this crowd tonight.

"So. I've been taking my lunch break with Meilani whenever I can. Most days, I bring my easel and paints too. I'm building this whole portfolio of her. I've painted more in the past three weeks than I have in the last two years. And she loves it! I swear she's posing and performing for me. It's so funny and makes me feel so good."

"Amazing!"

"Yeah but get this—this is the really amazing part—the other day, I kid you not, she let me know that she wanted to paint too."

"How did she do that?"

"Through the movements she was making. It was like she was mimicking what I was doing on the canvas. I know it sounds weird, but I ended up doing some research on it, and I learned that painting can be a good enrichment activity for sea lions. So I talked to Dana, and we're going to try it out with her this week."

"That is damn cool. Keep me posted on how it goes, will ya?"

"I will." She smiles. "Oh and the best news is, her trainers say she's putting on weight and being more responsive with them too. She's making some really rapid improvements."

"That's incredible. Sounds like you're making a real difference with her."

"Yeah." She lets out a breath. "I don't really understand why or how, though."

"When there's a connection, there's a connection," I say. "Sometimes these things are hard to explain."

I give her a wink and take a quick drink order from a woman in a purple dress.

"Truuuuue." Louise stretches out the word, then makes fun of my wink with one of her own. "But I mostly meant, it's not like I have a ton of experience with pinnipeds. I specialize in echinoderms. Though I did minor in psychology while getting my bio degree, so I'm sure that helps. I wasn't sure at first what aspect of marine biology I'd specialize in, and advisors usually say if you think you might want to work with cetaceans or pinnipeds, you'd be wise to study some psychology."

"Hold up. Echino-suh-tay-shuh-pinna-what? I don't think I caught half of that."

I hand a pinot grigio to the woman in purple.

"I'm sorry, I hate when people do that," Louise says.

"Do what?"

"Say fancy words to make themselves feel smart. I swear that's not what I was doing." She takes a quick sip of her drink, then explains, "Pinnipeds are marine mammals with four flippered limbs. So... seals, sea lions, and walruses. Cetaceans are whales, dolphins, and porpoises. But I mostly work with echinoderms: starfish, sea urchins, sea cucumbers.... basically, the weirdos of the ocean."

"Keep it weird, baby. That's what I always say." I hesitate. "Actually, I don't think I've ever said that, but whatever. I believe it. Weird is good."

She smiles. "Me too."

Her phone pings with a text, and she immediately pops to her feet. "It's Calliope. They're five minutes away. Brace yourself."

"Consider me braced." I laugh. "But why?"

"You never know what's going to happen when Calliope's in charge."

As it turns out, Louise is the one who should have been bracing.

Because when an older man walks in a moment later, her jaw drops.

And if looks could kill? This dude would be a dead man.

Chapter Fifteen

LOUISE

"Surprise!" the whole room shouts as Ralph and Calliope enter the bar.

I miss the big moment, though, because I'm cowering in the furthest corner of the room trying to calm my pounding heart.

Alright, cowering isn't completely accurate. I'm not someone who cowers. Currently, I am standing with one of Ralph's astronomy friends, trying my best to focus on his diatribe about black holes, when all I want is to be sucked into one myself.

What the hell is he doing here?

Who invited him?

The moment my dad walked in, I went into fight-or-flight mode. After quickly realizing that I didn't want to cause a scene on my brother's special night, I decided on flight.

I will stay the least amount of time necessary to be deemed a good sister, then I'm out of here.

Hopefully without having to talk to him.

"Oh man! You should see your face right now!" Ralph's astronomy friend says. "Am I freaking you out with all this black hole talk?"

I'm barely listening to you, buddy.

All my awareness is trained on my father, who is working the room, making small talk with strangers as if he belongs here. Perhaps these people wouldn't be strangers to him if he'd made any effort to be a consistent part of his son's life.

Or mine.

I thought we made eye contact a moment ago, but it was hard to tell in the dim lighting and all the revelry. Either way, it seems he's keeping his distance for now and waiting for me to approach him.

Well, he'll be waiting a long damn time.

Astronomy guy prattles on, "Don't worry. We are in absolutely no danger. Black holes are kind of like hippopotamuses. Sure, they'll mess you up if you wander into their mouths, but if you can avoid doing that, you'll be just fine."

"I'll um—I'll try to avoid that then," I say while watching Ralph across the room, happily slapping backs and shaking hands. "Though you may not want to use hippos in your black hole analogy moving forward."

"Oh no?"

"No. Hippopotamuses are aggressive and highly unpredictable animals. Studies have shown they kill over 430 humans every year. And believe me, those people didn't wander into their mouths. Those hippos charged."

"But they look so cute!"

"I assure you, they're not. They can weigh upward of four tons, they have lower incisors that grow to over a foot and a half, and they will run eighteen miles per hour in your direction to chomp you dead in a single bite. Especially if they're a mother and deem you a threat to their young."

It's at that moment, my own mother walks in, looking dressed to kill.

And kill she might when she realizes our dad is here.

I don't want to be here to witness the fallout, so...

"It was nice talking to you..." I search my mind for his name, but for the life of me, I can't remember it. "I gotta go."

I turn and run smack into Ralph, who envelops me in a hug. "Hey, where you running off to?"

I don't say anything. I answer by pressing my face into his shoulder and wrapping my arms around him.

"Just a sec," Ralph whispers. "Ben!" he says to astronomy guy, who I'm sure I've completely freaked out with my dark hippo turn. "Thanks for coming! Cool if I catch up with you in a little bit? I need to talk to my sister alone for a minute."

"Sure thing. Happy Birthday, Anderson. And nice to, uh—nice to meet you, Louise."

Ralph releases me from the hug. "By the expression on your face, I thought you might have needed a break from Ben. He can be chatty."

"Chatty is fine," I say. "I don't mind chatty."

When I look across the room, another chatty guy I know is pouring drinks and sending me a confused smile.

Can't blame James for being baffled by me.

One minute, he and I were connecting and sharing. The next? I hightailed it across the room like my ass was on fire.

"So you knew about this party?" Ralph asks.

"Uh... yeah." I give him a look. "And you knew about this too, ya dork."

He lowers his voice. "I did, but don't tell Calliope. I know she worked hard to keep this a surprise." Ralph beams at the room full of partygoers. "How cool is this, though? People from the museum are here, folks from grad school..."

"The guy who donated sperm to our mom..."

"What? Where?" Ralph's head whips left and right.

I nod in the direction of the high-top tables, where dear old Dad is now sitting with a group of scientists, chatting up a storm, like he doesn't have a care in the world.

"Did Calliope invite him?" I ask.

He shakes his head. "She wouldn't do that."

"Then who did?

At that moment, the bar music fades, and a live drumbeat starts to pound.

Drums? The performers brought drums?

Calliope and Mabel rush over to us. Calliope squeals and squeezes Ralph. "It's starting! Get ready for your mind to be blown, birthday boy."

"Callie," I say. "Do we know how that man ended up here?"

"Which man?"

"That one."

I try to subtly point in Dad's direction, but he catches me this time.

The drumbeats get louder.

He gives me a small wave. I turn away.

Calliope purses her lips. "I don't know. I don't know him." She pauses. "But he looks familiar."

Ralph leans close to Calliope and whispers something in her ear.

"Shit!" she says. "What the hell is he doing here?"

"You're breathing kind of funny, Lou. Are you okay?" Mabel asks, kind and considerate as always.

"Yeah, are you guys okay?" Calliope's eyes dart between Ralph and me, then back to our dad. "But also, can I say what we're all thinking? Or at least what Mabel and I are thinking?"

"How do you know what I'm thinking?" Mabel marvels.

"Your dad is sexy as hell," Calliope says.

I shake my head. "No. Ew. Stop that. Right now."

"Sorry, Lou, but he is! How could he not be? He looks like Ralph. Or Ralph looks like him. Point is, I'm seeing my future," she licks her lips. "And me likey."

"Callie?" Ralph groans. "Can we not go down this road right now?"

"You're seeing your future? In that man?" For a moment, I see red. "Calliope, a future with that man is heartache. It's chaos. It's thinking you're loved one minute, then knowing you're most definitely not the next. It's always wondering why you weren't good enough for him. Why he chose anything and everything else over you. It's constantly searching for love you will never have and answers you will never get. So if that's the kind of future you want for yourself, then, by all means, climb aboard and enjoy the fucked-up ride."

Ralph puts a hand on my back.

"I'm sorry, Lou," Calliope says. "It was a bad joke. I'm not going to jump your dad —

Obviously—as I fully intend to jump your brother and only your brother for the rest of our lives. All I meant was that I dig the whole rugged face, salt-n-pepper hair thing he's got going on, and if Ralph ages like that you won't hear me complaining." She pauses. "I'm sorry, though. Really."

I nod, then attempt to massage my own shoulders. They feel like rocks.

"Well," Ralph starts, "all I know is we'd better get Mom out of here before she sees him, and all hell breaks loose."

"Too late," Calliope says softly and nods toward where our mother is standing stock-still, her eyes shooting daggers at her former husband.

The drumbeats reach a crescendo, and a blinding beam of light cuts through the crowd.

Everyone shields their eyes.

"Billions and billions of years ago..." a seductive female voice says over a crackly microphone.

A man in a G-string enters the spotlight. He is covered from head to toe in silver body paint.

The sensual voice continues, "The universe as we now know it started as a single point."

Silver G-string guy emphasizes the word "point" with a pelvic thrust. That must have been a signal to the light operator because the light beam narrows to focus exclusively on his point.

"Wow," Calliope says. "I didn't realize their lights and sound capabilities would be so good. I'm impressed."

"What is happening?" Ralph murmurs.

"Magic, baby," she purrs. "Magic is happening."

The sultry voice continues to boom throughout the room.

"This point of infinite heat..."

The silver pointed pelvis pumps into the air.

"This steeeeeaming hot, sexy heat..."

The pelvis swirls.

"Was packed! Full! Of raw! Materials!"

Thrust. Thrust. Thrust. Thrust.

"Calliope," I whisper," I'm starting to think this isn't burlesque."

"For billions of years, this point was yearning and churning and burning..."

The performer's pelvis vibrates and shakes with vigor now.

"Don't hurt yourself, dude," I joke.

"It wanted to stretch..."

The man's silver hand teases his G-string while he gyrates.

"It wanted to growwwww..."

"Looks pretty fully grown to me," Mabel giggles.

"And when it reached the magnificent moment when it could no longer contain itself..."

The spotlighted hand pulls out an erect, silver penis and strokes it hard.

"Oh my God." Ralph covers his eyes.

"It BURST!"

Bright light flashes, then fills the entire bar.

The silver man is now surrounded by a troupe of naked people, all painted and accessorized to look like planets.

The same female voice proudly booms, "Welcome. To the Big Bang Bacchanal!"

With that, a literal big bang begins.

Chapter Sixteen

LOUISE

"Holy moly, they're really going for it!" Mabel starts taking off her own clothes. "This is a dream come true for a new nudist!"

Wally jogs over just in time and zips her dress back up. "How about we keep our skivvies on for now, babe?"

"You're right. This is their show. Don't wanna pull focus." She winks at her man.

My, my, Mabel's confidence levels have soared this summer.

"Did she say Big Bang *Bacchanal*?" Calliope whips out her phone and starts scrolling. "I thought the BBB stood for Big Bang Burlesque."

"Did you get a contract?" I ask.

"Yes. That's what I'm looking for."

"I feel like I should know this, but what is a Bacchanal?" Ralph's head tilts to the side as he stares at the carnal scene unfolding in front of us.

I'm doing the same.

"It's, um... It's a Greco-Roman cult party celebrating Bacchus, the god of wine. Otherwise known as...an orgy," I say.

"Wow, an orgy!" Mabel claps her hands. "That pretty one licking the big guy in the crown must be Saturn. Look at all the golden rings on her headpiece. And around her ta-tas."

"This is so scientifically inaccurate," Ralph says.

"Oh, ya think?" I mock.

"But, Mabel, for future reference," Ralph's teaching voice is in full effect, "the big guy in the crown is Jupiter."

"How can you tell?"

"His body paint is legit. I have to give them credit. They did do at least a minimum amount of research. Also, Jupiter is the largest planet in our solar system—often referred to as the 'king of planets'—so that explains the crown choice. But most importantly, see how his penis and its surrounding area is painted red and how he's committed to whipping it around and around like a helicopter blade?"

Mabel watches for a moment. "I do see that, yeah."

"He's trying to simulate Jupiter's Great Red Spot."

"What's that?" she asks.

"It's a high-pressure storm that's been swirling in Jupiter's atmosphere for over three-hundred years. It's so large it's visible from space."

"Welp. Not visible anymore," I mumble as Jupiter plunges into Saturn.

"Fascinating. Thank you for that teaching moment, friend." Mabel offers Ralph a fist bump.

"You bet."

Ralph accepts the bump, then he and Mabel go back to watching the action with renewed interest.

I huddle close to Calliope, who is scrolling through the contract like mad.

"What does it say?"

"I give up," she says and hands me the phone. "You know how these contracts are. So much mumbo jumbo."

"Let me see." I scroll to the bottom of the contract. "Did you read the fine print when you booked this thing?"

"Of course not. No one reads the fine print," Calliope scoffs.

"Always read the fine print, sister friend. Always! See? It says it right here: 'Big Bang Burlesque is code for Big Bang Bacchanal, a celestial orgy adventure.'"

Calliope grabs her phone back and squints. "Damn, that font is tiny."

"Aw, my girl got me a celestial orgy?" Ralph croons as he

gathers her close.

"She did." They kiss.

"Ugh."

Oops, did I "ugh" out loud?

"Lou, come on. Is this actually that big a deal?" Calliope huffs. "I mean, look around. People seem into it. The birthday boy certainly seems to have warmed up to the idea." She snuggles into Ralph's back while he watches.

"Is this legal, though?" I hiss. "Are orgies even legal?"

"Depends." Suddenly, James is beside me, also on his phone. "I just texted my, um, my lawyer friend. And we should be okay." He reads from his screen. "She says, 'Orgies are legal as long as they are a private affair where no entrance fee is charged, and all parties are consenting adults over the age of eighteen.'"

I can't believe I'm even having this discussion.

I put my head in both of my hands.

The last thing I want is to get James's business in trouble.

"Louise." He gently pulls my hands away from my face and places a warm palm on my cheek. "Everything will be okay."

I'm transported back in time to that first night with him. If I crane my neck to look past Venus and Mercury, who are currently stroking each other on barstools, I can see a direct path to the hall that leads to the walk-in refrigerator. I have to laugh at how funny it is that I want a redo of that truly bizarre night. I remember how warm and comforting his hands were, despite how cold it was. Something tells me, though, that I could be in subzero temperatures in the middle of Antarctica, and if James was standing next to me, I'd feel nothing but warmth.

Familiar voices arise from across the room.

Oh God. My parents have made it past their staring contest and are now full-on arguing.

"I'm gonna go," I say to James.

He hesitates, then asks, "Want company?"

Why does that question feel like such a relief?

Hell yeah, I want his company.

I nod.

He smiles. "Gimme a minute. I'll meet you up front."

He hustles over to the bar and starts talking to one of his employees, who is currently pouring drinks and chatting up customers.

I tap Ralph and Calliope on the shoulders.

"Guys? I'm heading out."

"What? Why?" Ralph says.

Call me crazy—but I don't relish the opportunity to watch a planetary orgy in a food and drink establishment while my big brother and estranged parents are within arm's distance of me.

I don't say that, though. I just give him a look.

"But we haven't done the birthday cake yet!" Calliope says. "I commissioned Bucks County Bakery to make me an Earth-shaped cake!"

"You did?" Ralph perks up.

"Yeah, baby. Don't think I didn't hear how horny you got talking about the teacher who threw you those geo parties! Tonight, I am going to make you forget Miss Thompson ever existed. We're talking about a perfectly spherical cake meticulously decorated with ocean and continent icing. And the layers inside are scientifically accurate!"

"That sounds awesome, Callie," I say. "But I'm still going to—"

"Well, accurate is likely too generous a term, but seriously, it's so fun!" She runs her index finger all over him, booping places on his body as she describes the cake. "There's a crunchy chocolatey crust, an orange sponge cake upper mantel, a lemon lower mantel, and a French vanilla inner core with silver flakes. You know, as an homage to the white-hot metallic center of our planetary home."

"My girl made me a space cake," Ralph rumbles and pulls her close.

"Well, my guy deserves the world, doesn't he?" she purrs.

When they start full-on devouring each other's faces, I take that opportunity to split. Clearly, I'm not needed here.

I find James waiting for me by the door.

"Are you sure this is okay? You're working." I gesture to the bar rag still in his hand and shrug on my coat.

"Not anymore."

He folds the rag and places it on a rack behind the bar, then tosses his keys to his coworker, who catches them with ease.

"Shall we?" He offers me his arm.

I take it, and we walk outside.

And run directly into a teenager who appears to be anxiously waiting for someone.

"Whoa! What the—"

"Hello!" she says excitedly. "My name is Marthy."

"Marthy?" I ask.

"Yeth. Marthy."

"Oh, Marcy!"

I have no idea who this Marcy person is, but she is high energy and has one hell of a lisp.

"Pleathe excuthe my articulation thith evening," she says. "I rethently got a palette exthpander in preparathion for long overdue brathes, and I'm not uthed to it yet."

"Not a problem," I say.

What is this kid doing outside of a bar on a Monday night?

James gently steps forward. "Do you need something, Marcy? Everything okay? You know this is a bar, and we don't allow unaccompanied minors inside."

"Oh yeth, things are more than okay, thank you. And don't worry, my mom ith in that Toyota Priuth you thee over there, waiting for me."

A woman waves at us through the windshield.

We wave back.

Okaaay.

"Well, then if you'll excuse us, Marcy, we need to get going." He looks at me and lowers his voice. "How'd you get here? The bus?"

"Yeah."

"I'll give you a ride then?" He nods toward his car.

"Please, yeah. That would be great."

Marcy whips out her cell phone, presses a button and holds it up.

Is she recording us?

"Oh no, you don't! You're not going anywhere, thinnerth!"

Thinners? Why is she calling us—Oh. Sinners. She's calling us sinners.

"Nicholath!" she calls toward her mom's car. "Bring over the boom!"

Another young teen who looks just like her bursts from the Toyota with a boom microphone and holds it high up in the air. Or as high as he can get it. He's not a tall kid, so it bonks me on the head.

"Sorry," he says.

"All good." I adjust my ponytail.

Marcy continues, "Ath you can probably tell, Nicolath and I are twinth. We work for the Willow Grove Gazette, a high thchool newthpaper dedicated to cracking the big thtorieth while they're hot."

"Good for you guys! Budding journalists. Very cool!"

"And we got a hot tip that thith ethtablishment ith hothting a planetary prothtitution party tonight." She shoves the phone closer to my face. "Can you tell uth what you exthperienthed while inthide thith den of debauchery?"

James tries to suppress a laugh and ends up choking.

I give him a slap on the back and inch us toward the car.

But these kids are on us like glue.

"Listen," I say. "I think it's awesome that you two budding journalists are out here chasing the hot stories! Keep it up! Follow your dreams! But I'm afraid I have to disappoint you. There's no 'den of debauchery' to investigate tonight. Nothing is going on in there other than a wholesome surprise birthday party for my big brother."

It's totally appropriate in this situation to lie, right?

Marcy gasps.

Nicholas drops the boom.

James's eyes widen.

"What?" I ask. "What did I say?"

I whip my head toward the building and quickly realize it's not what I said but what they're seeing that's causing all the fuss.

It's a sight I can never unsee.

It will be burned into my retinas for all eternity.

It's the globes of Jupiter's bare painted butt.

Mooning us through the bar window.

Chapter Seventeen

JAMES

We speed away from the scene, laughing our asses off.

I'm glad Louise sees the humor in this.

When we finally get control of ourselves and stop at a red light, she asks, "Should we call Ralph and Calliope?"

"And tell them what? That some high school freshmen from Willow Grove tried to crash their party? Nah. Besides, their mom got them back in their car as soon as we hopped into mine. I think she got more than she bargained for and won't be encouraging her kids to do these investigations anymore."

"How did they even find out about it?"

"Who knows?"

"Well, maybe we should at least text your buddy behind the bar. Give him a heads-up in case the cops show?"

"The cops aren't going to show, but yes." I lift my phone from its cradle. "I'll shoot him a text."

Ken is a longtime manager at the original Adventure Bar. Part of the next few months is making sure he's ready to take over managing the Manyunk location for me full time once I move back to Hawaii. What better way to give him a test run than to let him oversee a surprise celestial orgy?

A text alert sounds while the phone is still in my hand.

"My lawyer friend just following up. She checked with a few more of her colleagues, and she says Adventure Bar is all good on the legal front. This won't be a problem for us."

She exhales deeply. "That's good to hear."

It feels weird calling Eva "my lawyer friend." Calling her my ex never feels right either, though. I mean, she can't be an ex if we were never in an actual relationship. But she is one of my closest friends, and we have a kid together, so she certainly warrants a better description than "my lawyer friend."

I'm just not sure how to broach that subject with Louise without making it a whole thing, so "lawyer friend" will have to do for now.

The light turns green, and we start moving again.

"Where to?" I ask.

"Hm?"

When I peek over at her, she seems lost in thought. The lights of the nearby cars highlight her pretty face.

I'm so glad this is happening right now.

"Just wondering where I'm taking you. You want to go home? Or do you want to go somewhere?"

"I'm feeling pretty riled up," she says softly. "So can we just... drive?"

"Sure." I smile. "We can do that."

We drive quietly down Main Street as couples stroll hand in hand, and families mill in and out of restaurants and galleries.

After a few minutes of silence, I test the waters. "That older guy who joined the party. I'm guessing that was your dad?"

"I don't have a dad," she says.

Her eyes are glued to the windshield.

"Oh. I'm sorry for your—"

"Loss? No. I didn't lose him. He likes to disappear for long stretches of time, but he's most definitely alive." She sighs. "Yes, that was him at the bar. I'm just not sure he deserves the dad title from us at this point."

"Say no more." My fingers lift off the steering wheel, then relax back down. "Or, you know, do say more. Whatever you need."

"He left when I was a toddler. Called on holidays and birthdays for a while, until I guess he got bored of that. Last I heard, he was remarried and living in Cabo. But that must have fizzled out if he's back in the States and sniffing around us again. Thankfully, the BBB team created enough of a diversion that I was able to get out of there without speaking to him." She scoffs. "Cabo. Ugh. Do people even live in Cabo? It sounds like a fake place."

"They do. And it's not."

"You've been there?

"Sure," I say. "I've been most places."

"'Most places?' What does that mean? How many countries?"

"All of them."

"All of them?" she nearly shouts.

"Well, almost all of them. There are a few in Europe I still need to hit. And two in Africa."

"Excuse my language, but what the fuck, dude! How is that even possible?"

I laugh. "You make it a priority. Save some money. Create a plan. Keep it frugal. It also helps to have a job you can do from your laptop."

"Huh," she says. "Owning bars doesn't seem like the ideal job for a world traveler."

"Oh yeah, no. I did most of my globetrotting before starting Adventure Bar. I pretty much spent eighteen through twenty-five traveling and writing about it. I had a travel blog that did really well for a while."

"Wow, I'm impressed."

"Don't give me too much credit. I also had a small trust that opened up for me when I turned eighteen. That certainly helped. Plus, there's a whole network of travelers out there who are just waiting to lend a hand and help each other. It's a way of life."

"It's your way of life?"

"It was."

"But not anymore?" She urges me to go on.

"Yes and no."

"Way to be cryptic, dude."

"Sorry. I don't mean to be cryptic. I've just had some life changes over the past seven years or so, which have curbed my travels a bit. Not entirely, but a bit. Anyway, I am sorry about your dad."

She shrugs. "Don't be. He did me a favor."

"How so?"

"Taught me all the lessons I need to learn about men while I was still young. No offense."

I wince in a lighthearted way. "Aw, come on. 'No offense' is just as bad as 'don't take this the wrong way.'"

"True. You're right. Let me amend my statement. He taught me all the lessons I need to learn about most men. That better? It's taken me way too long to absorb those lessons and live accordingly, but better late than never, right?"

"Which lessons are we talking about?"

"One: Don't expect a man to take care of you.

"Okay."

"Two: Do not base your self-worth on what a man thinks of you."

"Fair enough."

"And three: Never, ever date a single dad."

Well, shit.

"Whoa. Really?" I say.

"I know. That last one feels judgy, but I stand by it. For me, at least."

"Why?"

"Well, once a guy has a child, that child becomes their world. Or at least that's how it should be. It certainly wasn't the case with my dad. With either of my parents, really."

"How do you mean?"

"After their divorce, they bounced around from partner to partner, always putting that shiny new person first, leaving my brother and me in the background. Then when their new toy inevitably lost its luster, they came back to us to playact being good parents, which only ever lasted a month or two until the whole cycle started again."

"That sucks."

"Yeah, it did."

"But... what does that have to do with you never dating a single dad?"

"I never want to be the person standing between a child and their dad. Ever. So I won't."

We start winding our way through the center of the city, and things get more touristy.

I consider playing devil's advocate.

I consider telling her it's one-hundred-percent possible to be an excellent dad and a great partner.

That she should give single dads a chance.

Correction: that she should give me a chance.

But who am I to say any of those things when my daughter and I are separated by thousands of miles and an ocean right now?

Why fight for a chance with this woman when I'm leaving in a few months?

"Hey, you want to go park at Penn's Landing and stare at the Ben Franklin?" Louise's voice snaps me out of my thoughts.

"The bridge or the man?" I joke.

"The bridge, ya dork."

"Louise Anderson, are you asking me to park with you? Is this a 1950s movie, and you are asking me to put aside my morals and park?"

She laughs. "Not like that. But yes, I am asking you to move your vehicle into that lot over there and to shift your car into park so we can sit by the water. Ever since I can remember, sitting by the water has made me feel calm."

"Still feeling riled up?"

"No," she says as she places her hand over mine on the gearshift. "Not anymore."

Parking it is.

Chapter Eighteen

LOUISE

After a quick stop at a 7-Eleven, we're sitting on a bench by the river eating Philly soft pretzels and sipping Gatorade while the Benjamin Franklin Bridge glitters overhead.

There's a small amount of space between us.

I'm not sure who put it there, him or me.

I wince and put my hand to my cheek.

"You okay?" he asks.

"Yeah, I've just been having this tooth pain lately. At least I think it's tooth pain." I massage a small circle on the hinge of my jaw.

"You should probably get that checked out."

I wave him off. "It's fine."

"Music okay?" he asks while a classic rock station plays. When we got here, he backed his car into the space right behind us and opened the hatchback so we can listen to the radio.

It's good, yeah." We watch a *Spirit of Philadelphia* party cruise boat float by. "So. No beer, huh? I figured when you were cool with an orgy taking over your bar tonight, you'd be wild enough to risk drinking a paper-bag-covered beer in public with me."

He takes a swig of his Gatorade. "Not a beer guy. But you should still have gotten one for yourself."

"Nah. I don't drink alone. You more of a cocktail dude then?"

"Nope. No cocktails either." He pauses. "I'm sober actually."

"Well, I should hope so. You drove me here," I joke.

He laughs lightly. "No, I mean I'm in recovery. Been sober for almost seven years."

"Oh."

Wow. I didn't see that one coming.

"Surprised?" he asks.

"Sort of? I guess?"

"Remember when I mentioned that money I got control of when I turned eighteen?"

"Yeah?"

"Well, that existed because of my mom. She died when I was young."

"I'm sorry."

He waves me off. "It's coming up on twenty years she's been gone, so..."

"So... people should stop saying they're sorry?"

"I don't know. Maybe? I mean, I've officially lived longer without her than I did with her. So when people say they're sorry now, it kind of feels like they're apologizing to someone else. To thirteen-year-old James who admittedly didn't handle things so well. That guy was way too cool to cry, so he started stealing cigarettes and wine coolers instead."

"Wine coolers?" I ask.

"Yeah," he says, full of mock offense. "You got a problem with wine coolers?"

"No, no problem."

I stifle a laugh.

Because apparently, I am a wildly inappropriate person.

The man just told me his mother died, and here I am giggling over his drink of choice while he was a grieving teen?

"I'll have you know that Bartles and Jaymes Fuzzy Navel wine coolers are a dangerous gateway drug, madam! They singlehandedly sent me down my teenage road to ruin and landed me in AA!"

This only makes me laugh harder.

"I don't know why I'm laughing! Oh my God, I'm so sorry. I should not be laughing!"

He laughs along with me. "It's okay. I'm just messing with

you. Life is like that, isn't it? Sad one minute, funny the next? But somehow it all blends together to create something beautiful."

I wish I had even an ounce of this guy's perspective.

His positivity and ability to roll with the punches are amazing.

A family of four walks by us. The little girl finds a tiny rock and throws it into the water.

"When your mom passed, you still had another parent I hope?"

"My dad, yeah. But he didn't do so well in the aftermath. He wasn't the warmest guy before it happened, but afterward? Forget it. He may as well have not been there at all. When he told me we were moving to Philly a few months after the funeral for a job transfer, it didn't take me long to figure out it was because he couldn't bear to stay on the island. Couldn't blame him for that. Everything there reminded me of her too. But my story sort of has a happy ending. I met Wally soon after starting high school here, and he helped me turn things around. Good friends have a way of doing that."

In a weird coincidence, *I Get By with a Little Help From My Friends* starts playing on the radio.

He chuckles, "Well that's a dose of synchronicity right there."

"Synchronicity?"

"You know, meaningful coincidences? Here I am talking about getting by with some help from my friend, and in comes Ringo to sing me a song all about that very thing."

"I know what the word synchronicity means. I'm just—" I pause. "You believe in that stuff? The woo woo 'universe' stuff?"

"My friend Kathleen asked me the same thing. I don't know if I'd call it 'woo woo,' but yeah. I believe the universe puts certain people and opportunities in front of us to learn lessons and help us become the next best version of ourselves. I also believe that sometimes we're so busy hustling and 'achieving that we don't see that life has an even better plan for us if we'd stay open and pay attention."

"Whoa. That was so... earnest."

"Too much?" He chuckles.

I surprise myself when I say, "No. Not too much."

I'm not used to openhearted, earnest guys like this.

The guys I'm used to do the whole mysterious, cool thing.

I'm starting to realize those guys are exhausting.

But James? James is refreshing.

"Haven't you noticed that sometimes life gives us these little... *coincidences* to let us know we're on track? Little nudges from the universe telling us it has our back?"

I scoff. "Not really, no. I'm a scientist."

"I would think you'd notice it even more then."

I don't know if the music actually gets louder or if it just feels that way.

James starts singing along and tapping his thumb on his thigh.

"Mind if we change the channel?" I blurt.

"Oh. Sure. Sorry, I can stop singing."

"That's fine. Sing all you want, just... a different song please."

"...Alright."

He climbs through the back of the car and presses a button on the dash. "She Loves Me" blares through the speaker.

Geez, aren't there any other bands in the world?

"Anything but The Beatles would be good," I shout from the bench.

He shuts the music off completely, slowly exits the car and sits down beside me. He looks at me like I'm from another planet.

"You don't like The Beatles?" he asks in disbelief.

"Not particularly."

"John, Paul, George, and Ringo."

"I'm familiar with the band, James. And yeah, no. Don't like 'em. Not my jam."

"How can The Beatles not be your jam!?" His voice ratchets up like he's swallowed helium. "Everyone likes The Beatles!"

"Clearly, everyone does not. Are you okay? Your voice is getting really high."

"Saying you don't like The Beatles is like saying, 'You know what? I don't really care for oxygen.'"

"Alright, you're being dramatic."

"No, I'm not! You can't even really categorize their music as music. It just... is. The Beatles didn't write songs. They wrote hymns on how to create a life well lived!"

I snort. "Yeah, that 'Octopus's Garden' anthem is chock-full of life lessons. 'Yellow Submarine' is also pretty inspiring. And 'I am the Walrus'! Wow. 'Goo goo g'joob,' am I right? Have you ever gotten such solid life advice before?"

"Rrrrrr," he growls. "You have a point. And don't think I missed the fact that you're only referencing ocean-inspired songs. But 'Live and Let Die,' 'Let it Be,' 'All You Need is Love?'"

I shrug.

"Come on, woman! Those are epic, soul-stirring anthems, all telling us to chill the hell out, breathe, and go on the ride of life!"

"You are nerding out so hard right now."

"You bet I am! For The Beatles? I'll nerd out until the end of time."

"I just think if you're going to praise the 'soul-stirring anthems,' then you also have to acknowledge that just as many songs were total—possibly drug-infused—nonsense."

He mimes stabbing a knife into his heart before settling back on the bench.

"Man." He blows out a breath and stares at the river. "I'm not sure we can still be friends after this revelation."

"Is that what we are?" I ask softly. "Friends?"

"Well, we *were*!"

We laugh.

"But I suppose it's an even trade. I tell you I'm an alcoholic, you tell me you're anti-Beatles. Somehow, together, we'll get through this."

He puts his arm around me.

I sink into him. Like we've done this a million times.

He makes it feel so easy.

"Wait a second." I lift my head off his shoulder. "You're an alcoholic who runs a bar?"

He nods.

"Should I be using that word? Alcoholic? It feels kind of mean."

He shrugs. "I usually say I'm 'sober' or 'in recovery,' but 'alcoholic' works too. One of the first things we say at meetings is 'Hi, my name is James and I'm an alcoholic.' I'm totally fine with that word."

"Isn't that hard? To run a bar?"

I take a sip of my drink.

"Not really. Think of it this way. It's not difficult being a heterosexual male gynecologist, is it?"

Gatorade sprays out of my mouth with my unexpected laugh.

"I wouldn't know, sir. I've never been a heterosexual male gynecologist. Have you?"

He looks out over the water, a devilish smirk on his face. "Have I been a heterosexual male? Yes. Still am, in fact. Have I ever been a gynecologist? No."

He rips off a piece of his pretzel and takes a bite.

"Are you sure you're not drunk right now? Because you're not making a whole lot of sense."

"Forget it. Hey, trivia girl, did you know that the invention Benjamin Franklin was most proud of was his 'glass armonica,' an instrument designed to replicate that spooky sound a wet finger makes when rubbed along the rim of a glass?"

"Of course I did. And are you flirting with me with that wet finger line?"

"Depends. Did it work?"

"No!" I laugh. "It's official. You have the weirdest flirt game I've ever encountered. And don't you dare change the subject on me! I'm invested in this conversation now. Tell me, sir, how is being an alcoholic bartender like being a heterosexual gynecologist?"

He slides down and rests his head on the back of the bench. "You're not going to let this one go. Are you?"

"Nope!"

"Sobriety and beer." He sighs. "Gynecology and vaginas."

"Meaning?" I gesture for him to continue, knowing where he's going with this, but really enjoying the process of torturing him.

"Meaning I can happily serve people beer all day without thinking about drinking. Just like a respectable doctor can attend to patients all day without thinking about..."

"Sex." I finish the sentence for him.

"Exactly."

"Well, I should hope so, you perv!"

I give him a playful slap to the shoulder, but when I go to pull my arm back, he catches it and holds.

Our eyes lock.

In one smooth motion, he hooks one arm under my legs, the other around my back, and slides me onto his lap.

"Well, aren't you slick?" I say softly when we're face-to-face.

"I have my moments."

God he smells good.

Like soap and sea breeze and everything delicious under the sun.

I whisper, "Just so you know, James. For the future? Gynecology jokes aren't usually the way into a girl's pants."

"I wasn't trying to get in your pants."

"Oh no?"

"No." He brushes the hair out of my eyes. "I was hoping for a kiss though. What do you think?"

"Just a kiss?" I say.

"Just a kiss."

When his lips touch mine, it feels like coming home.

Like there was a reason I threw caution to the wind and fell into his arms all those months ago.

Like there might just be some kind of future for us.

At that exact moment, another party boat floats by and releases fireworks into the sky.

James rests his forehead on mine and laughs softly.

"Let me guess. Synchronocity?" I say.

He gives a knowing shrug. "Could be. You tell me."

I answer in the only way I can.

I kiss him again.

Chapter Nineteen

LOUISE

I spend the next few days at the aquarium floating on a cloud.

For the first time in months, I don't try to get James out of my head. I let every sweet memory of our impromptu date play on repeat in my mind.

The way he kissed me in the car on the ride home every time we hit a red light.

The way he held my hand as he walked me to my door.

The fact that he didn't seem put out in the least when I told him I would not be inviting him inside. That was a hard one for me, but it was the right thing to do.

The whole evening was surprisingly wholesome for two people who essentially met while—as Mabel would call it—raw dogging in a refrigerator.

As has become my routine over the past six weeks, as soon as my aquarium shift ends, I put my staff badge in my locker, hop on a city bus, and scarf down a sandwich on the quick ride to UPenn.

So far, I'm loving all my classes. The workload is intense and the hours I'm maintaining are brutal, but it will all be worth it when I get that internship and I'm living the life in the Florida Keys, working side by side with Corbin Bellows and being a part of his coral conservation team.

Right?

I still haven't heard back about my application though, and I can't decide if I should be worried.

Who am I kidding? I'm worried. I'm a worrier. It's what I do.

When I hop off the bus by the Arts and Sciences building, I decide to check my email before going inside. The aquarium has strict rules about keeping our phones out of view of the guests, so I haven't checked it since this morning.

"Yes! Oh my God yes!" I scream when my inbox shows that Corbin's team has messaged me.

A flock of pigeons scatter, and a group of students give me the collective stink eye.

"Sorry!" I shout. "An email I've been waiting for just arrived and—" Why am I explaining myself to these people? "Whatever. Sorry for screaming. Have a blessed day!"

Have a blessed day? Who the hell am I right now?

I take a seat on a stone bench dedicated to a biochemistry major from 1971 so I can read the good news alone before heading inside.

Look at me expecting the best instead of the worst!

Progress.

The subject line reads: Urgent.

Huh. Maybe they want me to start right away instead of this spring?

That scenario would not be ideal, but maybe James is right, and the universe is looking out for me. What did he say? That sometimes the universe has better plans for us than we have for ourselves?

And maybe he's onto something with this synchronicity thing too, because as soon as I started stressing over the lack of response to the application... boom. There it was.

When I open the email and read it out loud, I feel my face immediately fall.

Dear Ms. Anderson—

We regret to inform you that although your application was one of the best we received, we will not be offering you an internship at the Center for Coral Conservation this year.

For more information as to what informed our decision, please review the linked article in this email.

Perhaps more importantly, we regret to inform you that The Corbin Bellows Foundation will no longer be acting as benefactor for your enrollment at The University of Pennsylvania's Graduate Studies in Marine Biology.

Your scholarship is rescinded effective immediately.

Best of luck with your future endeavors.

Sincerely,
Maria Costa
CB Foundation

Chapter Twenty

LOUISE

I am as surprised as anyone about where I end up next.

Am I on the phone with my wonderful, supportive brother?

No.

Out for a girls' night with Calliope and Mabel?

No.

I am at Adventure Bar, crying my eyes out while James pours me a drink and listens to every snot-infused word I have to say.

"The article has this huge picture of me with this dopey look on my face." I sniff. "Like I've been caught red-handed. But I'm sort of smiling too, like I love being naughty or something." I take a second to blow my nose. "And next to me, clear as day—seriously, it's like those kids took journalistic photography lessons or something—is a big-ass Jupiter ass smooshed up against the window."

"Oh God." James places my beer in front of me. "Damn, that sucks."

"I mean, how does someone get perfect lighting with a sneaky, nighttime cell phone photo like that?" I sniffle. "I couldn't do that if I tried."

"Kids today." Ralph shakes his head.

This gets a snorty laugh out of me. "Aren't you too young to say, 'kids today?'"

"I'm almost thirty-three. I think I've earned the right to say, 'kids today.'" He smiles.

"Oh and the headline reads: "Don't Be Like Moonshine Girl.""

"Are you 'Moonshine Girl?'"

"Apparently. I guess she was playing off the name of the liquor and the fact that there I was, in the moonlight... being mooned."

"That analogy needs some work."

"Agreed."

"Am I in the photo?" he asks.

"You're mostly cropped out, but you can see your arm. Your hand too."

What I don't say is that seeing his hand holding mine was the only part of the picture I liked. *More* than liked. Seeing his strong arm trying to guide me out of that weird line of fire stirred something in me.

"What does the article even say?"

"It goes on and on about the dangers of underage drinking and sexing, a message I support of course, but—"

"Tell me she doesn't say 'sexing.'"

"She says sexing. Many times. Turns out Marcy is a god-awful writer but an excellent marketer. Her article got into the exact right hands to ef up my life."

"A high school online newspaper? Come on. Who reads something like that?" James scoffs. "And you're an adult. Who cares what you do during your free time, whether it's drinking or sexing or whatever?"

"Corbin Bellows cares."

James looks at me, confused.

I take a sip of my beer.

"How's this for synchronicity? Corbin's grandson goes to the same high school. He wrote an article about pollution in the Schuylkill River on the same page and his proud grandpa recognized me in the photo."

"That's not synchronicity. That's just some shitty-ass luck. And okay, he doesn't want to offer you the internship? Fine. But to take away your scholarship too? What the hell?"

James is getting heated on my behalf.

"The follow-up email I got after I asked them—who am I kidding, *begged* them to reconsider—said that as a 'devout man with conservative values,' Corbin decided I wasn't 'the right fit' to be affiliated with his foundation after all."

"This is that *Deep Sea Discovery* guy we're talking about?"

"Yeah." I wipe my eyes with my sleeve. "Did you watch his show as a kid too?"

"Of course, who didn't? Doesn't he have like nine wives and a whole bunch of weird scandals going on?"

"Six wives. I mean, not all at the same time, but yeah, he's been married a lot. And yeah, he's got some not-so-secret skeletons in his closet."

"Fuck him, then! You really want to work with a guy like that? Someone hypocritical who makes quick judgments and breaks promises without getting the whole story?"

I shrug. "No? Yes? I mean, I certainly didn't want to lose my scholarship, James." I feel the tears welling again. "I'll have to drop out of the program now."

"No way! Then he wins! You gotta keep going!"

"How, though? I don't have that kind of money."

"So you take out a loan. I can help you with the ins and outs of that process if you want."

I shake my head. "Nuh-uh. If I can't afford it myself, I'm not doing it."

"Stop," he says. "You think everyone out there making things happen has hundreds of thousands of dollars in the bank when they start?"

"I refuse to put myself in debt."

"There's good debt and bad debt, Cold Brew."

Warmth floods my belly.

At what point did I actually start liking that nickname?

"Incorrect, James. All debt is bad debt."

"Mortgages, student loans, small business loans," he rattles off.

"Bad, bad, and bad."

He sighs and leans on the bar top, silent, waiting for me to continue.

"Loans need to be paid back."

"So you'll pay them back," he says matter-of-factly.

"Hey. Smart guy. Do you know what the starting salary is for a marine biologist?"

"No idea, no."

"Thirty-four thousand dollars a year."

"Thirty-" He can't even get the full figure out, he's so flabbergasted. "Shit. What? No!"

"Yes."

"But you're an expert on Muchinodrums!"

"Echinoderms," I correct with a laugh.

"Echinoderms, right! Sorry."

"And expert is generous, James. I'm just getting started."

He says hello to a regular customer and pours them their usual.

I talk to him while he works.

"You know, with all the diving you've done and this excursion company you're launching, I would think you'd know more of the sea-life terminology."

"Maybe you can teach me?" he flirts.

I give him a look.

He chuckles. "I guess my focus has always been more on people. And diving protocols. It's my job to keep everyone safe underwater. And to make sure no one is an asshole to the animals, of course. But yeah, I could definitely learn more about the specifics when it comes to marine life."

"Are people assholes to the animals?" I say in horror.

"Most aren't. But some of them? You'd be surprised. Enjoy, man." He hands the customer his drink and turns back to me. "I had this idiot once who tried to impress his girlfriend by riding a whale shark."

"What?"

"Yeah. Guy acted like the ocean was his own personal dude ranch."

I shake my head at the stupidity and feel a sharp pain in my jaw. I open and close my mouth a few times to give it a stretch.

"You still having that jaw pain?" James asks with concern.

"It's no big deal. Probably just stress."

What I don't tell him is that I'm pretty damn sure my wisdom teeth are impacted and I need to have them taken out. But a girl who just lost her school funding and whose health insurance hasn't kicked in yet for her new job can't exactly afford an epic trip to the dentist. So I'm riding this out for as long as I can.

I put the focus back on him.

"Wait. You scuba dived with whale sharks? Where? When?"

This guy never ceases to amaze me.

"For a few years in my twenties, I led an excursion in Isla Mujeres every June." A small smile curves his lips. "June is that awesome time of year when the whale sharks and mantas are making their way to the tip of the Yucatan Peninsula to feed in warmer waters. It's magical stuff. Though technically, we *swam* with them. You can't dive with whale sharks. It's fins and snorkels only since the scuba diving equipment isn't safe for them. They stay on the surface mostly and are actually really sensitive creatures." He pauses. "Sorry. I don't need to explain this sort of thing to a marine biologist."

"It's okay. I've actually never done that kind of thing before."

"What kind of thing?" He cocks his head to the side.

"Scuba diving, snorkling…" I say.

"What? How do you become a marine biologist without scuba diving?"

"There are ways around it. Besides, I generally consider myself a dry land marine biologist."

"Any particular reason?" he asks.

I look into his deep chocolate-brown eyes, and for the first time, I feel like opening up. "My unofficial therapist Gail says my fear of water comes from the fact that I felt like I was emotionally drowning during my entire childhood, which kind of pisses me off." I laugh.

"Why does that piss you off?"

"Because that dream analysis stuff is so literal! Someone who is emotionally drowning dreams about drowning? Come on! I don't think I need a professional to draw that conclusion for me."

"You dream about drowning?" he asks with concern.

"Sort of." I shrug. "Treading water in the middle of the black ocean, getting aboard the *Titanic* and *knowing* it's the *Titanic* — that's always a fun one. The dreams stop and start depending on what's going on in my life. And how close my parents are to me at the time."

"Understood." He nods. We watch the people chatting and laughing throughout the bar. "Maybe one day you'll get in the water with me."

I smile. "Maybe."

I decide to ask a question that's been on my mind for weeks. "Hey, that night when you brought food to Mabel's, you said something about Wally saving your life in the water. What was that all about?"

He sighs. "Back in high school, Wally and I and a bunch of buddies from the swim team took a dip in the river one night. They didn't realize how much I'd had to drink. The current was strong, and I got pulled under. Thankfully, Wally was there to pull me up. I started going to meetings the next day and haven't stopped since."

"Wow," I say.

"Everybody has a moment when they realize they need help, right?"

"I guess?"

"Well, that was mine." He grabs a rag and starts wiping the bar down. "Now, for the help *you* need..."

"Thank you for offering to teach me about loans, but I'm just not willing to go down that path. I spent my entire childhood watching my mom stress over money. It was a mess. There was always a mortgage payment or a car lease she couldn't pay off unless my dad sent her money, which he almost never did, and—"

"Well, he should have!" James says emphatically.

"I agree." I take in the anger that flashed on his face. As soon as I registered it, it was gone. "That said, I'm doing everything in my power to avoid that kind of lifestyle. I will not depend on a bank—or a man, for that matter—to get me where I want to go. Whatever I have—however small—will be mine."

"Fair enough." He nods and starts wiping down the bar. "Where *do* you want to go?"

"Huh?"

"Is there a goal you're working toward when it comes to marine biology?"

That's the question, isn't it?

I sigh. "There was."

I trace my finger around the circle of condensation my beer has left on the bar top.

I don't think I'm ready to admit this out loud, but a part of me felt relieved when I got that horrible email. It was almost like it let me off the hook. Took away this incessant need in me to be responsible. To always be pushing myself forward. I decided a long time ago that I wanted to work in coral conservation, but I'm having a hard time now remembering why.

I surprise myself when I say, "In a perfect world, I'd find a way to combine my love of the ocean with my love of art."

"Wow. That's—" He smiles. "Well, I don't know if we can call this a perfect world, but that sounds like an exciting and worthy goal."

"Maybe I'll just take a gap year while I figure things out." I laugh. "Can you call it a gap year when you're twenty-three?"

"Sure. Why not?" he says. "I'm sure people in their thirties and forties could benefit from a gap year too. Hell, we all could!" He pauses. "What *is* a gap year anyway?"

"It's the year some kids take between high school and college, isn't it?"

"Sure, but take away the age element for a minute. What is it actually *for*?"

I take a moment to think about that.

"Um. I guess it's a period of time you take away from the hustle and grind so you can just... experience."

My voice quiets as I realize what he's getting at.

"If you think about it, a gap is just... space, right? We all deserve to give ourselves space." He places his hand over mine. "Do what you gotta do and go easy on yourself. Okay?"

I look down at his thumb drawing small, comforting circles over my knuckles.

"My next step has to be finding a new place to live."

"Really? Why?"

"I took over Calliope's tenant agreement in the city because it's close to the aquarium and school. But it's right at the edge of my budget. Without my scholarship stipend, there's no way I can afford it anymore." I sigh and rub my hands down my face. "I guess I'll need to find a place in the burbs and figure out the commute somehow."

A funny look comes over James's face.

"What?" I ask.

"I may have a solution," James offers as he finishes wiping down the bar. "And it involves staying in the city."

"Dude, I told you. I can't afford—"

"You need to move apartments. Got it," he says. "But... you may not need to move as far out as you think."

"But—"

"Hear me out." He tosses a rag onto a rack of highball glasses, then grins. "I know someone who is open to a roommate. And I'm pretty sure you two would be a great fit for each other."

Chapter Twenty-One

LOUISE

"Rooooooomate!!!" Mabel charges me at full speed.

"Ooof," is the sound that comes out of me on impact.

She wraps herself gleefully around me like a squid.

I silently pat her back with both hands to confirm that she is fully clothed this time.

"Oh my gosh, this is going to be so much fun!" she squeals. "Are you as excited as I am?"

"I'm not sure anyone could be as excited as you are right now." I laugh. "But. Sure." I pause. "I mean, yes! Absolutely."

I pull back from the hug to find her beaming at me.

Mabel really is an adorable, amazing person.

I'm not going to lie, I was really looking forward to living on my own in the city, and I'm still reeling by everything that's gone down this week, but hey, sometimes life throws you a curveball. And if this kind, giving, enthusiastic woman is willing to help me get back on my feet, then I count myself enormously lucky.

I'm a little embarrassed to admit that when James first said he knew someone who'd be open to a roommate, I automatically assumed he meant himself.

Which is a ridiculous thing to have assumed.

Why in the world would he ask a woman he barely knows, a woman he had sex with once a few months ago and then made out with on a bench a few nights ago to move in with him?

But perhaps more importantly, why did I get such a pang of

disappointment in my gut when I realized he wasn't?

My brother steps out of the car, which is packed to the brim with my belongings.

"Ralph-alpha! How're you doing, buddy? I haven't seen you since the orgy!" Mabel purses her lips. "Hm. Is it okay to call you Ralph-alpha? Or is that strictly a Calliope sex thing?"

"It *is* a Calliope sex thing," Ralph says. "But—"

"Nope!" I say. "No buts! Mabel will never call you that nickname again!" I pull some duffel bags out of the trunk. "Also, Mabes, can we not talk about the orgy? I'm kind of trying to forget that night ever happened."

"Have Calliope and I apologized enough for that?" Ralph asks as he places some boxes on the car roof. "We really are sorry."

"You have. And I know you are. But for the future? You two might want to explore why you keep participating in public sex acts that get people fired."

"Touché."

"The word orgy doesn't really lend itself well to pig Latin. Have you ever noticed that?" Mabel asks as she grabs a small lamp and a garment bag.

What in the hell is she talking about?

"Yes," Ralph says. "Words that start with a vowel aren't a great fit for ig-pay atin-lay. But there are ways around that."

"Oh really? Do tell, *Ralph*." Mabel gives me a wink.

I give her a thumbs-up.

"Gladly, Mabel," he says. "When a word starts with a vowel, it's suggested that you keep the word intact and add "-hay" to the end. So in the case of the word orgy, you would say orgy-hay, though as an alternative, you can also use the suffix 'yay' as well."

I love my brother to the moon and back, but I swear, any opportunity to mansplain, and he is all over it. Even if the topic is something as inane as pig Latin. Something tells me, though, that he wouldn't dare ansplain-may with alliope-Cay.

"Thanks for that, Ralph. Orgy-yay is certainly preferable to orgy-hay. I mean, who wants to have an orgy-hay? Sounds itchy."

"Agreed! Orgy-yay it is!" I shout as I make my way to Mabel's—

or I guess, I should say *our*—front door with the first load of stuff.

Right away, I notice there's been an adjustment to the wooden sign.

It still says "Home is Where the Pants Aren't," but now an additional mini-sign swings below it that reads "But Only When My New Roomie Approves."

"I figured that would be a welcome addendum," Mabel says from right behind me. "Does the calligraphy look okay?"

"It looks great. And thank you. Not just for the sign. Or for keeping your clothes on, which is definitely appreciated. But for opening your home like this, Mabel. It's really... I'm just so..."

Against my wishes, my eyes well up with tears.

I put my bags down and let them flow.

"Aw. Don't cry, girlfriend." She gives me a hug, then pulls back and gently wipes my cheeks. "What's mine is yours! I couldn't be happier to bunk with you, biotch! And don't you worry about curbing my style, either. I'll still find plenty of Mabel Unleashed time when you're out of the house."

She smacks me on the butt.

Hard.

"Oh! Here's your key, baby!"

She reaches into her skort pocket and pulls out a small bronze key attached to a starfish keychain.

She's too much.

In the best possible way.

"You probably won't ever need this—I mostly use the code on the electronic keypad—it's T-I-T-Z by the way, or 8489 if you prefer thinking in numbers—but giving you a physical key felt more romantic. Not that we're going to be romantic with each other! I just wanted you to feel welcome. That's all."

"That's super sweet, Mabes. Thank you."

"Go on!" she says. "Punch in titz! By the way, we can absolutely change that to something you prefer later. It used to be bugz, but that felt too on-the-nose."

"Titz will be just fine."

I punch in the code, push the door open, and take in the small space.

Mabel really is an angel.

An openhearted, skort-wearing, bug-loving angel.

There is a big hand-drawn sign taped across the living room that reads "Rock on, Roommate!"

On the kitchen island is a big wicker basket with brightly colored balloons tied to the handle. I walk closer to it and find two bottles of my favorite pinot noir resting inside, along with bubble bath, takeout menus for seemingly every restaurant in the greater Philadelphia area, and a framed photo of her, Calliope, and me.

"Mabel, this is incredibly sweet."

"Don't mention it! When I was a little kid, my mom worked for this company called Welcome Wagon. When someone bought a new house, the Welcome Wagon would show up with a basket full of goodies to welcome them to the 'hood. And since you are moving into *my* little hood, I thought you deserved some swag!" Come on, let's dump those bags in your room!"

At that point, Ralph scoots in the front door, balancing too many things. "Look who I found!"

James walks in behind him, looking amazing as always. He's wearing that light gray Henley he wore the night we met. The set of bar keys that are always hanging from the belt loop of his low-slung jeans softly jangle as he comes closer.

"Hey," he says.

"Hey. I wasn't expecting you. I mean, I'm happy to see you. I just wasn't... expecting you."

He gives a small shrug. "Thought maybe you could use some help settling in."

"Oooooh. There's such crackly poppily energy between you two!" Mabel says. "Have you guys consummated your relationship yet or what?"

Ralph coughs.

James smirks and looks at the floor.

"Um. Consummation is for married people, Mabes," I say.

"This is a sex-positive home, Ms. Anderson," she scolds. "There will be no sex-shaming under my—forgive me, *our*—roof."

"Surrrrrrre, but the word consummate means—"

"I know what the word means. What I'm saying is, your raw dog refrigerator night doesn't really count, you know? Because you two didn't even know each other then. It's clear that the tides have changed, though, and there are real feelings between you guys now, so it's only a matter of time until you guys get down for real. With feelings this time. A consummation of the love brewing between you."

"Mabel," I hiss under my breath. "Could you not?"

Ralph hitches a thumb toward the door. "I don't have to be here for this, do I?"

"No, you do not. Thanks for your help, brother."

"Sure thing. Here."

He hands me a key. Everyone's handing me keys today.

"What's this for?"

"How do you plan on getting to work?" he asks.

"Bus?"

"Ugh. You know I hate buses."

"News flash, I've been riding them between school and the aquarium this whole time."

"Yeah, but this is a farther ride for you now. Seriously. Take her for a while. Till you figure things out."

I place the key back in his hand.

"Lou, you're my sister. My vulva is your vulva. You know that."

"Yeah, but what if you need her?"

James chimes in, "Hey, uh—I know I'm relatively new to this crew, but... anyone care to tell me what the hell is going on? Is there a reason you and your brother share a vulva?"

"His car," I explain. "It's the old family Volvo. When I was little, I pronounced it vulva, and it stuck."

"Ah." James exhales.

Ralph laughs. "Sorry to freak you out, man. My sister and I are close, but not that close."

"Would you say that?" I ask Ralph. "That we're close?"

"*Now*, I would. Hell yeah." He pauses. "Wouldn't you?"

"Yeah." I smile. "I would too."

"Good. Now shut up and ride my vulva, will ya?" He tosses the key in the air.

"Ew." I catch it. "You're disgusting."

"Back atcha, sis."

Ralph gives Mabel and James a little salute, then heads out the door.

I watch him go and feel unexpectedly happy.

And lucky.

I'm still getting used to having my big brother back in my life. I wouldn't say we were ever *estranged* exactly—I always knew we'd be there for each other if we truly needed one another—but we were living three thousand miles apart, and that solid year when we barely spoke to each other was rough on both of us.

"Well. Looks like I got myself a car for a while."

"Looks that way," James says.

"Come on, let's dump those bags in your room!" Mabel guides us to the second bedroom. "I did mention you'll be sharing the room, right?"

"Uhhhhh, no. You didn't. With whom?"

"Bonnie and Clyde."

"Who are Bonnie and Clyde?" James and I ask at the same time.

"My mantises," Mabel says proudly. "Bonnie's on the left. Clyde is on the right."

I cross the bedroom to the window where two clear cages rest on a low bookshelf. I approach them slowly and find a praying mantis inside each. Their beady little eyes are alert-as-hell and ready for anything. Their bodies are eerily still, so still I would think they were fake if it weren't for the occasional twitch of an antenna.

"I need to make one thing clear."

"Yikes!" I jump.

Mabel is suddenly super serious and whispering in my ear. She's so close I can smell the strawberry scent of her toothpaste.

"This is their room, and you're just living in it. Got it?"

"Uh..." I stifle my laugh and whisper, "Sure. Yeah, I mean, they were here first, right?"

"They sure were." She nods her head, totally missing the joke. "Aren't they beautiful?"

"They are, yeah." I nod emphatically, then look at James in the doorway to find he's doing the same.

Bonnie jerks her triangular head to the side and looks into my soul.

At least, that's how it feels.

Mabel says, "I was originally in a smaller unit, thinking we could share a bedroom, but... it became clear pretty quickly that wasn't going to be possible. Anyway, I was psyched when a two-bedroom became available, so they could have their own space!"

"Are you telling me you've been paying rent on a whole extra bedroom... for your bugs?"

"That's what I'm telling you." She purses her lips and sasses me right back. "Oh, don't give me that look! Like you wouldn't do the same if a manatee moved in with you."

So many strange things about this conversation.

I glance at my suitcases. "Mabes, if this isn't an ideal situation for you, I can definitely find another place to—"

"Don't be ridiculous!" She bounces up and down on the air mattress she blew up in anticipation of my arrival. "I'm beyond thrilled you're here. And Bonnie and Clyde will be too. As long as—" She hesitates. "Well, you, um... I mean, you don't plan on..."

"Spit it out, lady."

"You don't plan on having any... guests in here, do you?" She looks back and forth between James and me.

"Guests?"

"Yeah. Bedmates? Hookups? Bone buddies? Because I can tell you from my experience when Wally sleeps over..." She lowers her voice to a whisper. "They do not like that."

I'm sure it's just a well-timed coincidence, but at that moment, I swear the mantis on the right—Clyde—looks into my eyes and trembles.

When I turn to Mabel, she's stopped bouncing. She's sitting cross-legged on the air mattress, her eyes wide in expectation.

"Oh. You want me to actually answer that question?"

"I do. If I've learned anything while navigating the new relationship with my parents these past few months, it's that when dealing with humans, setting boundaries and expectations is key. So yes, please answer the question."

I look at James. He holds his hands up in surrender. He's not touching this conversation with a ten-foot pole.

"If... I end up having a... boning buddy," I say to Mabel. "I will do my best to... bone off the premises."

She leaps to her feet. "Oh good. That's settled, then. Not that I don't want you to have a fulfilling sex life because I really am gunnin' for you two crazy kids to consummate. I just think for your own safety, it's best that you don't do it here. So. Should we order some takeout?"

"Aah!" I say and cradle my cheek.

"I know!" Mabel says. "I'm excited too. So many awesome takeout options in this neighborhood. What are you thinking? Thai? Barbecue? Doritos Crunch Crust Pizza?"

"Alright, that's it," James says.

"The Doritos Crunchy Crust? Yay! Wally won't eat it with me!"

"I'll need to take a rain check on that one. Louise is in pain." He places a hand on my lower back. "We need to get you checked out."

"We?" I ask.

"Your jaw has been hurting for over a week now, and I can't stand by and watch you suffer when you don't have to." He brushes the hair off my forehead. "And yeah, we. Boning or not, there's a we here now. You know it, and I know it."

"And Mabel knows it," my endlessly peppy friend adds.

I hesitate. "I don't think I can, though. I think my wisdom teeth are impacted, and my insurance isn't—"

"Don't worry, Cold Brew. I know a guy."

"You know a guy?"

He winks. "I know a guy."

Chapter Twenty-Two

JAMES

Three hours later, I'm sitting in a waiting room at The Oral Surgery Center of Greater Philadelphia, waiting for word that I can go back and see Louise.

My buddy Alec took excellent care of her.

Louise was right. It was a wisdom tooth issue. Hers were so impacted she needed to be fully put under for the procedure. She was pretty nervous about that, but I told her I'd wait there with her and escort her home afterward. That seemed to calm her down somewhat.

My knee won't stop bouncing while I alternate between watching the clock and the door.

After what feels like an eternity, Alec finally opens the door and gestures for me to follow him. "You can come on back, kid. She's awake."

We walk side by side down a long white hallway.

How's she doing?" I ask.

"She's... interesting."

That's a weird thing for an oral surgeon to say.

"I agree, Louise *is* interesting," I say slowly. "But what do *you* mean by that?"

He stops outside of a private room and faces me.

I've known Alec for a long time. He was one of the first people I connected with at AA way back when I first started attending meetings as a teen. The guy hasn't had a drink in over twenty years. He's the epitome of steady and strong and is always willing to lend a hand to whomever needs it.

But right now, he looks shook.

He clears his throat. "Your girl seems to be having a reaction to the anesthesia. Which is not altogether uncommon, but..."

I don't correct him when he calls her my girl. Partly because I like the way it sounds, but mostly because the look on his face has me freaked out.

"But...?" I prompt.

"Her behavior could get me into a solid amount of trouble as a practicing physician."

"What did she do?"

"When she woke up, the first thing she did was smile, call me Alex..."

I shrug. "Everyone calls you Alex. Like you've always said, 'That just comes with the territory of being named Alec.'"

"And she grabbed my balls."

A nurse walks by pushing a cart of medicines and sends us a stern look.

Alec gives her a finger salute, and she keeps walking.

I lower my voice. "Oh. Well, that's... Yeah, that's not good." I pause. "I'm sorry?"

I'm not sure I should be apologizing for my not-girlfriend's actions, but this certainly wasn't the post-op discussion I was anticipating, so I'm a bit lost on how to respond.

"It's okay," he says. "Well, clearly it's *not* okay, but people do some strange things when they come out of sedation. Though, I have to say, this is definitely the first time I've been fondled!"

I wince. "Can you not say fondled?"

"You're right. Poor word choice. Anyway, I'll take you in now to see her, but I think it's best I keep my distance until her system settles a bit more."

"Roger that," I say.

"We'll want you to stay with her here for at least a half hour before she's cleared to go home. So give her a few minutes, then gradually see about getting her on her feet. Then I'll be by to check on her. In the meantime, if you need us, there's a call button next to her chair."

"Sounds good, doc. Thanks for everything. And you're, um…" I hesitate. "You're not going to press charges by any chance, are you?"

"Already did, pal." He places a hand on my shoulder. "Kidding. I'm kidding. It's all good. Go take care of your girl."

My girl.

He holds the door open for me, then promptly gets the hell out of there before Louise can assault him again.

I enter quietly and find her lying on a reclining chair in the center of the room.

She is a beautiful, puffy-faced vision.

Her eyes are droopy, and her mouth is full of gauze, but she still manages a bizarre version of a smile when she sees me.

"James! Hi, babyyyyyyyyyyy."

She called me baby.

"Hey, you. How are you feeling?"

I walk over to her and give her a kiss on the forehead.

"Amaaaaaaaaaazing."

"Oh yeah?" I chuckle. "Glad to hear it."

"Holdmyhandholdmyhandholdmyhand," she slurs.

I take a seat beside her and weave her fingers with mine.

"That feels amaaaaaaaaaazing."

"So," I start. "The doctor said everything went well, but he did mention that—"

"Ohmygosh I have to tell you what just happened. It was…" She closes her eyes momentarily and revels in whatever memory she's having.

"Let me guess. Was it amaaaaaaaaazing?" I smile and stroke her hair.

Her eyes pop back open. "It was! How did you know?"

"Just a guess. Go on. Tell me."

"Alex Trebek is my doctor!"

I look toward the door where Alec just left, then back at Louise.

"Ohhhhh," I say as the situation becomes clear.

His name is Alec.

He has gray hair.

And he has a mustache.

"Does Alex Trebek still have a mustache, though?" I mistakenly say aloud.

"It's back!" she says. "The mustache is back! And I'm so happy about that! Can we kiss? I'd really like to kiss you now."

She reaches her arms up and places both hands on my cheeks, ready for a puffy-cheeked, gauze-filled kiss.

Even in this state, she somehow manages to be beautiful.

I take her gently by the wrists. "Louise, listen. I'd love to kiss you any day of the week, but it's probably not the best idea right now."

"Awwwww. Whyyyyyy?" she whines.

I look at her adorable cheeks and marvel at how well she's articulating her words right now. Or maybe she's not, and I'm just tuned in to her and can translate the garble.

"Well, remember how you just had oral surgery?"

"I'd like to give youuuuuuuu oral surgery," she says, then cackles like a wild woman and grabs for my pants.

"Alright, alright, lady." I gently pull her hand away. "That can wait until you are fully consenting and not under the influence of an anesthetic."

"Awwwww." She rolls her head side to side on the reclining chair in a mini-tantrum of sorts. "I'm serious, though! You're so sexy. You're like the sexiest."

"Thank you. That means a lot coming from you." I hold back a laugh and glance up at the clock. "So. Here's the plan. We're going to stay here for a half hour or so, and then when the doctor says it's okay, I'll get you home safely so you can rest up, okay?"

It's clear by the look on her face that she's not listening to me and is on her own train of anesthesia-driven thought.

"Seriously, look at you, dude! Have I ever told you I want to lick your tattoos and rub my breasts all over your fuzzy buzz-cut head?"

"Wow. That's... Not in so many words, no."

"Well, I do."

"That's good to hear, Cold Brew."

"So you wanna?" She bats her droopy eyelashes at me.

I decide to go with honesty and sigh. "I do."

She reaches for her shirt button.

"But!" I continue, and still her hand. "The doctor will be back soon to check on you, so it's probably best to keep your breasts where they are. And the tattoo licking might want to wait as well."

"Dammit!" she shouts. "I'm pissed off by everything you just said!"

"Sorry." I shrug, then give her a smile. "Rain check?"

She makes a big show of squinting toward the window.

"Looks like a clear, cloudless day with a high of sixty-nine, big guy. No rain as far as the eye can see."

"No, I meant, can we do a rain check? When you're feeling more like yourself?"

"Only if you grow a mustache for me. You'd look hot with a mustache."

"I'll see what I can do."

"Yay!" She claps.

There's no way in hell I'll be growing a mustache anytime soon, but this doesn't seem like the right moment to disappoint her.

"I missed Alex's mustache sooooooo much. He had it when I was a super little kid, then he shaved it off, and I felt so confused and betrayed, ya know? Like he wasn't the Alex I knew before. This one was way too fleshy-faced. But I forgave him and got used to it. Because how can you not love Alex? Then when I was a teenager, he grew it back for a few weeks, and I was soooooo happy! But he let fans vote on whether or not to keep the mustache, and do you know what those motherfuckers did?"

Whoa, drugged-up Louise has a mouth on her.

"No. What did they do?"

"They voted for him to shave it off again!"

"Those motherfuckers!" I say in support.

"Exactly!"

I lean forward and take both of her hands in mine.

"What do you think, Louise, can we try getting you up on your feet?"

"Oh, hell yeah!"

With only the tiniest bit of assistance from me, she launches to her feet and presses her body against mine. Suddenly, we're in this sad, heavy hug, which morphs into a slow dance set to no music.

"He's been sick too. Did you know that?" she rests her head on my shoulder.

"I heard that, yeah. It's very sad."

"And he's still working! Even though he's sick! You know why?"

"Why?" I rub small circles on her back.

Is it wrong that I will soak up any chance to be close to her, no matter how bizarre the circumstances may be?

"Because he loves his fans and the work he does so damn much. He is the epitome of a good man. So smart, so kind. So strong. And now, such an amaaaaaaaaaazing dentist too. Is there anything he can't do?"

I take a breath in to say something.

She cuts me off. "No. The answer is no, James." She sighs. "It was a dream come true to meet him in real life, to have him in my mouth and to shake his hand."

"Is that what you thought you were shaking?" I ask. "His hand?"

We continue to dance.

"Yes? Why?"

"Because," I start softly, "and don't worry or feel bad about this because I already talked to him, and everything is fine, but... you grabbed the man's balls."

She stops dancing.

She lifts her head from my shoulder.

Her eyes widen like saucers.

And then she laughs.

And laughs and laughs.

"Hahahahaha. Oh my God, you are so funny! That's one of the things I love about you, James! You're so damn funny!"

"Thank you."

"And sweet. And sexy. Did I mention that you're sexy?"

"You did, actually. A few times."

"Sorry." Her nose scrunches up in this adorable way.

"You never have to be sorry for calling me sexy, Cold Brew."

She smiles and rests her head on my shoulder again.

"You're a lot like him, you know."

"Like who?"

"Alex Trebek. He's smart, kind, and comforting. Just like you. America's dad. Not that you're like a dad to me." She giggles.

"I should hope not." I try to laugh with her, but this shit is getting weirder by the second.

"But you are like nine years older than me, though. Is that old enough for me to call you Daddy? Like in the hot way?"

"Gosh, I-I don't know. Maybe we should table this discussion until you're—"

Louise lets out a huge yawn as she says, "I bet you'll be a good dad one day."

"I already am," I say.

This time, I'm the one whose body stills.

It just slipped out.

I didn't plan it.

But there's no way I can regret it.

I wouldn't deny my daughter for anything in the world. Truth be told, I want to talk about Iris every second of every day to whoever will listen to me. But every time I've tried to find a way to tell Louise about her, it gets hammered home that that will be the end of us. Realistically, I know there is a built-in end date to whatever this thing is between us. We're down to eleven weeks until I'm gone. But is it so terrible that I want it to last as long as possible while I'm still here?

It is. It is terrible. That kid is my heart and soul. Without knowing Iris, Louise doesn't truly know me. And what's that saying...? "A lie of omission is still a lie?"

Without meaning to, I've been lying to her all this time.

I close my eyes and brace myself for what comes next, sad but relieved that the truth is finally out.

Louise is so still and quiet.

"Louise?"

Nothing.

"Louise, did you hear what I said?" I stroke her hair. "I have a six-year-old daughter. Her name is Iris, and I love her very much. When I said I'm moving to Hawaii to start my new business, that was only partly the truth. The main reason I'm going is to be with my daughter because I can't stand being apart from her anymore."

The only response is a loud snore that rumbles directly into my ear.

Well. So much for pouring my heart out to the girl.

It's at that moment that Alec walks back in and finds us holding each other and swaying in the middle of the room.

"Is this a new kink your generation is embracing? Getting cozy in surgical suites? Should I prepare myself for more of this?" he asks with a laugh.

"Nope!" I say. "No kink. As soon as you give us the all clear, we'll get out of your hair. You've gone above and beyond for me today, man. Thank you."

I give Louise a vigorous rub on the back, and she wakes.

As soon as she spots the doctor across the room, she purrs, "I'll take 'What Women Want' for eight hundred, Alex."

"How about I go get those discharge papers," he says.

I nod. "That sounds like an excellent plan."

Chapter Twenty-Three

LOUISE

JAMES: Hey, Cold Brew. How are you feeling three days post-op?

ME: Pretty good. Apparently, I'm a quick healer. I still look a little chipmunky, but swelling is down so I'm back at work today.

JAMES: On hump day?

ME: Well, I don't have labs on Wednesdays anymore thanks to orgy-gate, so I'm free to hang with Meilani on hump day now.

JAMES: #silverlining

ME: Totally. How's Hawaii?

JAMES: Great. But I miss you.

*H*e misses me?

Should I say "Miss you too?"

Because I do.

But something holds me back from saying so.

I watch the little dots on James's side bounce, then stop. Bounce, then stop. Like he keeps changing his mind on what to say next. Just when I think he's not going to say anything else, another text comes through.

JAMES: How much do you remember from our conversation after your surgery?

ME: We had a conversation after my surgery?

JAMES: Say no more. I'll be back from my trip in five days. Think we could get together and talk? Like really talk?

ME: Sure. Just don't ask me to marry you or anything.

The little dots do their dance again until one last text lands.

JAMES: That'll be hard, but I'll do my best.

I watch Meilani swimming and sigh.

Why on earth did I say that?

I can't even commit to a real date with the guy, and suddenly, I'm busting out marriage jokes?

I'm getting oddly comfortable with him these days, and I find that I really like having him around. No, I *love* having him around. And when he's not in my general vicinity? I'm asking myself how I can finagle things to plant myself where he is. You know, in a not-so-obvious way. Who am I kidding? It's obvious to everyone at this point that I'm into the guy.

And it's a dangerous game I'm playing. Because I'm quickly growing attached, and he won't be here much longer.

But part of me is starting to think... what's the harm in enjoying his company while I can, ya know? I'm a big girl. I can handle it when he leaves. And maybe it would be good for me to see what it's like being with a truly kind and caring guy, even if it's for a limited time. Because let's be honest, that's something I've never truly experienced.

Take the other day, for example. What I said was true. I don't remember much from right after the surgery. The details are all fuzzy. What I *do* remember, though, is waking up at home, in bed—an *actual* bed, with everything I needed at my bedside to get better: my medicines, a water bottle, books and magazines, and a note that said "Feel Better, Cold Brew. Love, James."

Mabel told me later that he called her and Wally while we were at the surgery center and asked them to swap out my crappy air mattress for his actual bedframe and heavenly Tempur-Pedic mattress. The man literally gave me his bed. Who does that? He also gave Mabel instructions on how to play the role of my nursemaid while he was in Hawaii for another work trip and has been checking up on her to make sure she's up to the task.

James goes the extra mile for the people he cares about.

And for some reason, right now, that includes me.

And I'm grateful for it.

"No cell phones on exhibit."

A stern voice startles me out of my thoughts.

"Brendan, hi! How are you doing today?"

"No cell phones on exhibit," he repeats.

"You're totally right," I say. "However, we're not on exhibit right now, are we? As you know, guests aren't permitted back here. Also, technically, I'm not on duty right now, so..."

"Right," he says. "Well, Dana sent me to bring you these."

Disgruntled, he hands me three wooden T-shaped tools with paintbrushes on the end of them.

"Oh wow! Did you make these?"

I turn the brushes over in my hands. One look at them, and I know they'll be perfect for our experiment with Meilani today.

"I did. I do a lot of things around here," he huffs.

"I know you do. Thank you for this."

He nods and turns to leave.

"Hey, Brendan?"

He stops.

"I know we got off on the wrong foot when I started here. You were generous in wanting to welcome me and show me the ropes on my first official day, and I wasn't very receptive to that. I'm sorry. I'm not always the most... open when it comes to getting to know new people. But I'm working on it. And I appreciate this"—I lift the paintbrushes—"more than you know."

That apology was necessary, but I'd be lying if I said it didn't take a lot out of me. Brendan is no saint. He's still your typical old-school guy who carries around heaping doses of unchecked misogyny, but he has been making an effort to connect with me. And, like all of us, maybe there's hope for him too.

I think I was in so many bad relationships for so long that

once I figured out how good it feels to be on my own and to answer to no one, I got it in my head that I need to shut guys out the instant they show interest in me.

Maybe it's safe now to be a bit more accessible to people.

To men.

Platonic or otherwise.

"Would you like to stay and watch?" I ask.

Brendan's face lights up in an honest-to-goodness grin, not at all like the smarmy smiles he was flashing me on that first day.

"I would! Yeah!"

"Great. I'm really excited to see how she responds." I feel a giddy smile grow on my face too.

Dana and two sea lion trainers enter the space and say their hellos.

"So? We ready to give this a go?" Dana asks me.

"Yup!" I point up the short set of shallow stairs that lead to the rubber flooring at the top of the rehabilitation tank. "I set up a small easel on the upper level that should be a good height for Meilani, and all the paints I brought are water-based, non-toxic, and safe for animals."

The trainers assure me that all looks well, and we head up the stairs together.

Meilani comes right to the surface like she knows something exciting is about to happen.

The trainers place down two large buckets filled with fish and give Meilani the hand signal to exit the water and join us on the rubber flooring.

She slides onto the floor with grace and ease.

I've only seen Meilani out of the water a few times, and she takes my breath away every time. She's so powerful. So beautiful. So trusting even after having gone through so much.

The last time I worked with her trainers, they showed me the hand signal for "kiss." I do it now, and Meilani waddles right over to me and plants one on my cheek.

The trainers give her some fish, which she gobbles down happily.

"Good girl," I say with a smile and give her a rub behind the ears. "Are you ready to play?"

The trainers guide her over to the canvas and let her explore it for a moment. They show her the new T-shaped paintbrush Brendan made for her and place it in her mouth. She bites down on it like she's done this a hundred times, though we all know she hasn't.

They teach Meilani how to dip the brush into the paint. She "chooses" blue. I know that sounds crazy, but I swear to God, I watch this magnificent creature peruse the colors I've laid out in front of her and choose blue.

And then... she paints.

My heart fills to bursting.

Goose bumps cover my skin.

It takes everything in me not to cry.

When I look up at Dana and the trainers—even Brendan—they look just as delighted and moved as I am.

Dana walks over and pats my back.

"I think we've found your contribution to the arts festival, my friend."

Chapter Twenty-Four

JAMES

"Oh my gosh," Louise's excitement pours through the phone. "It's been so brilliant, I don't even know how to fully describe it to you. You'll just have to come see! Will you come?"

"To your arts festival?" I ask. "Are you inviting me?"

"As my date, yeah," she says sweetly.

I'm pretty sure she can hear my smile through the phone.

"Of course I will. Name the time and the place, and I'll be there."

"November eighth. It's a Monday night."

"Perfect. That's our slowest night at the bar."

What I don't say is that even if it was the busiest night of the whole damn year, I'd still be there in a heartbeat.

"It's called Brew at the Zoo. Isn't that cute?"

"A beer-inspired event where I don't have to work? *And* I get the hottest date in town? Sign me up."

"Awesome. Hey, did I tell you Dana looked at my portfolio, and she wants to auction off some of my work that night too?"

"No! That's incredible!"

"Yeah, she wants to pair my paintings of Meilani with the ones Meilani is doing herself. She thinks together, we can raise some serious money for the AZA."

Louise sounds positively giddy. The happiest I've ever heard her.

"Remind me what the AZA is again?"

"The Association of Zoos and Aquariums," she says.

"Remember when you said in a perfect world, you'd find a way to combine marine biology with your art? Looks like you're doing it."

"Wait. Are you home? Where are you? I just started talking your ear off the second you picked up."

"Yeah, I landed this morning. I'm at a meeting."

"I'm sorry! You should have told me you're working!"

"Not that kind of meeting. An AA meeting. Wally's actually here today as my guest."

Wally leans toward my phone. "Heyyyyyy, Louise."

"Oh hey, Wally," she says. "I'll let you guys go then. But..." She exhales. "Never mind."

"No. What were you going to say?"

"Is it too much to say that—if you're open to it—I'd like to go to one of those with you sometime? As your guest?"

"To an AA meeting?" I ask.

"Yeah. It seems like they're a meaningful part of your life. Would be nice to experience one with you."

To say I'm shocked would be an understatement.

Wally nudges me when I'm silent for too long.

"Yes. Yeah, um. I'd love that. Let's make that happen soon."

"Great," she says. "Talk soon."

"Soon, yeah," I say, totally flabbergasted.

I press end on the call and lean back in the folding chair in the community room.

Kathleen is welcoming some newcomers and guiding them to their seats. The room is bustling with folks sipping coffee and engaging in small talk before the meeting officially starts.

But my head is swimming with the conversation I just had.

"Dude." Wally smacks me on the back. "You okay?"

"She, um. She wants to come to a meeting with me. She said they seem like 'a meaningful part of my life,' and she'd 'like to experience one' with me."

"That's a good thing, right? You're not shy about sharing this part of your life with people."

"Yeah. No, you're right. Absolutely. It's just..."

"Just what?"

"I feel like I'm royally fucking things up with this woman."

"How so?"

"She doesn't trust people easily, and I'm—"

"The most trustworthy guy I know," Wally fills in the rest of the sentence for me.

I scrub my hands over my face, then rest my elbows on my thighs and hang my head.

"What am I missing here?" Wally asks.

"I haven't told her about Iris and Eva."

"What?" he nearly shouts.

"I know!" I gesture for him to keep his voice down.

"What the fuck, dude?"

"I know!" I repeat louder than Wally this time, and I capture the attention of nearly everyone in the room. I give them a sheepish smile and lower my voice. Wally huddles closer as I say, "Listen. It's not as bad as it sounds. I did tell her. But she was drugged at the time."

"Um, James? That's *exactly* as bad as it sounds."

"It was during the whole wisdom teeth thing," I explain. "But she doesn't remember me telling her. And before that, I just... I kept wussing out. It took so long for her to even give me the time of day—"

"One could argue that she gave you *plenty* in that refrigerator, you ungrateful bastard."

"May I continue?" I sigh.

"The floor is yours, sir."

"Thank you." I lean back in the chair and stare at the ceiling for a breath before focusing on my friend. "We started things off with her literally saying she didn't want to know anything about me. So I truly thought this would be a one-and-done kind of thing. But then... I learned pretty quickly that you can't do a one-and-done with Louise. She's fucking special, man. Little by little, she started letting me in, and I was so grateful for that that I just let things play out between us. Before I knew it, we were friends and—"

"Who fuck," Wally inserts. "You're friends who fuck."

"Way to be crass, dude. And no. That hasn't happened again since that first night."

"No shit!"

"It's true. We've made out a bit after the orgy, and she would've been all about a repeat performance in the surgical suite, but..."

Wally gives me a look like I'm a sick, sick man.

"Don't look at me like that. I put the kibosh on it right away. But we're getting off track here," I say, exasperated. "Sex isn't even the point. I just love being with her. Whatever time I get to spend with her is time I want to have. Doesn't matter to me one bit what we're doing."

Wally blows out a breath. "Damn, you've got it bad."

I don't disagree with him because the man isn't wrong.

He lets me continue.

"It took me a while to become friends with her. To gain her trust. Then—get this—she says the one thing she'll never ever do is date a single dad."

"Oh snap."

"I hate when you say that."

"Sorry. But this is an 'oh snap' moment if ever there was one. What did you say to her after that?"

"I froze!"

"Come on, man!" Wally scolds like he's disappointed in me.

"I mean, I said some stuff about how it's possible to be a great partner and an awesome dad, but she's got all this baggage with her own parents, and let's face it, our time together is limited anyway, so..."

"So what? You're just not going to tell her?"

"No, I am."

"You have to tell her."

"I know."

"Iris is your whole world, man."

"Believe me, I *know*."

Conversation in the room dulls to a soft murmur as Kathleen takes her position in the learning chair. The meeting is about to begin.

Wally whispers, "What are you doing tonight?"

"Working a shift at the bar."

"Get coverage."

"Why?" I whisper back.

Wally winks. "Because you've got plans."

Chapter Twenty-Five

LOUISE

"Why is this the first I'm hearing of this?" I ask Mabel as she hands me a bowl of popcorn.

"I talk about Family Movie Night all the time!" she says.

"You don't, though. You certainly have never invited me before."

Mabel busies herself with placing two Cokes down on the coffee table alongside a bowl of wings with little wet wipes and an empty bowl for the bones. I place the popcorn down beside it all.

"Well, up until recently, you've been an extremely busy person," she explains. "I didn't want to stress you out with extra invitations that you'd inevitably have to turn down."

I give her a look.

"Okay, truth be told, it's usually just Wally and me for movie night. But now that I'm wearing clothes at home—for the most part—we're opening things up to friends. The more, the merrier, right?"

"Surrrrre. So who's coming?"

"You know. Friends." I always know Mabel is up to something when she has a hard time looking at me.

It's then I realize that she only put two Cokes down.

The doorbell rings.

"Coming!" Mabel's voice echoes throughout the hallway as she runs gleefully for the door.

She flings it open to reveal James and Wally standing side by side like sexy soldiers.

James looks nervous.

"Hi," he says.

"Hi. Welcome home."

"Thanks."

"Okay, well have fun, you crazy kids, don't wait up for us, see you later bye!" Mabel rushes the words out as she grabs her purse from the hook and promptly pushes Wally outside while Wally pushes James inside.

The door slams behind them, leaving James and me alone in the foyer.

It's quiet for a moment.

"Do you hear crickets?" James asks.

"Oh yeah. They're not real crickets, though. It's that dumb bugfather clock over there."

"Bugfather clock?"

I point at the green, freestanding clock by the bathroom.

"Like a grandfather clock but all about bugs? Each hour it chimes with a different bug sound. Cicadas are at seven. Crickets at eight. Mabel loves it. I'm learning to tolerate it."

"Ah," he says and shifts from foot to foot.

"If you really want your ears to bleed," I joke, "then stick around until midnight. That's when a swarm of bees sounds. It damn near jolts me out of bed every night." I pause when he doesn't respond. "Not that you need to stay until midnight. Clearly, we've been set up, so you can totally go if you want to."

"Why would I want to go?" he says softly.

Is it possible that James is nervous?

Doubtful. He told me he was nervous the night we met, and that's what made him talk nonstop.

But he's not talking nonstop now.

He's barely saying a word.

"For the record, I had nothing to do with this," James finally says.

"Nothing?" I ask.

"I mean, Wally said we were coming here, and I knew I'd see you, but I didn't anticipate they'd ditch us the way they did."

"Me neither," I say. "But can I tell you a secret?"

"Of course."

"I'm not mad about it."

He smiles for the first time since he walked in.

"Neither am I."

He peeks at the little spread Mabel prepared for us on the coffee table.

"Take off your shoes and come on in, then. Relax. Have a seat."

Look at me hosting all of a sudden.

He slips off his sneakers and follows me into the living room.

"Is that a VCR?" he asks as he sits down on the floral couch.

"It is. If you haven't noticed, Mabel is pretty old school. Most of the stuff in our apartment are hand-me-downs from her parents. Oh and look, she left us some VHS tapes for our viewing pleasure tonight."

"Alright, what do we got?" James shoots some popcorn into his mouth and sinks back into the cushions.

He finally seems to be relaxing a bit.

I have to laugh when I see the many choices she curated for us and the obvious thread that connects them all.

I hold the tapes up one by one.

"We have... *10,000 Leagues Under the Sea, Dolphin Tale, Jaws, Splash,* and *Free Willy 1, 2,* and *3.*"

"She's a thoughtful friend, isn't she?" James says.

"I don't necessarily need to watch marine biology-inspired films in my free time, but yes. Mabel is a wonderful friend. "So." I wiggle the tapes in his direction. "What'll it be?"

"Oh, *Splash*, hands down."

"Agreed."

I pop in the tape and sit on the couch beside him. That "Wooly Bully" song starts to play, and baby John Candy starts looking up ladies' skirts.

"There are so many things wrong with this movie," I say. "I can't help but love it, though."

"Really? What can you find wrong with *Splash*?"

"Ohmygosh, where do I even begin?"

"Wherever you like," he says.

I launch in. "Alright. Why does the mermaid have pierced ears? How does her hair dry so quickly after exiting the water?

Why do people almost get hit by cars so often in this film? The Freddie character actually smokes a cigarette while exercising!"

"Well, it was the eighties," James says.

"True, and also, yes, I know it was the eighties, but holy crap, the amount of inappropriate male behavior in this movie blows my mind! The prepubescent peeping Tom on the boat, the fact that the *Schitt's Creek* guy tries to get Daryl Hannah wet to prove she's a mermaid. Oh and when Tom Hanks rejects her in that tank while he holds his little pee-pee? It's so freaking sad."

"You sure you want to watch it?"

"Oh, totally! I can hold two opposing beliefs at the same time." With that, I kick back and settle in to enjoy our movie night.

We watch for a few minutes, then seemingly out of the blue, James says, "You can?"

"I can what?" I say between crunches of popcorn.

"Hold two opposing beliefs at the same time."

"Oh. Yeah."

I thought that conversation was over. But whatever.

"Of course," I continue. "In this case, I'm totally comfortable holding the beliefs that *Splash* is both terrible and terrific at the exact same time."

"I'm, um..." James clears his throat. "I'm actually glad to hear you say that."

"Why?" I take a sip of my Coke.

He's acting so strange tonight.

Does he not want to be here or something?

"Because..." He shifts on the couch so he's in a more upright position and seems to switch tactics. "Can I mention something I've noticed about you?"

"Oh God."

"What?"

"Is this where you psychoanalyze me?" I laugh.

"Of course not, no! I wouldn't do that. Besides, you're the one with the psychology degree, not me."

"Well, I minored in psychology," I correct. "And to be honest, I'm not sure how much that has ultimately helped me with people. In my experience, animals are way easier to understand than people."

His mouth opens and closes a few times like a guppy.

But no words come out.

"What was the thing you noticed about me?"

"Huh?" he says.

"You said, 'Can I mention something I've noticed about you'?"

"Oh, right. You're, um, well—"

"Spit it out, sir."

"You're usually a bit all or nothing in your thinking."

"I am? Wait. How do you mean?"

"Like when you said someone can't be a single parent and be in a relationship."

"I didn't say that."

"You did. But listen, I just don't believe in a world where we always have to pick and choose. What if—sometimes—we really can have it all?"

"I simply said that I would never date someone with a kid. Which is my prerogative and not something I should be judged for."

"Nope, not judging you." He puts his hands up. "I just think the universe can surprise us when we open our thinking a bit. Take 1980s Tom Hanks, for example! If you asked him directly, 'Hey, Tom Hanks, would you like to have sex with a mermaid?' He'd probably tell you no."

"His character name in the movie is Allen, and are you so sure about that? I bet if we polled men in their twenties and thirties on whether or not they'd like the opportunity to have sex with a mermaid, most—if not all of them—would say yes."

"Okay, maybe that wasn't the best example." He scrubs a frustrated hand over his head. "What I'm getting at is—on paper—Madison and Allen weren't the best fit for each other. But they still found their way to each other in the end."

I pause the movie and smile, trying to lighten the mood. "Are you trying to tell me you're a merman?"

"Ha, no." He takes a deep breath. "Can I ask you a question?"

"Surrrrrre."

Movie night is starting to feel like some kind of grand inquisition.

"What do you want out of life?" he asks.

"What do I want out of life?" I repeat.

"Yeah. In general, I find it's helpful to focus on what I do want instead of what I don't want. So... what do you want?"

"I don't know. All the regular things."

I appreciate that he's trying to get to know me, but why? Why is he digging so deep when he's out of here in a few months? When there's no future for us.

"What are 'the regular things'?" he asks.

I sigh and put the remote on the table. Clearly, we're not watching this movie anytime soon. "You're difficult to talk to sometimes, you know that?"

"Me?" He slaps a hand to his chest.

"Yeah!"

"How? How am I difficult?"

"Just the way you're always..." I struggle to find the words. "I dunno, listening to what I say and and and... asking follow-up questions to make sure you understand, and you're so ugh, you're so... interested in how I feel and what I want and—"

"Yeah, I can see how that would be very irritating for you," he says with a scoff.

"Did you just scoff at me?"

"Maybe I did!"

His voice echoes throughout the apartment.

I sit and breathe for a moment to get my bearings.

"What is going on here?" I ask. "Are we fighting or something?"

"No. Why would we fight? We don't mean anything to each other, right?" he mumbles, almost so low I can't hear him.

But I do.

I hear him.

I take a leap of faith and say, "Of course you mean something to me."

"Really?"

I move closer to him on the couch.

We're sitting side by side.

So close.

"Yes. More than you know."

"So... why should it be this hard to reach each other?" he whispers.

I don't have an answer for that.

But I want to reach him.

So badly.

Without thought, I drop my head to rest on his shoulder.

He tilts his head to rest on top of mine.

I swear I can hear his heart pounding.

Or maybe it's mine.

He wraps a warm, strong arm around me.

I let him.

Before I can think better of it, I reach a hand up to cup his stubbled jaw.

He responds immediately by lifting his head and turning to face me. I can't bear to open my eyes to look at him, so I keep them closed, tilt my chin up in his direction, and thank God, his lips land on mine.

Our kiss is tentative at first, but things quickly pick up speed, and before I know it, we are a tangle of tongues and breath and touches. It feels like he's drawing me closer to him with his every inhale and breathing life into me with his every exhale.

He unbuttons my shirt, slides it past my collarbone, and devours the place where my shoulder meets my neck.

I almost come right on the spot.

No one has ever kissed me like this.

I want more.

I want as much as he'll give me.

I unbutton his pants.

He slides them down at the same time I'm lifting my skirt. He rolls a condom on in record time, positions himself right where I want him, and enters me in one long, delicious thrust.

I gasp.

Tears come to my eyes.

Not from pain, but from the sheer pleasure and relief of being with him again like this.

If I'm honest with myself, I've wanted this for so long.

"Oh my God, that's good," I breathe.

"Louise, you are fucking amazing," he moans as he begins to pump.

"Don't stop, don't stop, don't stop," I say and grip his ass.

"Why the hell would I stop, baby?"

He continues to worship that spot on my neck while I knead the muscles in his back and run my hands up to caress his skull.

He reaches under us and cups my ass, pulling me closer, deepening our connection.

It's like he can't get close enough.

I feel the same exact way.

All I want is more, more, more.

"I could live inside you, Louise."

"Fine by me," I pant.

"You are absolutely everything. The things I would do for you, if you'd let me."

He's relentless in his pace like he knows we're running out of time, and he wants to give me every ounce of pleasure he can before the clock runs out.

I feel the build swirling in me, curling my toes and shooting up my spine. My head presses back into the couch as my mouth opens in ecstasy. He seals his mouth to mine and swallows my moan as he pumps harder, faster, chasing and lengthening my release as far as it can go until it his own orgasm meets mine and we ride out the waves together, over and over, in an undulating sea of bliss.

His weight settles over me, his breaths rising and falling with mine. His heart beats a steady, satisfied rhythm against my chest.

I want to memorize everything about this moment.

Everything about him.

In that instant, all thoughts of a one-night stand evaporate.

I will take this man for as many nights as he'll have me.

Chapter Twenty-Six

JAMES

*L*ater that night, we're snuggling on the couch under a soft blanket, watching the rest of *Splash*, which is—as Louise mentioned—way more problematic than I remember when I watched it as a kid.

Her head is resting on my chest.

I'm stroking her hair.

Aside from the day my daughter was born, I can honestly say I've never been so happy.

I sniffle.

She lifts her head to look at me.

"Are you sniffling?"

"Nah." I joke and wipe the moisture escaping from my eye because it's clear I've been caught.

"You are!" she accuses with glee. "You're crying watching *Splash*?"

"Aren't you the one who said it's 'so freaking sad when Tom Hanks rejects her in that tank while holding his little pee-pee?'"

"That was me, yes," she laughs.

"I'd just like to mention—since Tom isn't here to defend himself—that there's no evidence leading me to believe he would have a 'little pee-pee.'"

"I dunno..." She purses her lips like she's deep in thought. "Something about the way he's standing there all shy and cupping his member? Seemed like the stance of a guy with a little pee-pee." She shrugs, then rests her arms across my chest and props her chin up. "But you wouldn't know anything about that now, would you?"

"Thankfully, no. I would not."

I kiss her softly on the lips.

"So, you're a crier, huh?"

"Hell yeah, I'm a crier!" I say proudly. "You gotta get that shit out."

"What shit?"

"All the shit we build up inside ourselves on a daily basis. If we're not careful, we layer it, and layer it, stacking one pile of unprocessed junk on top of the other until we become these thick, stony, immovable people who can't feel a single thing. I think the world, in general, would be better off if we all committed to having a 'cry of the day.'"

She laughs.

"I'm serious," I say.

"Oh. I'm sorry. You just—You always seem so happy-go-lucky."

"Maybe that's because I get in my cry of the day." I raise my eyebrows in a "gotcha" expression.

Her eyes narrow. "You're telling me you cry every day?"

I shrug. "Mostly. Yeah."

"That's so sad!"

"Nah. It's cathartic."

"And surprising!"

"Really? You're surprised?"

She sits up and wraps the blanket around herself. "Come on. You have to realize how rare that is. A man who not only cries on the regular but also proudly admits it?"

"I guess that's one thing my dad did right. He wasn't a guy who could deal with his own feelings, but he made sure I was hooked up with all the therapists after my mom died, so I could deal with mine."

"He wasn't?" She tilts her head to the side.

"Wasn't what?" I ask.

"You used the past tense when you talked about him just now. You said he wasn't a guy who could deal with his feelings."

"Oh yeah. He passed about seven years ago."

Right before I went on my last bender with alcohol and ended up getting my best friend pregnant.

Tell her, James.

As soon as possible, tell her.

"Am I allowed to say sorry this time?" she asks with a soft smile and a brush of her hand on my arm.

"Sure."

She links her fingers with mine.

"I'm sorry."

"Appreciate it. But I'm fine. Really." I lift her hand to my mouth and kiss it.

"I know you are. And lord knows I have my parent issues, but it must be hard when they're gone, knowing the chance to get it right with them is gone too."

"Well, now you're gonna make me cry, woman!" I tease her. "Any update since your parents were at the birthday party?"

Ralph ended up chatting with my dad that night. He wouldn't say how he found out about the party, just that "he's our father and he deserves to be there. Then he disappeared afterward like he was never there. Same old, same old."

"How about your mom? How was the rest of her visit?"

"She is still in town apparently. Ralph is trying to convince me to join them for dinner tomorrow night."

"Wow. How are Ralph and Calliope holding up with the extended house guest?"

"Just fine. Because Mom met someone—surprise, surprise— and she is currently staying with him until further notice."

The music swells on the screen and both of our attentions are drawn back to *Splash*, where Tom Hanks and Daryl Hannah are kissing and finally getting their happily ever after.

Like clockwork, my eyes mist up again.

She laughs. "You're killing me with this, dude!"

"Well, case in point! Crying isn't always about sadness. People also cry when they're happy, exhausted, surprised, relieved. It's a release. They cry when they're overwhelmed. When they take in the beauty of a new baby, the majesty of a sunset..."

"Ugh. I hate sunsets."

She what now?

"Care to repeat yourself, madam? I thought I just heard you say you hate sunsets."

"Then you heard me right."

I sit up taller and face off with her.

"Are you fucking kidding me right now?"

"Nope," she says. "I'm serious."

"You hate sunsets," I repeat, still in disbelief.

"I do."

"First The Beatles, and now this?" I shake my head. "I don't know, Cold Brew. If the sex wasn't so good, I might have to rethink this whole thing with you."

Her face falls.

It's an expression I never want to see on her face again. And I hate that I'm the one who put it there.

"I'm kidding, Lou," I rush to say. "I'm kidding."

A gentle smile quickly replaces the sadness that was there.

"You called me Lou," she breathes.

"I did, yeah."

"You've never called me that before."

"Is that...okay?"

"Yeah. It's more than okay."

She scoots close, sits on my lap, and wraps her legs around my hips.

Then she kisses me, slow and deep, and things between us start up again. But, because I'm an absolute moron, I can't help but break the kiss to ask again, "How does someone hate sunsets? Why?"

"Just do." She slides off my lap but keeps her thighs draped over mine.

"You have to give me more than that."

"Fine. I've always found them a little...depressing."

"Go on."

I will never not find this woman fascinating.

"When I was a young kid, we used to go to the Jersey shore once a year. It was such a different world than our landlocked little life in Nebraska. My grandparents on my dad's side had a house there. Even though my dad was basically out of the picture, they still invited us out once a year to spend time with them. They invited my dad too, and the big mystery every year was whether or not he would show. It sounds sad when I say that out loud, but it actually always felt like a hopeful time. Like this was the summer he'd join us there and spend time with us. Anyway, Ralph and I used to wake up early every morning and walk down to the beach. The budding astronomer in him wanted to watch the sunrise. I wanted to watch the water. I loved those mornings with him. Every morning, it looked like the water was giving birth to the sun. Like this ball of fire had been underwater, keeping its burn alive even when everything around it was trying to squelch it, drown it, soak it with sadness."

She shakes her head. "But it wouldn't let that happen. It stayed submerged every night, and then as soon as morning hit, it was like 'Hey bitches! You thought you could put out my flame? Well, you can't! Here I am, ready to do it all again!' That always felt so hopeful to me. It got me fired up and ready for the good things that I just knew would happen for us that day. And at the top of that list was our dad showing up, like he said he would. But every night when Ralph and I went back to that same spot, alone, and watched the sun go back down, I knew the possibilities for that day were over." She pauses. "I think most people are partial to the sunset. But not me. I want to see her rise."

The VHS tape has run to the very end, and that crackly fuzz fills the screen, but I can't take my eyes off her.

"No matter what, though," Louise continues. "During all those ups and downs, the ocean kept lapping at my feet. Almost like it was talking to me, reminding me that while people may let me down, nature never will. Nature never lies. It never abandons. It always comes back for us."

I run my hand along the length of her thigh.

"Is that when you decided you wanted to be a marine biologist? During those summers?"

"I think so? I remember sitting there, just marveling about how deep she goes, how many layers she has, and all the life that lives inside her. Sometimes I couldn't breathe thinking about how powerful she was. I decided I wanted to find a way to always stay close to her. If you ask me, there's nothing in the whole world as beautiful and as terrifying."

"I don't know about that," I say. "Ever looked in the mirror?"

She smiles sweetly and looks down.

I take her face in my hands, tilt her chin up, and whisper, "I'm going to make you rethink sunsets, Louise Anderson."

"Good luck with that," she whispers back.

We move into each other, and just before our lips make contact... the sound of bees fills the air.

I start swatting around us like a maniac, nearly knocking her in the face.

"Sorry! Sorry!" I shout. "Did I hit you?"

"No! I'm fine! James, calm down!"

At that same moment, the door opens, and Mabel and Wally saunter in.

"Oh wow! Are you naked under that blanket?" Mabel claps. "How fantastic! Should we stay or go? Stay or go, it's up to you!"

"Bees! Where the fuck are those bees?" I shout.

"It's midnight!" Louise shouts back and throws me my boxer briefs. "Remember I told you the bugfather clock chimes with bee sounds at midnight?"

"Right, right, right," I say.

"Yeah, just give it another five seconds," Mabel shouts over the noise. "And...5, 4, 3, 2, 1!"

Silence.

"There we go." Louise pats my thigh. "All better."

"You had sex on my childhood sofa, huh?" Mabel says, and it's hard to tell how she feels about that.

"Uh, maybe?" Louise says. "Are you mad?"

"Are you kidding? I'm ecstatic! I'm so glad he told you about his daughter and that you're clearly okay with it!"

Shit.

That look I didn't want to see on Louise's face again?

It's back. But a hundred times worse than before.

"Louise," I start. "I can explain—"

She shoos me away like my words could sting her.

"James told me about what, Mabel?" she says in a hard, cold tone.

Mabel's eyes widen in confusion when she says slowly, "About his daughter, Iris? In Hawaii?"

"Funny. He forgot to mention that."

Chapter Twenty-Seven

LOUISE

"Louise, will you open the door, please?" The knocks on my bedroom door are growing louder by the second. "Louise, please, let's talk."

"No, thank you," I say and shove my legs into my pajama pants. "You lied to me. I don't talk to liars."

"I have never lied to you. I just hadn't found a way to tell you yet that I—"

"Have a daughter?" I shout.

"Yes." I hear his sigh, even through the door. "Will you please open up so I can see you?"

I ignore his request. "You hear how terrible that sounds, don't you? You didn't tell me you have a daughter! A daughter, James. That poor girl! What did Mabel say her name is?"

"Iris."

"Iris," I repeat. "How old is she?"

"She's six."

"Six years old." I shake my head and go silent for a few moments.

"Louise, if you're going to break up with me, please open the door so you can do it to my face."

That's it.

"We can't break up if we never were together!" I say as I fling open the door.

And find him still shirtless and in his boxers.

"Would you please put some clothes on?"

"Mabel and Wally went back to his place to give us some privacy."

"That won't be necessary since you're leaving." I charge past him into the living room, grab his jeans and T-shirt, and shove them into his chest.

He dutifully slides his pants on, and like a love-sick idiot, I watch him.

How does he manage to make putting clothes on look sexy? Focus, Louise.

"So what do you do, James? Hide her from all the women you date?"

"No. I do not." He pulls his shirt over his head. "You are the first woman I've dated in seven years. And yes, we have been dating. That's what they call what we've been doing, whether you want to admit it or not."

"Seven years? I call bullshit."

He blows out a puff of air. "Louise, I am trying very hard to keep my cool right now."

"So am I!"

"No. You're not. You're jumping to conclusions, and you're assuming the worst of me. You're also being damn insulting by insinuating I'm somehow ashamed of my daughter."

"Aren't you, though? Daughters are such a buzzkill for dads! Especially when they're young and have so many inconvenient needs! Believe me, I should know."

"Baby." He reaches for me.

"Don't call me baby."

He takes a deep breath.

His brown eyes pour into mine.

"I'm sorry for the dad you had growing up, Lou. You deserved so much better. But my situation with Iris couldn't be more different. I promise you that. And if you could just find a way to calm down and listen to me, I will tell you everything."

"You should have told me right away."

"When?" he huffs. "When you declared that all single dads are the enemy and incapable of holding down a relationship? Or when we first met, and you told me you were only using me for sex and didn't want to know anything about me?"

I stumble over my words. "That's... that's—"

"Exactly what you said, Louise." He fills in the blank for me.

When I don't say anything to refute his words, he lowers his voice and repeats softly, "It's exactly what you said."

Despite my best efforts, a single tear breaks free.

Silently, he watches the tear roll down my cheek. Then he traces its trail with his thumb.

I swallow and take in a breath.

I can barely hear my own voice when I say, "I said that when I... It was before I..."

"Before you what?" he whispers, eyes locked with mine like he's trying to coax my next words out of me.

Before I started falling for you.

But of course, I don't say that.

Instead, I close my eyes.

I shut him out.

The sound of his breathing gets closer.

He places a warm hand on my shoulder.

The heat of it radiates throughout my entire body.

"I'm sorry I didn't find a way to tell you sooner. But I am not sorry for who I am or the life I have with my daughter. If that part of my life makes us incompatible in your eyes? Well then, there's nothing I can do about that now, is there?"

I want to say, "this is my issue, not yours."

I want to say, "I'm an adult now, and my relationship with my parents shouldn't affect me this way anymore."

And more than anything, I want to say, "can you be patient with me while I work through this?"

But I don't say any of those things.

Instead, I keep my eyes sealed shut and whisper, "I guess not."

"I guess not," he repeats, then slips his hand off my shoulder.

His footsteps move away from me.

"I'll see you around, Cold Brew. You know where I am if you need me."

The door clicks shut behind him.

Chapter Twenty-Eight

LOUISE

"Isn't Calliope coming?" I ask Ralph as we drive through the suburbs on our way to Bucks County Tavern.

"No. Mom said family only."

"So why is she going to be there?" I mumble.

He pats my leg. "Lou. Come on. Let's do the best we can. She says she has exciting news to share, and she wants us to be happy for her. It doesn't cost us anything to be happy for her."

"Speak for yourself." I scratch my head a few times. I swear, family interaction makes me itchy. "Is she bringing the guy? She better not be bringing the guy."

"I have no idea," he says as he signals to turn left into the parking lot.

He pulls into a spot and shuts off the engine.

I lean back, not ready to unbuckle my seat belt yet.

"How are you so okay with her these days?"

"I don't know." He shrugs. "I feel like if she knew how to do better, she would. And I guess one day I woke up and realized I'm a grown-up now. My life is pretty great. And maybe I don't need to hold on to all the anger and disappointment I feel for the little kid I used to be. Maybe that kid grew up and knows how to take care of himself now. Holding on to all the negative feelings I have—or had—for them only hurts me in the long run."

Wow. How did I get surrounded by all these self-aware men?

Then it hits me for the hundredth time today that I'm no longer surrounded by James. He walked away from me. Correction: I pushed him away from me.

Ralph hands me back the key to the vulva.

"Thanks for driving," I say. "I've just been a bit scattered since…"

"Are you going to talk to him?" he asks, then clarifies, "I overheard some of your late-night phone call with Calliope."

More like late-night sob fest.

"I don't know. One drama at a time."

He puts his hand on the door.

"Ready to go in?"

I sigh. "Yeah. Let's get this over with."

Ralph walks into the restaurant first, and I trail him. It takes everything in me not to sulk like a little kid being forced to go to a boring adult gathering.

Like Ralph insinuated, I'm the adult now. I don't need to keep repeating my patterns from when I was a child.

Ralph stops short, causing me to smack straight into his back.

"Oof. Geez, dude, a little warning would be nice," I grumble.

"A little warning would be nice," he says under his breath.

I step to Ralph's side and take in the scene in front of him.

It turns out, Mom did bring a guy.

And not just any guy.

The guy.

Sitting next to her, snuggled up on the same side of the booth, is our father.

"Hi, kids," he says.

"Hi, kids!" Mom repeats with a squeal. She shimmies out of the booth to give us hugs. My arms dangle to my sides as she squeezes me. I'm not intentionally withholding affection from her. I just can't seem to make myself move.

"Surprise!" she says as she reaches high to wrap her arms around Ralph's neck. "Are you surprised?"

"To see you here with Dad?" Ralph asks. "A bit, yeah."

"Sit. Sit, sit, sit." Mom points at the opposite side of the booth, then tucks herself under Dad's arm. He kisses the top of her head.

I think I'm going to be sick.

Ralph pulls me into the booth. I flop next to him like an out-of-water fish.

"So. Forgive me for stating the obvious, but…" She does a drumroll on the tabletop. "Your father and I are back together!"

"What?" Ralph asks. "How? Why?"

Mom beams and cuddles closer to Dad. "I guess sometimes things just happen for a reason!"

Ralph and I just stare at her.

"Okay, no, you're right. You two deserve an explanation. Before your birthday, Ralphie, I called your father to give him a piece of my mind—"

"Like she does every few months." Dad chuckles.

Mom swats him in the arm. "Well, can you blame me? You've been a real stinker for a very long time, mister!"

She giggles.

What in the hell is happening here?

"That's a fair assessment," Dad says and takes a swig of his beer.

"And I let it slip that I was in town visiting you kids for Ralphie's birthday. Little did I know, your father was back in the States working on a new truck route and wasn't too far away. So do you know what he did? He drove all day and all night to be with us at the party! To be with me."

Her face goes all shmoopy as she gazes into his eyes.

They kiss.

I resist the urge to throw up.

"You were the one who invited him?" Ralph asks.

Dad laughs. "I wouldn't say she invited me, but she did let the cat out of the bag. And boy was she mad when she first saw me there!"

"Oh, I was! But…" Her voice slows, and she curls a lock of hair at the nape of his neck around her finger. "One thing led to another, and now we've got a little local apartment together. He's still on the road a lot with work, but it's nice to have a home base little love nest."

"Are you fucking kidding me right now?"

It's the first thing I've managed to say since we walked in.

"Louise! Language," Mom scolds and looks around at the other patrons in apology.

"No." I hold up a hand. "Don't 'language' me. You used more language when I was growing up than anyone. I am a grown woman now, and I will use all the language I like!"

Ralph places what he must think is a comforting hand on my knee. I immediately swipe it off. "Lou—"

"Ralph, this shit is insane! What? We're supposed to be happy about this?"

"Of course!" Mom says and places a hand over her heart. "We're putting our family back together. How can that not be a good thing?"

"Back together implies that we were ever a family in the first place. We were never a happy family. Never!"

"Sweetheart, that is not true. We had our moments." Mom's voice warbles. Her eyes well with tears. When Dad takes his hand in hers, I want to scream.

"We"—I point at Ralph and me—"had our moments. Lots of moments. A lifetime of moments. We were all each other had. Because you"—my eyes dart back and forth between our parents—"were so involved in your own dramas and dumpster fire of a relationship, you couldn't even concern yourselves with what your kids were going through."

"What were you going through, Wheezy?" Dad asks like he's suddenly ready to have a father-daughter fireside chat.

"Don't call me Wheezy," I seethe.

"I'm sorry. What were you going through, Louise?" he corrects.

"Life, dude! We were going through life! Didn't you want to be a part of that? Witness that? I mean, come on! James lives four thousand nine hundred and eight miles from his daughter in Hawaii, and he travels there every single month for an entire week to be with her."

When I calmed down enough after my blowup with James, I realized that his daughter has been the main impetus for his monthly trips to Hawaii. And for his move in... how many weeks? Are we down to ten now?

I also may have calculated the exact mileage between there

and here, though I'm not sure why.

"James, the attractive bartender?"

"Yeah, Mom. James, the attractive bartender."

Of course, she noticed him and knows him by name.

"Oh sweetie, are you two dating?" she chirps. "He seems like a lovely man!"

"No, Mom, we're not dating. Wanna know why?"

"Why?"

"Because after a lifetime of watching you in action, I can't function in relationships! I've watched you dangle yourself like shark bait for my entire life, allowing yourself to be devoured by anyone who would have you. So I've done the same! Over and over again. And now, when a 'lovely man' is finally interested in me, I push him away because I'm terrified of being like you!"

"Louise. Show some respect," Dad rumbles like I'm an unruly teenager in need of redirection.

"You're right, Dad. I apologize. That was unfair to sharks. Most of them are peaceful creatures who are unjustly maligned by a fearful media determined to paint them as villains."

"But the real villain is me?" Mom sniffles. "I thought you kids would be happy for us. I'm trying to put our family back together."

"Take a breath, Lou," Ralph says.

I take his advice, slow down, and try to speak sense.

"Mom. How many family dinners did we have before tonight?" I look at Ralph and Dad as well. "Anyone have a total? Because I can count the number on one hand, and nearly all of them involved passive-aggressive parental digs at each other and dramatic details that we *children* should never have been privy to. For you to act like this is some sort of happy reunion is maddening. I'm sorry, but you can't reunite something that was never united in the first place."

I gather my purse and stand.

"Sweetie, don't go. Let us help you."

"With what? My homework? You were too busy for that. Want to cook me dinner? That's something else I always did for myself—once Ralph was out of the house anyway. Don't even get me started on the unfair weight that got placed on his shoulders!

Or maybe you want to help me pass my driver's test or pick out my prom dress or visit colleges! All things that would have been really helpful to me when I was a kid and I needed you. News flash, I don't need you anymore. I think my own thoughts, I make my own money, and I live on my own terms."

"And we're so proud of you, baby." Mom sniffles some more. "I may have made some mistakes as a mother, but we still have time! You know my friend Miriam? She and her daughter are the best of friends! They do everything together. Do you know how sad and embarrassing it is for me to see them going to the movies together, getting pedicures, and hitting happy hour at Sam's while knowing I don't have that with my own daughter?"

I shrug. "I'm sure Miriam and her daughter would be happy to have you tag along."

Mom's mouth drops open.

Who am I right now?

I take another moment to breathe.

"I don't want to hurt you, Mom. I just—"

I take in her sad eyes, looking at me to make everything better, but...

"I can't."

I move toward the door, expecting Ralph to follow. He doesn't.

"You coming?" I ask.

His eyes dart back and forth between our parents and me.

"I'm actually—" He pauses. "I'm going to stay."

Better him than me.

"Have fun with your little performance, everyone," I say. "I'm out of here."

Chapter Twenty-Nine

JAMES

"You seem sad, Daddy. Are you okay?" Iris's little face lights up on the small screen, and I'd give anything to reach through the phone and hug her right now.

I place the phone on its holder while I wipe down the bar.

"Yeah, Rissy Roo, Daddy's fine."

But Daddy is not fine. Not at all. I can't stop thinking about how I left things with Louise last night. I'll see you around, Cold Brew? I may as well have put the final nail in the coffin of our relationship myself. This is a woman with obvious abandonment issues, and I just walk away from her the moment things get tough?

"You know what, Iris? I'm not fine. Sometimes grown-ups try to put on a happy face for their kiddos because we don't want you to worry, but you're a big six-year-old now—"

"Six-and-a-quarter-year-old," she corrects.

I laugh. "That's right. Excuse me. You're a big six-and-a-quarter-year-old now, so I think it's important that I always tell you the truth. I'm having a bit of a hard day today. Do you ever have hard days?"

"Totally! Yesterday, Marco, this boy in my class, said I smell like a pomegranate."

"Is that a bad thing?" I ask.

"Of course! It's a terrible thing!"

Who knew? Last I checked, pomegranates smelled damn good.

"Oh. Well, I'm sorry that happened, sweetie."

"It's okay. I told him he smells like a papaya."

"Good comeback!"

Am I supposed to encourage comebacks? Hell, if I know. This parenting shit is hard. She's only six, and I feel like we've already been through at least seven different stages of development since she was a toddler. Each one seems to require a different set of rules and guidelines.

"What caused your hard day, Daddy?"

How to phrase this so she can understand?

"I, um. Well, I got in a fight with a good friend."

"Oh! Kind of like me and Marco!"

"Kind of." I nod.

"What's your friend's name?"

I sigh and try to keep my smile. "Louise. Her name is Louise."

And just like that, as if I summoned her out of thin air, Louise walks into my bar.

She stands in the doorway a moment, like she's unsure if she's still welcome here.

"Took ya long enough," I attempt a joke.

She smiles.

"Pull up a chair, won't you?"

"You sure?"

"Absolutely."

"Ooh, a customer! Let me talk to the customer!" Iris's excited voice peals through the speakerphone.

Louise freezes mid-sit. "Oh. I didn't realize you were... I can come back later when..."

"Don't be silly," I say. "Please. Sit."

She still looks extremely uncomfortable, but she settles onto the stool and hangs her purse on a hook.

"Hawaii is six hours behind us," I explain to her. "Iris and I always have a post-school-day-wrap-up phone call around this time. She loves to say hi to the customers. She knows all the regulars. Don't you, baby girl?"

"I do!" Iris says proudly. "And they all love me."

"I'm sure they do," Louise says with a smile.

"Would it be okay if I...?" I gesture to the phone and mime turning it in Louise's direction.

"Um, yeah. I guess. If you're okay with it, I'm okay with it."

"I'm great with it," I say.

Louise tucks her hair nervously behind her ears and leans forward as I turn the phone fully around to face her.

"Hi!" my little girl's voice says. "I'm Iris. What's your name?"

"Hi, Iris." Louise waves. "My name is Louise. It's nice to meet you."

"Ohmygoodness, we were just talking about you, Louise!"

"You were?" Louise asks, then looks up at me, panicked. "You were?"

"Rissy and I were talking about how sometimes friends have fights and say things they don't mean."

"Louise is a pretty name!" Iris is fully committed to her conversation and not paying attention to me at all anymore.

"Thank you." Louise laughs. "Iris is very pretty too."

"Do you know what Iris means?"

"Hm. I don't know for sure, but... maybe flower?"

"Ding, ding, ding! How did you know?" Iris is awed.

"Just a lucky guess." Louise chuckles. "Hey, Iris, I have a new friend named Meilani, and—"

"Oooh, I like that name!"

"Me too. Meilani is actually a sea lion. Your daddy told me her name means heavenly beautiful or heavenly flower. So my two new friends both have flower names. How cool is that?"

"So cool!" Iris squeals.

Louise is a natural with her. Not that I'm surprised in the least.

"How did you become friends with a sea lion?"

"I work in an aquarium, and that's where she lives."

"Can I come meet her sometime?" Iris nearly shouts with excitement.

Louise looks at me for guidance.

I nod and mouth, "Sure."

"Sure!" Louise says.

"Yay! Because I'll be there again to visit Daddy in..." She pauses. "How many weeks, Daddy?"

"Five weeks," I answer.

"In five weeks! So when I'm there, I'd love to meet Meilani and you and do all the Philthy-delphian things together with Daddy!"

"That, um. That sounds good?" Louise says and looks at me with uncertainty.

"You're fine," I whisper. "You're doing fine."

"Well, this has been fun, Louise, but my mom has my after-school snack ready to rock, and I'm freaking famished, so I gotta go, love you Daddy, see you at bedtime, bye!" Iris says in one breath and signs off.

"Bye, kiddo." I laugh and say to a blank screen.

It's silent for a moment.

"I've gotta work on that 'freaking' thing. Keeps popping up in her speech. Probably not the best habit for a six-year-old, right?"

"Gosh, I don't know." Louise breathes.

"What can I get ya?" I ask. May as well start with the easiest thing on the agenda: getting this woman a drink.

Sergeant Pepper's Lonely Hearts Club Band starts playing over the speakers.

"Do you mind if we...?"

"Change the station? You got it." I switch the music over to a nineties playlist I made recently.

"How about a Blue Moon?" she asks.

"Coming right up."

As I pour, she says softly, "I never explained The Beatles thing to you, did I?"

"No, but that's—"

"When I was little—before my dad left—he loved listening to Breakfast with The Beatles. I guess it was a thing the local radio station did every Sunday morning. Anyway, no matter what was going on in our house or how much fighting there was between him and my mom, that was something we'd always do together. I'd eat my Lucky Charms. He'd read his newspaper and drink his coffee. And we'd listen to The Beatles." She sighs. "Gosh, it's wild I can even remember that. I had to have been just under three."

I place her beer in front of her.

"Thanks," she says.

"Thank you. For coming back."

I place my hand over hers. I don't know if it's too much too soon, but I'm dying to touch her. To make some kind of contact with her.

To my surprise and relief, she doesn't move her hand away. She just looks deep into my eyes.

"I can't stomach lying, James. I just can't."

"Good. Neither can I."

"Withholding the truth feels like lying sometimes," she says in an almost whisper.

I drop my head toward my chest.

"It does. You're right. And I can't tell you how sorry I am for how this all came out."

"Well, Mabel has a big mouth," she jokes. "And you've already apologized. I didn't come here to make you grovel."

"You didn't?"

"No." She pauses. "But I would like to understand."

I pull up a stack of crates I keep behind the bar and sit on them so we're on the same level.

I clear my throat and begin.

"This is not an excuse—I promise you that—but when you said you'd never in a million years date a guy who was a father, that felt an awful lot like judgment to me. It especially stung being that—I'm not sure you've gotten the memo yet—I'm reeeeeeally interested in dating you."

This gets a laugh out of her.

"You don't know the circumstances of how I became a dad. You don't know what my relationship is like with my daughter or with her mom. Seems to me that if you lump me in with the bad examples of parenting you've seen in your past, then you might miss out on something pretty damn good. We'd miss out on something good."

She nods.

I take a big risk and say, "I'm not your dad."

She scoffs. "I know you aren't."

"I'm not the other guys you've dated either, who, I'm getting the distinct sense didn't treat you very well."

"I know that too."

"But you don't," I argue. "Not really. You've never given me a chance to get past that wall you've erected."

"Why you go and say the word 'erect?'" She takes a long sip of her beer.

"Are you kidding me right now?" I laugh.

"No, I'm not! I can't take anyone who uses that word seriously."

"In fairness, the word has multiple uses. You can stand erect. You can erect a building. You can erect an empire. A wall. A monument. Your spine can be erect."

"Alright, alright, stop, please." Her laughter softens. We listen to the Goo Goo Dolls play through the speakers. "Here's a little sidebar for you: never google 'erector set.'

"Oh no?"

"No. You'll get a mishmash of pictures of children playing with cranes interspersed with diagrams of handheld pump thingies for elderly men. It's confusing and disturbing."

"Noted. I promise to never google 'erector set.'"

"I think that would be best."

After a few moments of silence when neither of us seems to know how to move forward, she says, "So tell me."

"Tell you what?"

"You said I don't know the circumstances of how you became a dad or what your relationship is like with her mom. So... tell me."

"Eva and I—that's Iris's mom's name, Eva—we grew up together in Hawaii. She was my literal girl next door. We did everything together. The best friend I ever had. Until Wally, that is. Those two are pretty much neck-in-neck now for the people who have had the most influence on my life. Not that it's a competition or anything."

God, I'm rambling and justifying.

Why should this be so hard to talk about?

I check in with Louise, and she's just waiting patiently, sipping on her beer and hanging on my every word.

I continue, "You know I moved here after my mom passed, and that's when the drinking started becoming a problem."

She nods.

"Well, Eva and I stayed in touch throughout it all. We wrote letters, made phone calls, and supported each other as friends as best we could from afar. And that's all it ever was. A friendship. The best kind of friendship. Fast-forward a bunch of years, and between my AA meetings, Eva and Wally's support, and the sense of purpose I felt with the traveling blog, I had the drinking under control for a really long time. But then about eight years ago, my dad got sick, so I curbed my travel and put down solid roots in Philly again to be close to him. I started Adventure Bar, and that took off in an exciting way. But when my dad died, it brought up all kinds of stuff that I thought I'd dealt with, but apparently not enough. I had my first drinking relapse in years. Eva traveled up here for the funeral and to help get me back on track, but I don't know... the emotions got mixed up and confused, and we ended up having this one drunken night."

"Which resulted in Iris." Louise can obviously see where this is going.

"Yeah. We knew the next morning we were better off as friends, and it wouldn't happen again," I say. "But then when we found out Eva was pregnant, we agreed to do everything in our power to co-parent this baby the best way we could. Eva moved up here with me, and we raised Iris here full-time until nine months ago, when we decided they'd be happier in Hawaii, close to Eva's family. I have to tell you, the whole experience has never been anything but joyful."

"That's good," Louise says with a gentle smile.

"Is it. I feel incredibly lucky for that. But I do need you to know something."

"What's that?"

"There's absolutely nothing romantic between Eva and me. She's moved on, and so have I. But she and Iris are my family, and I'm committed to that. To them."

"You think that's going to scare me away?" she asks with a smile.

"Um. Yes? Learning about their existence pretty much sent you running and screaming from me last night."

"I felt lied to."

"I know. I promise I won't let that happen again."

"And I didn't want any part in keeping you away from your daughter. She's adorable, by the way. Seems like you and Eva are doing an amazing job with her."

"Thank you. That—" I swallow. "That means a lot."

"James. You telling me that you're committed to your family is exactly what I needed to hear. Don't worry, I'll keep my distance when they visit in a few weeks."

"Please don't," I say. "With me leaving after the holidays, I only have so much time here with you. And you heard Iris, she wants to meet you! And Meilani too."

She winces. "But aren't you only supposed to meet someone's kids once the relationship is serious? What do we tell her about us?"

"What I already told her. That we're friends."

"Is that all we are?" she asks softly. "Friends?"

What I want to say is hell no we're not just friends. I don't spend every day and night fantasizing about my just friends. I don't obsessively brainstorm things I can say or do to make my just friends smile. And I certainly don't agonize over the ticking of the clock because every minute that goes by is one less I get to spend with my just-friend.

"How about friends who fling?" That's the boneheaded compromise I come up with.

She laughs. "Friends who fling?"

"Would that work for you? That's what you said you were looking for in the very beginning right? Just a fling?"

"It would, yes," she says. "But..."

"But?" I prompt.

She sighs. "I know this sounds crazy, and it's not really synonymous with the definition of a fling, but... I kind of sort of don't want you flinging with anyone else."

"That won't be a problem for me."

"You sure?"

"Never been surer."

"Surer isn't a word." She smirks.

"It is now."

She laughs.

"Good," I say. "It's settled then."

We shake hands like we've signed a business arrangement instead of agreed on a super tenuous understanding of the future of our relationship.

But things are moving in a hopeful direction.

And I am here for it.

I lean over the bar to whisper in her ear.

"Get ready, woman. Because I'm gonna fling the hell out of you."

Chapter Thirty

LOUISE

"*I* missed you," he pants between kisses.

"It's only been a day." I laugh.

I tear off his shirt.

He does the same to mine.

When I'm standing in front of him in only my bra and panties, he scans the length of my body with a hungry look on his face, and says, "Longest damn day of my life."

"Why are you still wearing pants?" I ask.

"Not a clue, Cold Brew."

He shucks off his jeans.

I push him down on the bed and climb on top of him. He instantly responds, and just like that, I crave him inside me.

One of these days, I imagine we'll take our time with each other, but so far, every time we've been together, it feels like we're on this mutual race to pleasure. Like we're incapable of controlling ourselves or slowing things down.

I am certainly not complaining.

After our heart-to-heart at Adventure Bar, he asked me the telltale *You wanna get out of here?* question. My answer was a one-hundred-percent, absolute, hell yes.

His co-manager Ken saves the day yet again. I really need to buy that guy a thank you gift at some point.

I tear open a condom and roll it down his length with my mouth.

He sucks in air through his teeth. "Fuck me, that was hot."

"I'm about to, James. Have you ever heard of patience?" I pretend to scold him, but it's hard to keep a straight face when he's lying on my blue-and-white-striped comforter, looking so desperate for me.

"I have no patience where you're involved, Lou."

He sits up just enough to grab me by the back of my neck and pull me on top of him.

Holy shit.

He was wrong a moment ago.

That was hot.

I don't waste any time straddling him and sinking down on his cock.

"So good," he says as he fills me. "So fucking good."

"You're telling me," I breathe and start to find my rhythm.

We move together like we were made for each other.

"I'm so glad this is happening," he says.

"Me too."

"It feels different than the first time, doesn't it?"

"Well, yeah." I laugh. "The first time, you had me up against a beer keg, and my left ass cheek went numb. This whole being in a warm, comfortable bedroom scenario feels pretty boring and vanilla if you ask me."

"Oh damn, well, we can't have that, now can we?"

With supreme finesse, he lifts me off him, turns me around on all fours, and enters me from behind.

I gasp.

"You like that?"

"Yeah, I do," I say in a throaty voice that doesn't even sound like me.

I lower my head and chest to the mattress which allows him to go even deeper. I swear I see stars.

"Do you feel that?" he asks, but his tone has suddenly shifted from sexy to actual concern.

"Yeah, I do." I reach under us and cup his balls while he continues to thrust, but his movements are a little less confident now. "It would be next to impossible not to feel that, big guy."

"No, no, I mean—" His voice climbs up a few notches. "Do

you feel like...?"

I press my palms into the mattress again and look over my shoulder. "Like what? Do I feel like what?"

He blows out a breath.

"Goddammit, you're sexy when you look at me like that."

His hands grip my hips tighter, and his eyes fill with renewed lust.

"Cool," I say, right on the edge of frustration. "Can continue then?"

"We can, yeah."

He picks up the pace again, and I'm right back on that ride to heaven.

Thank God.

"I just feel like maybe someone's watching us?" he says.

Ugggggggh.

"What? No. No way. Are you serious?"

"I am, yeah."

I try to talk sense to him. "Listen. I know Mabel is newly 'unleashed' and everything, but I don't think she's full-blown voyeuristic creep."

"Does it hurt to double-check?" he asks.

I sigh. "I suppose it doesn't. Mabel?" I call out. "Mabel, are you home early?"

We freeze and listen for a response.

Nothing comes.

And at the rate we're going, neither of us will tonight either.

"She's not home, James."

"I don't know, Lou. It's just this feeling I'm getting. Like there's an... energy in this room. Don't you feel it?"

Clearly, things were progressing way more nicely when I was steering this sex ship, so I inch forward and separate us for a moment. I turn around on the mattress and stand on my knees to mirror his position. I'm just about to put him back where he belongs when I realize... he's right.

Someone is watching us.

And that someone is perched right on top of James's sexy, prickly skull.

Mabel didn't call this the mantis room for nothing.

"James?" I whisper. "Don't move."

"Why? Don't move why? What's going on?" he says at full volume.

His panic rises at the same time his dick lowers.

"You're not going to like what I'm about to say, but you have to promise me that you won't freak out."

"I'm absolutely freaking out!" he says. "Tell me what's going on."

"Bonnie is on your head," I whisper so low, I barely hear myself.

"What?" He squints, like that will help him hear better.

I try again, a little louder this time. "Bonnie is on your head."

"What?"

"THERE IS A PRAYING MANTIS ON YOUR HEAD!"

"Fuck! Shit! Oh my God!"

James flies into an instant frenzy, running, swatting, and screaming.

"Don't swat!" I yell. "Don't swat at her! You'll hurt her!"

But it's too late.

Bonnie's tiny but powerful body soars across the room and lands on the plush carpet.

She's still.

So are we.

Oh God, please tell me we did not just kill Mabel's mantis.

Please, please, please, please, please.

"What do we do?" James whispers.

"I don't know, but if Bonnie is dead, you're the one who's telling Mabel," I threaten.

"How the hell did she even get out of her cage?"

As soon James asks the question, the answer becomes clear.

Bonnie twitches a few times, then gets back on her mantid feet.

"She's alive! She's alive!" I clap and cheer.

My cheers are instantly silenced when Bonnie marches her insect self right back to the low bookshelf, scales it, drops into her cage, and... pulls the lid on top.

That. Was. So. Damn. Freaky.

This has been a lovely experiment living with my pal Mabel these past few weeks, but clearly, this is not a long-term solution.

"I've gotta get the hell out of here," I say to James.

"Yeah, you do."

Chapter Thirty-One

LOUISE

CALLIOPE: Sister friend, is it true that you and James have moved in together?

MABEL: It is true. They almost killed my praying mantis last week with their irresponsible at-home sexcapades, so I kicked her out.

MABEL: Kidding. She left because she couldn't take the heat. #MabelUnleashed

ME: Hey, bitches. No, James and I did not move in together. I am simply staying at his place for a little while until I figure out my next move.

MABEL: A little mantis told me your preferred "move" is doggy style. #YouGoGurl

CALLIOPE: Could you cool it with the hashtags, Mabes?

MABEL: I'm not sure that I can. But I'll certainly try.

ME: Gotta go, guys. James is taking me on our first official date.

CALLIOPE: First date, my ass. You're practically engaged at this point.

ME: No. We are not. And all of our dates so far have sort of spontaneously happened. Tonight, he's planned some kind of surprise. He's picking me up and everything.

CALLIOPE: How's he picking you up when you live together?

ME: For the last time, WE DO NOT LIVE TOGETHER.

CALLIOPE: Geez. You don't have to shout. Have fun, sister friend. Don't do anything I wouldn't do.

ME: Callie, there isn't anything you wouldn't do.

CALLIOPE: Truuuuuuuuuuuuuth!

I walk out of the aquarium and find James leaning against his car, waiting for me. He's dressed super casual tonight in low-slung gray sweatpants, a "Kiss Me I'm a Bartender" T-shirt, and a soft black hoodie.

"The bartender wants a kiss, huh?" I ask as I sidle up beside him.

"He does indeed."

I give him a long, slow kiss until a catcall whistle stops us. I turn to find Dana and Brendan making their way to their own cars and giving me cheesy thumbs-ups. I've gotten closer with these two over the past few weeks. Seems that all Brendan needed to—mostly—drop his attitude was a sense of community. Surprisingly, he's gotten really inspired by this painting project with Meilani. He's crafted us a dozen more custom paintbrushes for her to use, and he even assists me with her on Wednesday afternoons after he leads the weekly penguin parade. He told me the other day that he's also brainstorming ways to get his penguin crew painting.

Art really can bring people—and animals—together.

I wave to them both and move to the passenger side of James's car. He's right there to open my door and usher me safely inside.

I snort. "A little much, don't you think?"

"What?" he balks. "As this is our first official date, I thought some extra chivalry was in order. You're not going to resist my charm all night, are you? I've got a whole thing planned."

"Oh, there's more?"

"Of course, there's more! There's a duffel bag by your feet. Open the front zipper pocket."

He shuts my door and walks around to the driver's side while I reach into the bag and pull out...

"A blindfold?" I squeak. "Remember when I told you my brother was fired for fornicating on museum premises? I'm sorry James, but I'm not getting kinky with you in the aquarium parking lot."

He starts the car and turns on some tunes.

"Damn. My master plan is ruined." He laughs. "While I'm down to fornicate with you at any time, in any place, no. That's not what I had in mind. The blindfold is so you don't guess where we're going before the grand reveal. The road leading up to it is pretty recognizable."

I give him a look.

"You game to play along?" he asks.

"I guess so," I say nervously and place the blindfold over my eyes.

He kisses my nose and starts to drive.

"How long will it take to get there?"

"Not long. Ten minutes or so."

He takes my hand and places it under his on the gear shift, so it's almost like I'm controlling the car while blindfolded. It's wild. The sounds around me come alive in a new way with my eyes temporarily out of the equation. The rumble of the car engine. The flow of his breath. The beating of my heart.

"So. Fornicating, huh?" he says, seemingly out of the blue. "What a word choice."

"It comes from the latin root fornus meaning a brick oven of arched or dome shape."

"Are you inviting me into your oven, Louise?"

"Ew." I laugh. "You're being weird. Why are you being weird?"

"Sorry," he says. "I'm a little nervous, I guess. I want to make sure this night is good for you. There's a fifty-fifty chance my idea could be a disaster."

"You're nervous?" I ask.

"Don't sound so shocked. Of course I am. Everyone gets

nervous around things they care about, don't they?"

I shrug, not sure how to answer that question.

"Can I mention something I've noticed?"

"Uh-oh," I laugh. Last time you said that, you told me that I have all-or-nothing thinking."

"This is good. I promise."

"Go ahead." I hold my breath.

"You haven't done the Jeopardy thing in a long time. This little brick oven fornication interlude just now was actually the first bit of trivia you've busted out in over a month."

Huh. He's right.

"I guess I… haven't needed to," I say. "When I'm with you, I feel…safe. Understood. I don't need to work so hard to impress you or keep you."

It's quiet a moment until James says softly, "I know I asked you to wear the blindfold, but would you mind taking a quick peek at me?"

I lift the bottom of the blindfold up an inch and am treated to the most brilliant smile on his handsome face. He's beaming.

"I really liked hearing that," he says. "Thank you."

He lifts my hand to his mouth and kisses it. Goose bumps erupt all over my skin.

"Alright, back into the blindfold you go. We're getting close."

How did I not notice this before? That ever since I've gotten close with James, that nervous need in me has quieted. I never really questioned how that whole trivia thing started and what drove me to do it. But now that I'm thinking about it, it's all becoming clear.

"That whole *Jeopardy* thing I do—or did—I'm realizing it's kind of sad. Night after night I would sit at my tray table eating the microwavable meal I heated up for myself, and get the comfort I should have found in my parents from a game show host. Isn't that sad?"

I don't actually need him to answer that question.

Somehow, he knows that and just listens.

"Game shows are supposed to be fun. But have you ever noticed the name of that one? *Jeopardy*? Do you know the definition of the word *Jeopardy*?"

"Sure, I guess. It means—"

"Exposure to or imminence of death, loss, injury."

"Yikes," he says.

"Yeah. And that's how it felt. Like it was life or death whether or not I got all those answers right. Especially after it became a little parlor trick for my parents. 'Do the thing, Wheezy,' Mom would say proudly whenever one of her new 'friends' was around. Rattling off all those facts and information always got me their approval. Their attention. So I made sure to keep it up." I pause. "But maybe I don't need to do that anymore."

"Yeah," he agrees. "I don't think you do."

A Beatles song comes on the radio, and James immediately changes it.

"Not to get too heavy," he says. "But as a kid who lost his mom young, I can tell you there is a real tendency in me to 'live for my mom.' She was awesome, and that approach sounds good on the surface. Because people suggest things like that all the time: 'you get to live for her now,' and 'go out and do all the things she didn't get a chance to do.' But living our lives for other people gets dangerous real quick. We lose track of what we want and who we are while we're trying to honor them." His tone shifts. "It goes the other way too though."

"What do you mean? What other way?"

"I just mean that our parents don't have to die to overly influence our lives. If we disagree with how they raised us or how they're living, without realizing it, we can launch this quest to do everything the opposite way they did, or we can make all of our life choices in an effort to spite them. That's no road to happiness or authenticity either."

Is that what I've been doing? Letting their shortcomings steer the decisions I make in my life?

"Alright, Cold Brew. We've arrived."

He shifts the car into park and shuts off the engine.

"You ready?" he asks.

"I have absolutely no idea."

"Here, let me help."

He exits the car and walks around to my side to open the door. He guides me out, then stands flush against my back, his arms around my waist, his breath on my neck.

"Moment of truth," he says. "May I?"

His warm fingers brush my ear as he reaches for the blindfold. I nod.

He lifts it off me and... what I see in front of me is the last thing I expect. I'm not exactly sure what I anticipated. Maybe I thought we'd have a romantic dinner? See a cool show? Go to an outdoor concert? But this?

"Splash City?" I nearly shriek. "You brought me to Splash City?"

"Yeah!" he enthuses. "Have you ever been?"

"No, dude! Because I hate getting in the water!"

"Right, yes. I know. You've mentioned that. But I thought this could be a way to get over that fear while having a stupid amount of fun!"

My heart starts pounding.

"But I don't even—I didn't bring a suit."

"In the bag."

I reach for more excuses. "It's almost dark out. They have to be closing soon."

"Tonight's a special late-night event. They light up all the water slides. They bring in a live band. It's awesome."

"What do you say? Give it a try? I'll be with you every step of the way."

I just stare up at the sign, frozen.

"Listen." He turns me to face him and holds both of my hands in his. "If you really don't want to do this, we'll turn around right now. I told you there was a good chance this idea would be a disaster. I just hate to see an ocean-loving girl like you missing out on all the joy that comes with actually getting in the water. I thought this could be a fun baby step in the right direction."

"Alright, let's do it," I say.

"Yeah?" James squeezes both of my shoulders and bends his knees to look right into my eyes. "You sure?"

"I'm sure."

Ten minutes later, we're standing at the top of The Swirling Sidewinder, a curly water slide designed so two people at a time can go down in a double-seated raft.

"Isn't the name Swirling Sidewinder redundant?"

"A bit, yeah," James says. "But I thought this one would be a good fit for your first time. You don't have to go alone, and the fact there's a raft involved means there is far less potential for a wedgie occurrence."

I look down, where the slide deposits a set of squealing kids into the pool below.   "If a wedgie is the worst thing that happens, I'll be fine."

James scoffs, "Spoken like someone who's never had a wedgie."

Oh my God, we're next.

The ride attendant sets our raft in the launching station and gestures for us to climb aboard.

James gets in the back and opens his legs wide so I can sit between them.

I settle in front of him and grip the rubber handles while jets of water pour down the tube in front of us.

"Wedgies," I say, suddenly out of breath. "What a weird way to bully someone, right? Like 'hey come here, kid. I'm going to yank your underwear between your butt cheeks until you scream. I mean, how did this practice even begin? And do people even attempt wedgies anymore? These days, wouldn't a wedgie constitute assault?"

"There's no turning back now," James says and wraps his arms around me. "Lean back. I've got you."

I sink into his hold and keep my eyes wide open as James gives us a gentle push and sends us zooming down the slide, water splashing all around us.

Chapter Thirty-Two

JAMES

We've been unofficially living together for three weeks.

Going to sleep beside her every night and waking up to her each morning has me feeling like I'm living in a dream. A heart-bursting, mind-blowing, sex-filled dream.

There's an ease between us now that I never would have predicted when we first connected all those months ago. Back when she requested—no, demanded—that we be a one-and-done.

I'm so damn grateful she changed her mind.

She's slowly getting to know Iris too. A few times when I've been doing my late-night phone call to Hawaii to "tuck Iris in," she's joined us. She's even come aboard our Marla the Mermaid writing project. After helping us with some sea facts and terminology one night, Iris gave her the title of "Marine Biology Consultant" and insisted that we put her name in the acknowledgments when we finished.

Internally, I'm freaking out that I have to give this all up in seven weeks.

Outwardly, I'm doing my damnedest to keep up the "friends who fling" façade.

But it's getting harder by the day.

Because I'm falling for this woman. Fast.

And those feelings show no signs of dissipating any time soon.

Or ever, if I'm being honest with myself.

I'm walking through the parking lot of the Philadelphia Zoo when I spot her sliding through a side exit to come greet me. As a key player in making this event happen tonight, she arrived hours ago to get things set up and then got ready on-site.

The vision of her literally takes my breath away.

She's wearing a formfitting blue sequined strapless dress that hugs her around the knees and sports a daring slit up the back.

"Don't you clean up nice?" she says and gives me a kiss on the cheek.

"Woman, I want way more than a kiss on the cheek right now. You look fucking incredible."

"Yeah? The lighting in the staff bathroom wasn't the best. I'm calling it Sequined Mermaid Chic." She spins.

I look her up and down and break out in applause.

"Oh stop." She smacks me playfully on the shoulder, then takes my elbow when I offer it.

We walk past the gates, arm in arm, pick up our seating card and make our way down the lit path toward the gazebos set up for the event.

"Thanks for coming with me tonight," she says.

"Are you kidding me? I wouldn't miss it for the world."

"People will bid on the paintings, right?"

"Of course they will. Your work is phenomenal and Meilani's is..." I search for my words. "Well, I don't think I can classify a sea lion's painting skills as phenomenal, but she really did some... cool splatters."

Louise laughs. "She did, didn't she?"

"You and Meilani make a good team."

She nods, but her smile fades.

"They're sending her back to California. Did I tell you that?"

"No. Why?"

"It's a good thing. A great thing, actually. She's not in the running to re-release into the ocean, but there's this great team out in Monterey creating prosthetic limbs for marine life and they think Meilani's a good candidate for a new flipper. They sent out a prototype last week for her trainers to try with her. You should have seen her light up when she wore it. It was... it was beautiful." She takes a deep breath, then lets it out. "So they're going to send her to The Center for Marine Mammals after Thanksgiving to work with that team. Build her strength up even more. Give her the best life possible."

"I imagine there are some mixed emotions about that."

"Yeah. There are." She wipes a tear from the corner of her eye before it can drop. "I mean, they'll send me videos, and I can visit, but..."

"It won't be the same," I finish the sentiment for her.

"Yeah. It won't be the same."

Without realizing it, we've stopped in the middle of the path, surrounded by trees strung with twinkle lights. We're looking into each other's eyes and feel like neither of us is talking about Meilani anymore.

I place my hand on her cheek.

"Lou," I start. "You know, people make things like this work. The distance will be an issue, but we can find a way to—"

"I'm not ready to sit down yet." She cuts me off. "Want to peruse the auction with me?"

"Um, yeah. Sure."

She links arms with me again and steers me toward Raptor Ridge where the items for auction are displayed.

Okay. I clearly didn't pick the right time to have that discussion.

We walk in silence while taking in everything the auction has to offer.

"My station is right over... there." Her voice trails off like she's seen a ghost.

"You okay Cold Brew? What's going on?"

Her eyes are fixed on someone standing in front of her largest painting of Meilani. It's one of her best. Painted in what I've come to recognize as her signature style, it uses bright blues and yellows and greens and can be enjoyed from a distance, but when you get closer, you see the hundreds of tiny squares that make it a masterpiece.

She has a true gift for this.

"Humans are six times more likely to be killed by this domestic animal than a shark."

Her voice sounds hollow when she says it, her eyes still glued to the man's back at the canvas.

"What?" I say.

"Play along. Please. Humans are six times more likely to be killed by this domestic animal than a shark," she repeats.

"Of course, of course. What are cows?"

"That's incorrect. The answer is domestic pigs. The sound of this fictional character's iconic breathing was developed by studying scuba divers."

"Oh, I know this one! Who is Darth Vader!"

"Correct. These brainless, umbrella-shaped marine animals have been known to shut down nuclear power plants on more than one occasion."

"The answer is 'What are jellyfish?' but Louise, seriously, tell me what's going on."

At the sound of Louise's name, the man turns around.

I don't like to judge a book by its cover, or a man by his ascot, but at first glance, this man has asshole written all over him. Though likely, my instant aversion to him has less to do with his choice of neckwear and far more to do with the fact that Louise is practically shrinking into herself in his presence.

"Louise! Long time no see! Your work has really... moved along."

He scans the painting again, then turns back to her with a phony grin.

"What are you doing here?" she says.

He looks at me and extends a hand. "Hi. Trent. And you are?"

"James." I accept his handshake, but I don't like it.

"You Louise's current playboy?"

"Excuse me?" My internal temperature immediately rises.

Please don't punch this guy and cause a scene. "Trent," he repeats, placing a reverent hand on his chest, like that name alone should ring important bells for me. "Louise's first love. After our breakup, I heard she went on a bit of man-spree trying to forget me." He looks me up and down. "I guess that's still ongoing."

Louise's voice is low when she says, "I didn't go on a man-spree, I just—I was experimenting for a while, and—"

I stop her right there. "You don't owe an explanation to me. Or this guy. Or anyone for that matter. You could have 'spreed' with an entire squadron at fleet week, and that wouldn't change a thing about how I feel about you." I pause. "Nothing could change the way I feel about you."

"Awwww," Trent coos. "You two are so sweet."

"What brings you here tonight, Troy?" I ask.

"It's Trent," he says, offended.

"My apologies. Louise has just never mentioned you before, so."

He scoffs. "I find that hard to believe."

"Believe it." I take Louise's hand in mine.

His eyes dart down to where we're connected.

"I came here tonight because I'm working for a gallery now in the Berkshires. I came across an article about a girl who's helping to rehabilitate marine animals through art. I was impressed, Louise. Seems you learned a lot from your time with me."

He turns his back on her to study the painting again.

"Wait a damn second," she says, but then shuts her mouth as quickly as she opened it.

Her body tenses beside me. I see the emotions welling up inside her, but she's trying to keep a lid on them.

"You want to say something to this guy?" I lean closer to her.

"It's not worth it," she seethes.

"Sure it is," I say. "Not for him, but for you."

Her eyes narrow while she considers her next move.

"I can give you some space if you want, or I'll stay right here with you. Whatever you need."

"Stay," she says. "I want you to stay."

Music to my ears.

I nod and take just a single step back to let her do her thing.

She taps Trent on the shoulder.

He turns.

"You're right, Trent. I did learn a lot while I was with you."

"I learned everything I don't want in a relationship. I learned what the opposite of a good man is. And I learned how I will never let a man treat me again." She pauses and shakes her head. "You made me feel so small."

Trent huffs. "Now Louise, no one can make you feel small. Your feelings about yourself are yours and yours alone. It's not my fault that your artistic skills were lacking while we were together. But you've improved. You should be happy."

"I am happy, you condescending prick."

He actually stumbles back a step at her words. Clearly, she's never spoken to him like this before.

She lowers her voice. "You found a way to criticize and belittle every piece of art I ever made. I lost years of my creativity because of you. But that's over now. As you can see"—she gestures to her paintings—"I've taken my creativity back. No piece of me is yours anymore."

He adjusts his ascot and grabs a glass of champagne from a nearby server with a passing tray. "Goodness, you've gotten dramatic, Louise. I simply wanted to come here and celebrate your night. If you can't handle some good old-fashioned criticism, then you'll never make it in the art world."

"It's time for you to leave."

"Excuse me?" he says between sips.

"Like you said, this is my night. Not yours. And I'd like you to leave."

"You heard the lady," I say.

Louise's lips tighten when she looks at me. It's an expression I can't read in the moment.

"But I purchased a ticket!" Trent puffs up his chest.

"And we'd be happy to reimburse you for that, sir," Louise's coworker Brendan says with a customer service smile. Seems he'd be watching the escalating tension from a few feet away. "I'm sorry to hear you're not feeling well tonight, sir."

"I feel just fine!" Trent argues.

Brendan continues as if Trent didn't say a word, "Dominic here is working security for us tonight, and he'll gladly escort you to the exit where I'll process your refund."

Dominic—who is apparently six-foot-five and looks like he could bench press a small country—steps out from a golf cart with the word SECURITY emblazoned on the front.

He doesn't have to say a thing.

"Fine," Trent huffs and dutifully climbs into the golf cart with Dominic and Brendan. As the vehicle pulls away, he shouts, "Your shadow work is still atrocious!"

"So is your ascot, asshole!" I shout back.

Louise giggles and shoves me in the shoulder.

"I couldn't help myself," I say. "I hope you don't mind."

"My favorite part was, 'you heard the lady.'" Louise does a terrible impression of me. "Way to go all old-school Clint Eastwood on him, ya dork."

She wraps her arms around my neck and sinks into me.

"That... was awesome," I say. "How do you feel?"

"Like you're too good to be true," she whispers.

"Nah. I'm the real deal. Kiss me?"

"I thought you'd never ask."

Chapter Thirty-Three

LOUISE

I'm peering through the window at Adventure Bar, watching James chat with a gorgeous woman and wondering how the hell I got here.

She laughs at something he says.

He beams back at her, like making her laugh is one of his greatest joys.

They're so at ease with one another.

So in sync.

The scene sends a pang of jealousy straight to my gut.

I know it shouldn't.

But it does.

The Brew at the Zoo event was a success on so many levels. We ended up raising over twenty-five thousand dollars to combat ocean pollution. A staggering percentage of those proceeds came from my paintings of Meilani, a fact that still blows my mind. And I was flying high the entire night after finally exorcising Trent from my system in such a satisfying way.

But, James named his excursion company The Highs and Lows for a reason. Oftentimes, those two things go hand in hand.

When we arrived back at his place that night, we learned that Alex Trebek had died. I sobbed. For hours. I felt silly in a way because I'd never met the man. I didn't know him, but in a bizarre sense, he'd been there for me over the years in a way my parents never had. It felt like a major loss.

James didn't make me feel silly for a second though. He held me the whole night while I cried and told me how sorry he was. How everything was going to be okay.

This is ridiculous. I should just go in there and say hi. What did I expect? That they would hate each other? That she wouldn't be beautiful? Iris is stunning, so why wouldn't she be gorgeous too?

On the count of three, Louise.

One... Two... Three.

I press the door and draw James's attention right away.

"Lou! Hey! Get over here!" he shouts.

Eva swivels on her stool to face me with a warm smile. "Hi, Louise! I'm Eva. I've heard so much about you."

"Likewise." I shake her hand. Then like a doofus, I say, "You're, um. You're so pretty."

"Oh gosh, thank you." She swings her long curtain of shiny black hair over her shoulder. "You too. Obviously." She chuckles. "You don't need me to tell you that. Here. Sit next to me, sit next to me." She pulls out the stool beside her.

"Okay." I take the offered seat and am surprised when James leans across the bar to kiss me. Right in front of her.

He whispers in my ear, so only I can hear, "Relax. You have nothing to prove."

I realize then that he had a Blue Moon waiting for me and my favorite nachos.

"To the woman who's stolen James's heart!" Eva lifts her glass and gestures for me to do the same.

"Eva. Can you chill out with that?" James lovingly scolds. "You're gonna scare her off."

"Oh buddy, if you haven't done that already, I think we're in the clear. Cheers!"

I hesitantly lift my glass and clink it with hers.

"So" I say. "How was your flight?"

"Long, but good. Iris is at an age now where she can amuse herself on the plane and I can actually get some sleep or do some work. A big change from the baby days! But, if I'm being honest, she's always been a great traveler. Lots of practice with this guy as her daddy."

I smile and look around. "I expected to see Iris here. Where is she?"

"Potty break," Eva says.

James lifts his chin. "Here she comes now."

A little girl with Eva's hair and James's eyes saunters down the hallway like she owns the place, trailed by a tall handsome man with tan skin and shaggy blond hair.

"Louise!" she squeals and runs straight into my arms. "It's you!"

"It is! It's me." I laugh. "And it's you too!"

I check in visually with Eva to make sure this is okay. I'm still uncertain of the rules when meeting the daughter of your "friends who fling" partner.

She gives me a sly thumbs-up, signaling I don't have anything to worry about.

Eva really is cool as hell.

I'm not sure what I expected, but to say I'm pleasantly surprised would be an understatement.

"This is Ron, my boyfriend. Ron, this is James's girlfriend, Louise."

"Good to meet you, Louise," Ron says and offers me a handshake.

"You too!"

I don't correct Eva's use of the word girlfriend. Something tells me that would ruin the whole positive vibe we have going on here.

"James tells me you two are heading up to Vermont tomorrow?" I try to make conversation.

"Yeah, we're going to spend a long weekend there before heading home. We hear it's gorgeous this time of year. We got ourselves a cozy little cabin with a woodburning stove." Eva wraps her arms around Ron's waist as he sidles up next to her barstool. "A total one-eighty from our life in Hawaii."

"I bet."

Ron kisses her on the top of her head. She squeezes him a little tighter. They're a super-cute couple and look very much in love.

"Daddy, can I make a Shirley Temple?"

"Course you can, kiddo. Get back here," James says.

Iris squeals and pushes through the swinging saloon doors that lead behind the bar. James plops her on top of a stack of crates at the end of the bar, and the two of them get to work.

"Iris has been very excited about meeting her marine biology book consultant in real life," Eva says.

"And to visit her aquarium!" Iris shouts and swings a maraschino cherry around by its stem. "Don't forget that part, Mom!"

"How could I forget? You're going to learn all about crustaceans, right?"

"Cetaceans, Mom. Daddy signed me up for the 'What's the Purpose of a Porpoise' Workshop. Crustaceans are lobsters and crabs and a bunch of other stuff. Cetaceans are dolphins, porpoises, and whales. I told you that, geez!"

"My bad, my bad." Eva laughs, then says under her breath, "She gets saucier by the second."

"I'm gonna step out to take a work call," Ron says and holds up his ringing phone.

"Okay, babe, we'll be out as soon as she's finished her Shirley Temple."

"Nice to meet you, Louise," Ron says, then gestures to James that he's heading out.

"Have a great trip, man," James calls out from where he and Iris are pouring syrup into her glass filled with bubbles. "Thanks for bringing me my baby girl."

"You bet," Ron says with a finger salute, then heads out the door.

Wow.

This little modern family is so... functional.

"She likes you," Eva says quietly as she sips her soda.

We both watch Iris and James playing at the end of the bar.

"I like her too. You have a really sweet kid." I hesitate. "Not that I know her very well. James has just put me on the phone a bunch of times and—well, you know that. Of course, you know that. You're her mom. You're with her 24/7, monitoring her phone calls and who she's talking to, and—"

"Louise?" She places a gentle hand on my arm.

"Yeah?"

"You can relax with me. It's okay."

"It is?" I breathe.

"Yeah." She chuckles. "This is not the moment I give you the 'if you hurt him, I'll kill you' speech. I mean, I certainly hope you don't hurt him. But you two are grown-ups. You'll figure it out." She pauses. "Listen. I'm sure this is a strange time for you: navigating a new relationship, juggling the complications of dating the father of a young child… And, gosh, doing that all while that new guy is in the midst of moving across the country? It can't be easy."

She's right about that, but I do my best to school my features.

"So I thought I'd offer you something—in the event it helps."

"What's that?" I ask.

"You don't have to worry about me." She looks right in my eyes when she says it. "I trust James completely. Always have. Always will. I want him to be happy, so I will give him the same grace he gave me when I was falling in love with Ron. You have my full blessing to have a blast with those goobers these next two weeks."

Iris cackles at the end of the bar as James dramatically covers his ears when she makes empty-glass slurping noises through her straw.

"That—" I swallow the lump in my throat. "That means so much to me Eva, thank you. But you should know that this is temporary. We're not falling in love like you and Ron. We're just— Well, we're… having fun until it's time for him to go."

She gives me a knowing look. "Okay," she says, not the least bit convinced by me.

I can't blame her, though.

Because right now, I'm having a really hard time believing that myself.

"Rissy?" Eva calls out. "Time to go, boo boo. Let's go have some fun in that fancy hotel before I bring you back to Daddy's place tomorrow morning."

"Yay! Hotel! I love hotels!"

"I know you do."

"See you tomorrow, Daddy." Iris gives James a quick squeeze, then runs around the bar to her mother. "Is it the hotel that gives you warm chocolate chip cookies at the front desk?"

"Is there any other?" Eva ruffles her daughter's hair.

James places a drink down in front of a customer, then makes his way over to us and tosses a rag onto the bar.

"Nine o'clock sound good for a drop-off, Evie B?" he asks.

"Sounds perfect, thanks."

They bump fists.

Eva gives me a hug and whispers, "See you again soon, I hope."

I return her squeeze. "I'd like that, yeah. Have, um... Have a great trip."

"We will, thanks."

A moment later, Iris and Eva are gone, and James and I are leaning toward each other across the bar.

"So," I say like a total doofus.

"So," he repeats.

"Eva. She's..."

"What? What is she? You okay?"

"Fine, yeah. I'm... great. She's great."

"You sound surprised." He laughs.

"I guess I am. I didn't expect that to be so easy."

"Not everything in life needs to be hard, Cold Brew."

"I'm starting to see that."

He kisses me softly on the lips.

"Can I get you another drink?"

I shake my head. "I was actually hoping we could go back to your place."

"Oh really?" he flirts.

"Watching you with Iris was..." I hesitate to say this next part, but what the hell? Apparently, all bets are off tonight."...it was all sorts of sexy."

A cocky grin spreads across his face. "Oh, was it now?"

"Yes. It was," I say and instantly hold up a finger in warning. "But do not take that to mean something it doesn't. I am by no means saying I want to procreate with you. Or with anyone for that matter. Ever."

He tips his head up to the ceiling and laughs.

God, I love that sound.

"Alright, yuck it up, dude. I am just as surprised as you are by my reaction, but…" I drop all the sass from my voice and get real. "The way you speak to her, with so much respect and love. The way you crouch down to look her in the eye. The way she clearly adores the ground you walk on and hangs on your every word… well, it… it moved me." I exhale. "You're an incredible dad, and that's sexy as hell."

"Thank you, Lou. That means everything to me."

"You're, um… You're welcome."

He reaches his hand across the bar and takes hold of one of mine.

I look down at our knuckles braided together so comfortably, so perfectly.

I don't ever want to let go.

He gives my hand a squeeze and rumbles, "I'm on two full weeks of daddy duty starting tomorrow morning, so it'll be a lot of early nights for me. Tonight however…"

"Yeah?" My voice sounds breathy as I lean closer to him.

"Tonight, I'm all yours."

Chapter Thirty-Four

JAMES

"Who would like to touch my purple sea urchin?"

A sea of grubby hands shoots to the sky, including my daughter's.

Louise is leading a "Creatures of the Coral" workshop at the aquarium this morning, and these young minds are eating it up.

She's a natural with kids.

"Alright." Louise laughs at their enthusiasm. "I promise you will all get a chance. But first, I need you to show me these two fingers."

She holds up her second and third fingers on her right hand and brings them together. The kids mirror her pose.

"Those are the only two fingers we'll use to touch Mr. Spike, okay? And we'll do it just like this."

She demonstrates very softly stroking the sea urchin's spines.

"Can I see everyone practice in the air? Good, everybody, good! Sometimes people think sea urchins are scary because they look so sharp and pointy, but I assure you that Mr. Spike will not hurt you. He's not venomous and doesn't sting. But a lot of urchins do, so if you ever see one in the ocean when you're on vacation, be safe and don't touch it, okay?"

"Okay," the kids answer in chorus.

She smiles. "Fun Fact: In most languages, the word urchin translates to sea hedgehog. How cute is that?"

The kids start to crowd and shove to get a better look at the creature.

"Alright, everyone, let's form a peeeeaceful line now—no shoving, please—and you'll all get a turn to touch him."

Iris and I follow orders and hop in line. I can't take my eyes off Louise as she works with each kid one by one. It's clear she enjoys what she does, and she's great at it, but my gut tells me this isn't the exact right place for her.

Ever since the night of the arts festival, a brainstorm has been forming in my mind.

She was practically glowing that night. Joy was emanating from her every pore. The idea I'm cooking up could keep that smile on her face permanently. And selfishly, it would keep the smile on mine too. Because it would mean we can stay together after I move to Hawaii.

I haven't found the right time to talk to her about it this week with Iris in town, and I have no idea if she'll be open to the idea, but I have to give it a shot.

And soon.

Because departure time is in less than a month.

"Hey, Rissy!" Louise beams when we reach her for our turn. "I'm so happy to have you in my workshop! How was 'What's the Purpose of a Porpoise?'"

When did she start calling Iris by her nickname?

I love it.

"It was awesome!"

I lean to whisper in her ear, "I was peaceful and patient in line, Miss Anderson. Will you stroke my Mr. Spike?"

"This an educational setting for children," she whispers back. "Get your mind out of the gutter, sir."

Louise insisted on moving her things back to Mabel's for the two weeks that Iris was here. She thinks it would be confusing for her to see her dad essentially living with a woman he's not seriously dating.

I appreciate her care and consideration for my daughter more than she knows, but if Louise thinks I'm not serious about her, then she's not paying attention.

Iris giggles as she explores the sea urchin.

Louise

"And what is the purpose of a porpoise?"

"That title was actually a bit misleading," Iris says like a tiny, introspective adult. "The instructor never really answered that question. But anyway, isn't everyone's purpose just to be happy?"

This kid floors me with the things that come out of her mouth.

If that is her current six-year-old life philosophy, then maybe Eva and I are doing something right after all.

"That's, um... That's a nice way to look at things, sweetie." I may be imagining it, but Louise seems to get choked up at the interaction and tries to hide it.

"Hey, Louise! Did you know that my daddy is Santa Claus?"

Louise's eyes go wide as she looks around at the other children. "Isn't she a bit young to know that?" she whispers to me.

"Don't worry," I whisper back. "She's still a believer."

Iris prattles on. "I don't mean he's the real Santa Claus. Duh, how could he be the real Santa Claus? I mean he's going to dress like Santa Claus next Saturday."

"The aquarium asked me to fill in as Scuba Santa next weekend," I explain. "She's excited. I know Saturday is your day off, but I was hoping maybe you'd be game to watch her while I'm in the tank? Should only be two hours tops."

She pauses before answering, and for a moment, I'm afraid I've overstepped.

"I'd be honored," she says with a smile.

"Great," I say, relieved. "Thank you."

Louise gently lifts the sea urchin away from Iris. "Alright, girlfriend, you know I'd talk to you for hours, but I gotta make sure everyone in line gets a turn. Before you go, though. Psst." She gestures for Iris to come closer. "My boss said I can do a half day today so I can join you and your daddy for your Philthadelphia date. Does that sound good?"

"Yesssss," Iris hisses. "That sounds great! Daddy and I have all the plans planned."

"You do?" Louise looks at me.

"*We* do," I say. "We have all the plans."

Chapter Thirty-Five

LOUISE

James and Iris weren't kidding. They made all the plans.

We visited the Liberty Bell.

We rode the carousel in Franklin Square.

We got ice cream at Bassett's and strolled through Longwood Gardens.

And that was just the first afternoon and evening we spent together as a trio. The rest of the week, I joined them for everything I could too, and I ended up having the time of my life.

I saw corners of this city I didn't even know existed.

I saw a parent-child bond that I didn't know was possible.

And I saw a happy family-focused version of myself I never anticipated.

I resisted going on adventures with them the first week Iris was here. I told James I didn't want to intrude on their father-daughter time, which was true. Mostly, though, I was terrified of getting attached to her. To them.

But let's face it.

I was smitten with Iris the first time I met her.

And James? I've been head-over-heels in love with him for months now, but I'm too prideful and stubborn to say it.

We'll put Iris on a plane back to her mom tomorrow. James will stay back here to tie up loose ends, but then he'll join them in Hawaii two weeks later.

Permanently.

And if I'm not careful, he'll go never knowing how I feel.

"Louise? Are you crying?" Iris asks as we sit hip to hip in the aquarium amphitheater waiting for her father to appear in the shark tank.

"No, sweetie, I'm not. Just got a little something in my eye." I dab it away with the corner of my sleeve.

I tuck my arm around Iris's shoulder and pull her close.

Her little arm reaches around my belly and squeezes me back.

"Can I tell you a secret, Louise?"

"Um. I think so?"

"You have to promise not to tell anyone."

I've never seen Iris so serious.

"Hm. On second thought, no, Rissy. I'm sorry. I can't do that."

"What? Why not?" she whines and scrambles out from under my arm.

"Because you're a kid, and I'm a grown-up. When you're with me, it's my job to make sure you're safe and protected. What if your secret is that someone hurt you, but I've already promised you that I won't tell anyone? Then I'm in a real sticky situation, don't you think? Because as the grown-up, it's super important I tell your dad and your mom if someone said or did something to you that they shouldn't have. But sadly, that would mean breaking your trust. And I wouldn't want to break your trust for anything in the world, kiddo, because you're precious to me."

"Oh my gosh, you grown-ups need to chillax," Iris says.

"Do kids your age say chillax?" I laugh.

"They do now! My mom said it once, and I liked the sound of it. Anyway, I'm not going to tell you something too serious. I hope you won't tell my dad or mom, but if you have to, whatever, dude. I'll deal."

This kid cracks me up. She's innocence and maturity all rolled into one.

"Alright then, dude. What's your secret?"

She watches the fish in the massive tank in front of us for a few moments, then whispers, "I'm really sad to be going home tomorrow."

"You are?"

She nods and blurts out in one breath, "It's not that I'm not excited to see Mommy and Ron—because I am—but it's been so fun being with you and Daddy, and I wish I could have all four of you with me all the time."

Not what I was expecting.

At all.

I swallow a lump in my throat. "Well, your dad will be there for good in just two more weeks, right? So you'll have your mom, your dad, and Ron. That's going to be pretty great."

"But not you, right? You're not coming with us too?"

God, I wish I could. I'd be lying if I said I hadn't considered how great that could be. But what am I going to do? Invite myself along? Insert myself into a family where I don't belong?

Even if that was something James wanted too, I refuse to repeat my past mistakes with guys. I won't lose myself in a relationship again. I don't know where I'm supposed to go or what I'm supposed to do next, but whatever it is, I know I have to walk my own path, not follow some guy on his.

But he's not just some guy.

Not anymore.

"No, sweetie," I say as kindly as I can. "I'm not coming too."

"You'll stay in touch, though, right? And you'll visit?"

"I'm not sure, Iris. I hope so? But I'm just not sure."

I just finished telling her I won't make her promises I can't keep. So I'm sticking to that. As much as it pains me to do it.

Iris nods sadly. "I'm going to miss you."

"I'll miss you too."

I open my arms to her for a hug. I wrap her up in a tight squeeze just as Christmas music starts to blast from the speakers accompanied by a boisterous "Ho ho ho, welcome to the show show show!" voiceover.

"That's the cue for the kids to go down to the front!" I say and pat her on the back.

She squeals and hurries down to the front row where an usher is opening up a "kids only" section.

My phone pings with an email notification. I quickly check

my email as the announcer runs through the safety rules and emergency exits available inside the amphitheater.

"Holy shit," I say out loud when I see who the email is from.

A woman to my left covers her sleeping infant's ears and shoots me a glare.

I wince. "Sorry, I'm sorry."

The email is from Corbin Bellows.

Not from someone on his team but Corbin Bellows himself.

I peek down where Iris is standing at the glass. She looks up at me and waves. I give her a big smile and a thumbs-up back, then dive into reading the email.

> *Dear Miss Anderson,*
>
> *I'm reaching out to you to right a wrong, and I hope you will be amenable to the discussion.*
>
> *Two months ago, I rescinded your scholarship funding after learning of an incident you were involved in that I deemed troubling.*
>
> *This was my mistake, and I am deeply apologetic. If people gave up on me every time I made a dubious personal choice, I would have no career. And I think we both know, I've made plenty of dubious choices in my personal life.*
>
> *I recently learned about the work you've done with the sea lion training team at Philly Aquarium and how it's led not only to increased funds for combatting ocean pollution—a cause I am deeply committed to—but to a promising partnership between the aquarium and the CMM prosthetics team in Monterey.*
>
> *I find it inspiring and heartening seeing a young mind like yourself combining your passion for art and science to make a better world for marine life and for people too.*
>
> *I hope you will accept my sincerest apologies for my misstep. Should you like to return to the marine biology program at UPenn, your scholarship will be reinstated in full, effective immediately. Furthermore, should we*

still have your interest, the "Keys to the Coral Kingdom" internship you applied for in Florida this spring is yours.

It would be our pleasure to welcome you aboard.

With Respect,
Corbin Bellows

Iris is suddenly back beside me.

"Rissy, don't you want to watch from the front?"

"No. I want to watch with you." She points at the top of the tank. "Look! It's Daddy!"

Right on cue, James lowers in the center of the tank in a cloud of bubbles, waving to the excited crowd of kids and parents. He's decked out in full Scuba Santa gear. He even has a sack of "presents" on his back.

He spots us right away and makes what I think is the "hang loose" sign he gave me all those months ago outside Mabel's apartment. But when I look closer at his gloved hand, I realize his index finger is extended as well.

It's the sign for "I love you."

I know it's for Iris and not for me, but when I look down, I see that my hand involuntarily formed the same shape, like my body knows my heart better than I do.

I lift the shape and move it side to side, silently saying two things at the same time.

"I love you" and "goodbye."

Chapter Thirty-Six

JAMES

It's a dark December morning with just a sliver of the sun starting to rise.

Louise was all smiles and hugs while saying goodbye to Iris, but since we got in the car, the vibe between us has been tense and eerily quiet.

We head farther away from the airport and follow the signs toward Valley Forge.

"That was hard," she says softly.

"You'll see her again," I say and place a hand on her thigh.

"Will I?" she asks.

"Won't you?"

"Are you really asking me that question?" she fires back.

"I am, yeah."

The only response this gets is her sighing and looking out the passenger window.

"Lou," I start. "At some point, we do need to talk about this. We've been pretending this countdown isn't happening for months now, but pretending doesn't change the fact that I'm moving to Hawaii in ten days, and we still don't have a plan."

"What kind of plan can we possibly have, James? You leaving was the deal from the very beginning. That is the plan. That is the only plan."

"Okay, but moving doesn't have to mean leaving."

"That makes no sense."

"Come with me," I say.

"Come with you where?"

"To Hawaii. Come with me."

She turns to look at me.

"Are you serious?"

"Never been more serious in my life." I peek up at my rearview and make a quick decision. I veer off an exit at the very last second, causing the guy in the truck behind us to honk and shout profanities at me through his window.

"What the hell are you doing, James?" Louise shouts and grips the passenger door.

"I can't have this conversation while I'm driving." I turn toward the entrance for Valley Forge National Park but immediately pull off on the side of the road. "I'm sorry. You okay?"

"This isn't a parking spot," she huffs. "You can't just stop here."

I shut off the engine.

"Well, I just did."

She shakes her head, silent.

"Can we have a conversation about this?" I ask. "A real conversation?"

She only shrugs, but she doesn't try to shut me down.

I suppose that's something.

I unbuckle my seat belt and turn to face her as much as I can.

"Yes, I have to leave. But I have absolutely no desire to leave you. Let me rephrase because that doesn't begin to capture what I'm going through over here."

I take her hand.

She lets me.

"Every time I even think about being thousands of miles away from you, I lose my damn mind. I want to throw a fucking hissy fit and scream at the universe about how screwed up it is. That after seven years, I meet the woman of my dreams basically five minutes after I promised my daughter I'd move across the country. It's maddening. It's frustrating."

"But you want to go."

"I want to be with my daughter. And I want to be with you." I pause. "Both things can be true."

She closes her eyes and leans back into the car seat.

"You said we have no plan," I say softly. "And you're right. But this seed of an idea planted in my brain the night of the arts festival, and it's been growing ever since." I reach over and cup her cheek. "Louise."

She opens her eyes and focuses on me.

"What if you were a part of The Highs and Lows with me?"

"Your excursion company? You're running scuba diving adventures and hiking mountains, James. Just because I've ridden a few waterslides with you doesn't mean I'm ready to plunge sixty feet into the ocean for fun. And I don't even own a pair of hiking boots."

"So we'll get you some. I'm creating experiences for people, Cold Brew. And I'm just getting started with this thing. It can be whatever we want it to be."

I pull out a plane ticket with her name on it and place it in her hand.

"We can be whatever we want to be."

Her mouth drops open as she stares down at the piece of paper.

I continue, "There's going to be boat rides and beach parties and... what if we offered painting workshops too? You could do that, Lou! Can you imagine? You on the beach, combining art and the ocean like you've always wanted to? It would be amazing. You could—"

"Corbin Bellows sent me an email yesterday giving me my scholarship back and offering me the Florida Keys internship this spring." She cuts me off.

I let that sink in for a moment.

"That's—That's, um—" I swallow. "What did you tell him?"

"I told him thank you. And that I accept."

I nod in understanding.

But I'm not a guy who gives up easily.

Not on her.

Not on us.

"Tell him you've changed your mind," I say.

"Excuse me?"

"Tell him you've changed your mind! Lou, I saw you juggling

those long hours at school and simultaneously working full-time at the aquarium. You weren't happy."

"What, I shouldn't work hard?" she scoffs.

"No, of course you should—if that's what you want—but you weren't happy! You were stressed. You were unsure of yourself. You were in near constant *Jeopardy* mode and dragging yourself from one obligation to the next." I soften my voice. "When you started experimenting with Meilani, though? When you built up that amazing portfolio? When you auctioned off those paintings at the arts festival and raised all that money for a good cause? Baby, you glowed. You were shining from the inside out. We could create that kind of life together. Full time. You could feel that way every day."

"I need to get out of this car," she says and flings the passenger side door open.

"Fine. Yeah, let's take a walk." I exit my side of the car and hustle behind her down the dirt road.

"Alone, James! I want to be alone!"

"I don't believe you," I shout. "You don't want to be alone. I don't want to be alone. We want to be together. Really together this time. We can make that happen!"

She stops walking and whips around to face me. "You were supposed to be one night! That's all I ever wanted from you. But you had to keep pushing it!"

"Pushing what? When did I ever push you into anything?"

"Um. Every second?" She throws her hands up.

"That's bullshit, and you know it, Lou. Every step of the way, I have been taking my cues from you."   She shakes her head. "Don't gaslight me. Don't do that."

"Gaslight you? Cold Brew, I'm—I don't know what you're—"

What the hell is happening here?

"Take a breath with me, will ya? However you're feeling is one-hundred-percent valid, but I need a minute to catch up with where you're at right now. Can we just... take a breath?"

"How I'm feeling is one-hundred-percent valid?" she says quietly, like those words are completely foreign to her.

"Yes. Of course. How you feel is how you feel. I might just

need a little help to get on the same page and understand."

She stares at the ground and kicks some tiny pebbles with her boot.

"You're angry that I bought this ticket for you without talking to you first?"

She nods.

"Okay. I get that. I knew it was a risk, but I wanted you to know how serious I am about you. And... maybe I've watched too many movies, I don't know." I try to make her laugh. It doesn't work this time.

"I can't just change my whole life for a guy," she says.

"Of course not. I don't want you to change a damn thing."

"Just where I live, what I do for my career..." she says with a healthy dose of sarcasm.

I place my hands on her shoulders and run them down her arms.

I take both of her hands in mine.

"So we do this long distance," I say. "Forget the plane ticket. We'll tear it up. We'll forget I ever mentioned it. I've been making monthly trips across country for almost a year now. I'll keep doing it to be with you. However you want to make this work, baby, I'm in."

"I'm going to text Calliope to come pick me up," she says.

"What? No. We can talk some more on the drive back to Mabel's. Or not talk. Whatever you want. Let's just get back in the car and—"

"No, James. I need some space. Now."

She drops her hands from mine and sends the text.

I look up at the sky and blow out a breath.

A few seconds tick by.

I respond as calmly as I can. "Fine. I'll, um—I'll wait in the car until I see her pick you up."

"You don't need to do that."

"I'm not leaving you on the side of the road when it's barely daylight."

"I don't need you to take care of me." Her energy ratchets up again.

"I love you, Louise."

Her breath cuts off.

Her eyes go wide.

Not a single sound comes out of her mouth.

Not exactly the response I was looking for. But I'm in so deep at this point, there's no sense in holding back.

"You don't want to hear that, huh? Well, guess what, Cold Brew? I don't care. I fucking love you, and I need you to know that. These feelings I have for you have been building up inside me since the moment I saw you. They get more intense every minute I spend with you, and if I don't let some of it reach you in a way you can understand?" I tap my palm on my chest. "I'm gonna burst. You say you want something casual, something 'on the surface.' But you don't. Not with me. With me, you want it all."

A tear rolls down her cheek.

It absolutely kills me not to wrap her in my arms and comfort her.

But I don't know how many more times I can handle her pushing me away.

"What are you afraid of?" I ask gently.

"Nothing."

"Everyone is afraid of something."

"Spiders. Home invasions. Creepy kids who talk about their past lives," she snarks.

"Oh really? I love that creepy kid stuff. Iris told me once that she used to be an old brick mason in Palm Springs during the 1950s. Now every time I look at her, I want to call her Mort."

She laughs through her tears. "Really?"

"Yeah." I shrug. "She told me her name used to be Mort."

Her smile is brief, but it means everything to me.

It means there's still hope.

I risk stepping forward and brush a tear off her cheek.

"You're afraid that if you let yourself fall in love with me, you'll lose yourself. Like you did when you were with Trent and with the guys before him. Like your mom does whenever she's in a new relationship. But Lou?" She tilts her chin up so her blue eyes meet mine. "I promise you, I will never let that happen."

I kiss her.

So softly.

Because I'm afraid of something too: That if I press too hard, she'll step away from me.

Permanently.

"I'll give you your space," I say.

And then I walk away.

As I get in my car, I look east and see the sun rising higher and higher in the sky.

At that moment, it feels like a sign that despite how low I feel right now, everything will be okay.

Or maybe that's the last I'll ever see of her, and I really am that idiot "woo woo universe" guy.

Chapter Thirty-Seven

LOUISE

I wake up in a cold sweat and turn to see two pairs of compound eyes staring at me.

"Yeah, yeah, I know. I should really talk to someone about this."

Is it weird that since returning to Mabel's, I've found comfort in Bonnie and Clyde?

They're always freakishly attentive to my sounds and movements, which has me feeling a little less alone this week. And Bonnie's I-do-what-I-want-when-I-want attitude is helping me get out of my head and connect with what *I* actually want and need. When Bonnie feels caged in? She literally finds the lock and frees herself. She apparently only does this when someone in the vicinity is having sex, but that's neither here nor there.

Point is, if Bonnie is a bug and she can free herself, then so can I.

And Meilani's doing it too. An actual shark ripped off her flipper, and how does Meilani respond? By learning to trust those around her, trying new things, and seizing unexpected opportunities.

Why are animals so much smarter than we are?

I fire off a text to my tried-and-true confidant, who I haven't spoken to in way too long.

> **ME:** The dreams have started up again. Oh and I broke up with refrigerator sex man, which I'm sure you would say is related. Got time to talk?

GAIL: Call you in five.

I exit my room, pluck a taped pink number three off my door, and throw it in the bathroom wastebasket, then start brushing my teeth.

Mabel has been finding little ways to remind me that James is leaving soon. Each morning this week, I've found a little note on my bedroom door with the number of days left until he flies away.

The reminders are completely unnecessary.

I could tell you the number of minutes left before he leaves.

Because he's all I think about.

All day, every day.

I finish brushing and rinse.

True to his word, James has given me the space I asked for. And it sucks.

Calliope was kind to me that morning when she picked me up. The girl who always crosses the line knew from one look at my tearstained face that I wasn't up for answering questions or taking any advice. So she didn't push me.

At first.

Now, however, I'm getting constant texts from her that look like this:

CALLIOPE: Have you called him yet?

ME: No.

CALLIOPE: Are you going to?

ME: No.

CALLIOPE: Woman, are you crazy?

ME: No.

In my heart, I know I'm not crazy.

I'm doing what I have to do to look at myself in the mirror.

I've sold myself short so many times over the years. I've let myself believe that who I am and what I want out of life isn't as important as whatever man is in my life at the time. I've let them define me. It started with my dad, then continued with every single guy who came into my life after him.

So if I were to take James up on his offer to go with him to Hawaii—to partner with him in his company—wouldn't I be doing the same thing all over again? Giving up my identity to be a part of his?

My phone rings. The screen lights up with Gail's name.

"Hi," I answer.

"Hey, girl, hey. You okay?"

"Yes? No? I don't know. Let's talk about you, though. We always talk about me, and I hate the idea of having a one-sided friendship with you."

"Lou. You texted me because you needed support, didn't you?"

"Yeah." I sigh.

"So lay it on me."

I give her an abbreviated version of everything between James and me over the past three months as I make myself a coffee and shuffle out to sit on the front stoop.

When I finish, Gail says, "I only have one question. Why the hell aren't you packing your bags for Hawaii right now?"

"Did you hear anything I said?"

"Yeah! I heard every word. Did you? Louise, you're so in love with this guy you can barely see straight." She pauses. "I'm about to say something big and profound. Are you ready?"

"I'm ready," I say.

"Are you sure? Because I don't think you're ready for this jelly."

"I'm ready for the jelly!" I laugh. "Please, say whatever you need to say."

"You can stop punishing yourself now."

"Punishing myself? For what?"

"For the way other people have treated you."

Tears well behind my eyes. "I don't know what you're—"

"Your dad's shortcomings aren't your fault."

"I know that," I scoff.

"Neither were Trent's or Aidan's and whoever the hell came before them. Louise, the only thing you're guilty of is giving too many chances to people who didn't deserve them. They didn't deserve *you*. Seems to me that finally a guy comes around who is more than worthy of you—I mean, with everything you've told me, even *I'm* considering taking Mr. Adventure Bar Refrigerator Man for a spin—"

"I'm going to tell Hannah you said that!" I laugh.

"Just trying to get you to laugh, Lou. Mission accomplished." I can hear her smile through the phone.

"Shouldn't I be able to be on my own, though?" I ask quietly.

"You should, yes. And you are. But when you find the right person..." Her voice softens. "Why should you have to?"

I watch the sun rise while I sip my coffee and let that sink in.

Then I surprise even myself when I say, "I'm sorry for the way I treated you sophomore year. It wasn't right."

"Whoa, Nelly! Where did that come from?"

"I've owed you an apology for a long time, Gail."

She pauses. "Are we really talking about this right now?"

"Yeah. We are. I am." I swallow. "I said I didn't know you had feelings for me. And I believed that at the time. But some part of me knew. I think I was just... afraid to lose that feeling.

"What feeling?" she asks.

"Having another person really see me? It was intoxicating," I say. "I fell in love with that feeling."

"While I was falling in love with you."

"Yeah. I'm truly sorry, Gail."

"Water under the bridge, lady. We came out on the other side just fine, didn't we? The question is, what are you going to do now? Because... Refrigerator Sex Man sees you too."

"Oh my God, you really have to stop calling him that!" I laugh.

"Excuse me," she fires back. "You literally texted me the words 'I broke up with refrigerator sex man.'"

"I know. He just..." I watch the sun rise higher in the sky as an idea forms. "Somewhere along the line, he became way more than that."

So much more than that.

He's everything.

"Gail? Thank you so much for this. But there's someone else I need to call."

"Make it happen, baby," she says. "Make. It. Happen."

Chapter Thirty-Eight

JAMES

" *I* 'm gonna miss you, buddy." Wally slaps me on the back and pulls me in for a hug.

"Guys, you know this isn't goodbye forever. I'll be back to check in on the business, and I'm sure you two will be throwing a wedding bash or popping out a baby I've gotta meet sometime soon, won't you?"

"Whoa!" Mabel says. "Give us a minute, will ya? We've been dating less than six months!"

"Well. When you know, you know, right?" I say and give Mabel a squeeze.

I thought I knew.

I'm back at the airport about to head through security, and while I'm touched by the crew that sent me off—Wally, Mabel, my pal Kathleen and even Alec are here—I can't help being disappointed someone else didn't make it.

"I'm sorry she's not here," Mabel says softly in my ear before I release her.

"It's okay. I respect her decision. She knows what she wants."

And what she doesn't want.

"Look out for her for me though, will ya?" I ask.

"Of course," Mabel says sadly.

Kathleen puts a hand on my shoulder. "What did I tell you, Jamesy? Any girl who can't recognize the wonderful man you are isn't worth your time or energy."

"I'm sorry to hear it didn't work out, kid," Alec says. "You two seemed like a great fit to me."

"Boyo, are you telling me Alec met this girl, and I haven't?"

"Intimately," Alec says under his breath.

Kathleen narrows her eyes.

"She was coming down off a high and grabbed Alec's balls," I explain. "No big deal."

Kathleen gasps. "Are you sure this girl is the right one for you, boyo?"

I thought she was.

Alec waves off Kathleen's skepticism. "She wrote me a very nice card after the incident. Poor kid was really embarrassed and apologetic."

"We were making a plan for her to join me at a meeting," I say to Kathleen. "And I was looking forward to you getting to know her, but... well, sometimes things don't work out, I guess."

It's not that I had high hopes Louise would change her mind and use that plane ticket after all, but I did think she'd find it in her heart to say goodbye. Over the past two days, it's taken every bit of strength I have inside me to resist reaching out to her. But she very clearly asked me for space. And being that I didn't exactly honor her wishes the first time she asked me to keep my distance way back in the summer, I had to give it to her this time.

I open my arms to Kathleen for a hug.

She rocks me side to side. "You'll find a new group there, won't you?"

"Of course I will. I pop into a great group every time I'm there to visit. They'll be my homebase now."

"Good. I'm glad to hear that." She steps back from the hug and puts her hands on my cheeks like I'm a little kid. "Because you know the drill, boyo. With big disappointments like this, there's always a chance of a relapse."

"Seven years sobriety, Kath. Don't worry. I'm not letting that go." I place my hands over hers. "Not letting you go either, lady. You know that, right?"

"What's that I hear? Is that an open-ended invitation to join you in paradise?"

"You better believe it! I have a guest room with your name on it anytime you want to use it. That goes for all of you," I look at Wally, Mabel, and Alec. "You're welcome anytime."

"You better go, buddy."

I look at the time on my phone and know Wally's right. I check it one last time for new voicemails, then put it in my pocket. She's not coming, and I need to make my peace with that. After a few more goodbyes and good wishes, I make my way through security and board my flight.

Something about being up in the air, suspended between time zones, helps me clear my mind. By the time I touch down on the Big Island, I'm ready to focus on everything this move is bringing me instead of what it requires me to lose.

"Daddy!!!"

The best sound—and girl—in the world crashes into me as soon as I exit the revolving doors leading to the passenger pickup area.

"Baby girl!" I drop my suitcases and spin Iris around and around.

"You're here for realsies now, and I get to see you all the time!" she squeals.

"That's right!" I give her an extra tight squeeze and kiss the side of her head. "I'm so excited to be here with you, baby. For good this time."

I put Iris back on her feet and maneuver my suitcases to the curb, where Eva is leaning against the car, smiling at us.

"How're you feeling, Jay Bear?"

"Oh, you know..." I sort of half shrug, half smile.

She gives me a hug and says softly, "You know, it's okay not to be a hundred percent right now."

"Thanks, Evie B."

I've kept Eva up to date on all things Louise. She knows I'm hurting.

"But..." Eva raises her voice for Iris's benefit. "We're really excited you're here. Aren't we?"

"Yes! And we don't have a surprise for you!" Iris jumps in the back seat and hides her face.

I toss my suitcases in the trunk, then stick my head in the open back window. "You don't have a surprise for me, or you do?"

"Don't!" she squeaks. "We don't!"

"Okay." I laugh as I get in the passenger side and buckle up. "She has a secret for me, huh?" I whisper to Eva.

"Iris?" Eva says in her sternest mom voice, which isn't very stern at all. "Buckle yourself in and..." She mimes zipping her mouth and throwing away the key.

I turn around to find Iris doing the same gesture and fighting a fit of giggles.

They're up to something.

Alright.

I'll let them have their fun at my expense.

"So." I drum my hands on my thighs once we're on the road. "Where are we heading, ladies? Should we hit Iris's french fry place? Ooh, or should we get some bubble tea?"

Eva hesitates. "Um. We thought we'd drop you off at your new place right away."

"What? Why? Don't you want to find a place to grab a bite? We always grab a bite after I fly in."

"Yeah. I know, but... I think today it's best you get settled in at your new place first."

"You guys going to stick around? Obviously, I'm not set up with food yet, but whatever, we can order in. Wanna call Ron and tell him to swing by and join us?"

"Ron's working late tonight, so he'll have to pass, and you're probably tired after the long flight, so Rissy and I will get out of your hair."

"What are you talking about? You could never be in my hair."

"James!" Eva laughs. "You know I'm a terrible liar. Will you put me out of my misery and just trust me on this one? Believe me, you want to be dropped off alone."

The last thing I want to be is alone right now.

But she asked me to trust her.

So that's what I'm going to do.

It's a quick ride to my new place, which is just a few streets over from where Iris and Eva live. And if I was a betting man, I'd say that any day now Ron will be joining them there too.

We pull into the empty driveway, and I think of all the things that need to happen before this house will feel like a home.

"Hey Rissy, do you and mommy have plans tomorrow?"

"Mommy, do we have plans tomorrow?" she asks.

"She's got school," Eva says. "But after that, we're free."

"Cool if I take her shopping so we can set up her new room?"

"Oooh! Say yes, Mommy! Please say yes!"

"Of course, yes!

"Yay!!"

"And James, you don't need my permission to take our daughter shopping. We're in this together, right?"

"Right." I exhale. "I think it may just take me a minute to get back into our flow now that I'm here."

"That's understandable." She pauses. "Welcome home, Jay Bear."

I lean over and kiss her on the cheek. "Thanks for everything."

"Back atcha."

"Can I have a squeeze from my girl?" I say over my shoulder.

Iris attacks the back of my seat and wraps her arms around my neck. I make a big production of acting like I'm choking.

"Can't breathe," I wheeze. "Daughter. Is. Too. Powerful."

"Alrighty, Rissy. Buckle up again. Daddy has to go," Eva says.

I get out of the car and haul my suitcases out of the trunk.

Eva reverses out of the driveway way faster than necessary and shouts out the window, "Have fun tonight and call us tomorrow!"

"Yeah, Daddy! Have fun and say hi to—"

"Iris!" Eva scolds before Iris can finish her sentence and peels down the street.

I'm left standing alone in the driveway.

Geez. Welcome home, huh?

It's like they couldn't get away fast enough.

I start dragging my suitcases toward the door when something stops me in my tracks.

The faint notes of a familiar song carry on the ocean breeze.

I leave my suitcases right where they are and slowly make

my way to the side of the house, where a rocky path leads to the beach.

I slip off my shoes and walk steadily forward.

The rocks dissipate and the soil turns to sand.

The music gets louder.

The lyrics of *Here Comes the Sun* by The Beatles fill my ears.

My heart begins to pound, and I don't even know why because this can't mean what I think it—

"What took you so long?" A voice washes over me.

And I think I've lost my damn mind.

Because the fiery orange sun is dipping toward the horizon over the water, spilling into reds and pinks and peach, but all I can see in front of me is Louise wearing a yellow sundress and the most brilliant smile I've ever seen.

I'm speechless.

And confused.

"I thought it was time I reclaimed The Beatles," she nods toward the speakers on the soft blanket spread out under her feet.

"How did you—? Why are you—?"

"You make me rethink sunsets," she says with tears in her eyes.

I run to her as fast as humanly possible and scoop her into my arms.

We kiss like our lives depend on it.

"I love you," she says between kisses. "I love you so much. I'm sorry."

"You don't have to be sorry for a damn thing." I rain kisses down her throat and back up, then run my fingers through her hair. "Thank you." I kiss her lips. "Thank you." I kiss her nose. "Thank you." I kiss her forehead.

"Thank you," she says. "For being patient with me."

"Always. Forever."

But then I realize I may be getting ahead of myself.

"So what's going on? Are you visiting? Are you staying? Are you –?"

"I'm staying. If you'll have me."

"Cold Brew, I will have you until the end of time." I kiss her again. "But what about Corbin and your scholarship and—"

"On pause. They said they'll hold it for me while I explore the 'exciting entrepreneurial opportunity' I have in front of me. They're even interested in investing."

"What exciting entrepreneurial opportunity is that?" I ask.

She reaches down and grabs a binder.

"I took your brainstorm for my potential contribution to The Highs and Lows and built on it. You, sir..." She shoves the binder against my chest. "Have some reading to do tonight."

"That's not the only thing I have to do tonight." I wrap my arm around her and pull her close.

"You can do both." Her sweet breath cascades over my skin.

I nuzzle into her neck. "Can I?"

She responds with a soft moan.

"Sure can. A wise man once told me we don't always have to pick and choose. Sometimes? You really can have it all."

Epilogue

LOUISE

I'm floating in the middle of crystal clear blue Pacific Ocean.

This time it's not scary.

This time it's not a dream.

When life is this wonderful though, I do sometimes worry I'll wake up any minute to find it was all in my imagination.

But so far, so good.

We're six months into life on the Big Island and I've never felt so free. So... on purpose.

I've been "doing the work" as Gail would say, and tackling the emotional stuff that still rears its head from time to time.

Going to AA meetings with James has been a big part of that. I'm constantly amazed at how open and honest the people are there. I go to support him, but every single time, I walk out feeling like their stories have supported and inspired *me*.

And I'm working on healing things with my parents. It's baby steps for sure. But in an astounding plot twist I certainly didn't see coming, they are still together and seem happier than ever. We're even talking about them flying to visit us here in Hawaii this year. I don't kid myself into thinking things will ever be perfect with them, but moving the relationship into a healthier place is doing wonders for my head and my heart.

I snorkel my way toward the boat just as a school of Redfin Butterflyfish create a burst of colorful movement in my periphery. That's right, I'm snorkeling. James may have literally pushed me to confront my fear of the water, but since then I've been dipping my toes in every chance I get and allowing myself to go deeper every day.

To my left, a manta ray flutters past me. Below me, a green sea turtle soars over the coral. I've been studying these creatures for years in textbooks and watching them through fish tanks, but to actually be swimming among them now, without fear and whenever I want?

It truly feels like magic.

Today is our test run for our big grand opening bash happening next week and all our most important people traveled here to help us celebrate.

When I reach the ladder of the boat, James is already onboard and reaching out a hand to pull me up.

"Last one on board again," he chuckles and draws me in for a kiss.

"Really?" I look back to the water and see that he's right.

Once again, it was just me and the sea.

Perhaps the way it was always meant to be.

I peer toward the shore and spot a pod of Hawaiian monk seals resting on the beach, and of course they remind me of Meilani. I miss her a lot, but her team in Monterey emails me updates on her at least once a month, which definitely helps. Sometimes we even set up video calls so Meilani and I can "chat." And James, Iris and I just got our plane tickets to California to see her in person at the end of the summer.

So we're still connected.

Like James said all those months ago, "When there's a connection, there's a connection. Sometimes these things are hard to explain."

"Ready to see your students' work?" James asks.

"Of course!" I say.

We pad over to the main deck area and find our whole crew dutifully filling their canvases with color. The painting workshop I'm running is called "The Flow." We put people in some of the most beautiful, nature-filled spots in the world and encourage their creativity. It's amazing to see what people create when you give them the freedom to just... be.

My heart fills as I take in all of our people's creations.

Mabel and Wally are painting portraits of Bonnie and Clyde to hang in their new home. Calliope and Ralph are designing cover concepts for their next series of dinosaur love story collaborations.

And Iris, Eva, and Ron? I have to put my hand over my heart and regulate my breathing when I see what they've made. An image of Iris is the biggest in the center, with all four of her "parent people"—as she calls us—surrounding her.

"I think my heart might explode," I say.

"I think you'll be okay." James laughs softly and cuddles me from behind.

"Toast!" Wally shouts. "It's time for the toast!"

He distributes champagne glasses and fills them with bubbles: Sparkling Nature's Nectar for Iris and James, prosecco for the rest of us.

"To The Highs and Lows!" Wally leads.

"To The Highs and Lows!" we all respond.

And it's then I realize that James is right. Whatever highs and lows come our way, with this incredible guy by my side, everything will always be okay.

The End.

Backstage Pass

The journey of writing a book is a wild one! And from what I'm starting to understand, that's always going to be the case. I saw a social media post the other day from a well-known, undeniably successful romance writer that said something like "Every time I write a book, I need to learn how to write a book." My initial thought was "What? Youuuuu?" But then I thought about it and realized that she never seems to repeat herself. Each book feels like its own little world – even inside of the same series – and I dig that about her.

So, of course she feels like she's learning how to do it every time. She's letting the book find *her*, instead of the other way around.

I feel like that happened to me here with *Sharkbait*. I set out to write a book full of silly sea shenanigans. I assumed it would carry a vibe pretty darn similar to the dino humor of *Flirtasaurus* and the broad bug jokes in *Lovebug*.

But then Louise asked me for something a little bit different.

The humor is still the driving force, but it's maybe not quite as in-your-face here as in previous books. And that's okay with me. Because that's not who Louise is.

We met her briefly in Book One as Ralph's cool-headed semi-estranged sister. Then we got to know her better in Book Two as she found her way into the Calliope and Mabel friend group. In both books she was the person of reason. The one who people came to when they needed to be talked off the ledge. She gave *other* people perspective and comfort. So, when she starts wrestling with her own stuff in *Sharkbait*, she needed someone to be *her* go-to person.

Enter James, the guy who started speaking so loudly (and in Teddy Hamilton's voice, audiobook fans!) that he demanded he get his own chapters.

I resisted it for a bit, because you can't do single POV for the first two books in a series and then suddenly switch to dual POV for the third, can you?

Well, I guess you can, because I did!

Alright, time to thank a few people!

Big thanks to Erin Hazell, a member of my Reader's Group and real-life marine biologist who spent time on the phone with me giving me the skinny on what day-to-day life is like working in an aquarium. Note: If I screwed up any details, don't come after her and her scientific brilliance! I took what knowledge I could gather, then freed myself to write some fiction. Thank you to Cindy Warschauer for entering the contest to name my sea lion and coming up with "Meilani." I loved it the moment I heard it. Lots of gratitude goes to the amazing Patty Villali Koett and Julia Heudorf for being brilliant beta readers who always offer such valuable feedback, and to the wonderful Jenny Sims for her editing prowess and for never making me feel bad about my morphing deadlines.

What's up next, you ask? A lot! I thought *Sharkbait* would be it for this series, but I wasn't quite ready to let this crew of characters go, and I wanted to have some fun seeing all three of their Happily Ever Afters overlapping a few years in the future. So... *The Natural History Novellas* are coming!

Here's what you can expect from The Natural History Novellas:

- A "where are they now?" two-year flash forward!
- Calliope and Ralph's working relationship as a "dino porn" author/narrator duo!
- A book signing event gone wrong in Las Vegas!
- Mabel and Wally selling syrup at a redhead convention in the Netherlands!
- All three couples together at Lou and James' place in island paradise!
- An anniversary!

- An engagement!
- A wedding!

After that... who knows?

Well, *I* know. But I'm going to keep the new series I'm writing under my hat for now while I keep tapping away at my keyboard. Thank you for all of your support!

xoxo,
Erin

Other Titles by Erin Mallon

The Natural History Series
Flirtasaurus
Lovebug
Sharkbait
The Natural History Novellas

Scripted Stories in Audio
These Walls Can Talk
These Walls Can Talk 2: The Narwhal Strikes Back!
These Walls Can Talk 3: Rise of the Machine
The Bromantic Comedies
The Net Will Appear
Skin Hungry
Come Find Me
Branched
Pale Blue Dot(s)

Novellas
Showmancing the Bone